Claimed by Three

A Dark Protectors Fantasy Romance

Coveted Prey
Book 9

L.V. Lane

Cover by Three Spires Creative

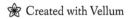 Created with Vellum

Contents

Chapter One

Dede

As I near the open door to my chamber, the sounds of rutting greet me—grunts, groans, giggles, and the slap of meeting flesh.

Should I be angry?

I recognize the grunts and groans, although I assuredly wish I did not.

The giggles? I can make a guess. It's likely a fool maid thinking to curry herself favor, deluding herself that she is more than a willing hole.

I'm not angry, I realize. Two emotions assault me—one is relief that someone else draws his attention, and the other is deep-rooted exhaustion with the direction my life is taking.

I consider turning around. It would be the sensible thing to do, but for the first time in many days, a little of my former spirit rises to the surface. Why should I walk away from my own chamber? Shoulders squared, I continue into the room like I don't know what is happening.

He has her bent over the small dining table of my suite. Her rough skirts are thrust up, while his pants are down, white ass on display. With another deep grunt, he stills.

My timing is impeccable.

The maid notices me first, and her short, sharp squeal rouses the man behind her from the final throes of his climax.

"Fuck!" Killian hisses.

"Anna," I say, never taking my eyes off the young blonde woman, who I admit is comely. "I would appreciate it if you would clean the room, given you are already here. It has not been thorough of late."

"Dede," Killian mutters, stuffing his flaccid cock into his pants. Meanwhile, Anna thrusts her skirts down and scurries off to clean the chamber, her face bright pink.

"No need for vexation, my lord." Killian is not a lord. He is merely the king's chancellor, who sees himself as more through me. "A virile man is free to take pleasure where he may. I do not hold you at fault."

A flash of anger sparks in his eyes before a timely knock upon the open door. It is a day for interruptions, it would seem.

"Killian, you are needed at the gates!" the guard announces.

Killian snatches up his sword, scabbard, and belt, and with a glare in my direction, quits the room.

In his absence, I exhale a tight breath, my hands shaking. This stress is a dark, oppressive cloud following me around, one that cannot be endured forever. For two years, I have been living under this shroud.

Two long years.

I'm interrupted from my melancholy by the return of the maid. "I am sorry," she says. Anna is pretty, and Killian has ever had an eye for the lasses of the keep.

I wave a dismissive hand. Anna is the least of my concerns.

"He said you were a..." she starts, and I raise a brow. "A lady without passions."

An inelegant snort escapes me. "A 'frigid bitch' is his preferred choice of words, I believe. No need to coat it in honey, Anna. I am all that and more."

I am small and unremarkable, with hazel eyes and hair somewhere between blonde and brown. Few men would notice me were I not the sole heir and unwed daughter of a weak king. "Leave," I say, losing all pretense of patience.

Bobbing a curtsy, she gathers the bucket, clothes, dustpan, and brush, then scurries out of the room. The *click* as the door shuts is a blessed relief.

Once upon a time, my chamber brought me joy. The spacious suite is decorated in lilac and green, with gold details on the swags of my charming four-poster bed. A wide window overlooks a corner of the courtyard and the meadow and river to the south. Much has changed over the years since I was a child, space for toys giving way to a long reading couch and a small table that can be used for dining or work. It is my retreat, a place of my own, where I can read or sit upon the high stool and peer out at the goings-on around the castle.

But everything changed after my mother died. My father withdrew from life, and a year later, Grady, the man I was ready to commit my life to, quit his position as commander of the army, heading north to where his familial estate was besieged by the Blighten, taking fifty warriors with him, most of them alphas. Ours wasn't the only kingdom losing men to the war, and raiders soon found easy pickings among kingdoms short of soldiers.

Two years on, and the once-respected commander has still not returned.

I don't know if Grady still lives, and I am torn by guilt that in his absence, I sought protection and comfort with Byron.

Still, it is hard to regret Byron, who while young, has more virtue in his little finger than can be found in the whole of Killian.

My room is not only my room, for I am forced to endure Killian's increasingly less subtle marking of my space. He fucks maids over my furniture and has seeded my bedding more than once. My bed is no longer my sanctuary, but a place where I suffer lingering scents no amount of cleaning or changing of covers can ever fully disguise.

This is coming to a head. In the eyes of the court, I belong to Killian.

Killian, who many people view as the savior of Langetta after Grady left us.

Killian, who everyone presumes to one day claim me as his wife.

Killian, my father's chancellor, an alpha and an excellent swordsman, with raiders in his back pocket.

Killian, who likes to rut women in my room and defile my personal things.

My father turns a blind eye to what his chancellor does to his daughter. I stare out the window, through which I can see a smattering of clouds in an otherwise blue sky. I'm still waiting, I realize sadly, for Grady to return, bitter, angry, lost, desperate, and yet childishly hopeful in the dark of night, when dreams of him haunt me.

"*I will return,*" Grady said that fateful day as he brushed tears from my cheeks with the pad of his thumb. I was only eighteen then, barely a woman, still wide-eyed with wonder at the world and in love. Oh, fool me, I'd been so in love.

Killian, who was suspiciously absent when the alphas left for the war, returned. Shortly after, our former chancellor mysteriously died, and Killian took his place. Raiding increased. Killian threatened to leave if he wasn't given his dues, and my father, in a moment of weakness, relented, making Killian the commander of the guard in addition to his chancellor duties, citing that we needed stability within the castle. Soon after, Killian began his seduction, which turned into persuasion, which deteriorated into thinly veiled threats to abandon us and take half the remaining guards with him if I didn't show him favor.

Guilt assaults me.

That my father isn't a stronger man, lost still as he is to his grief.

That a young alpha is the only thing between me and the more powerful Killian.

That the rumors about Killian having the cutthroats and raiders in his pocket are true.

That I am too young and naïve and believe still that Grady will return and save us all.

Ticktock. Ticktock.

Time is running out, I sense it as assuredly as I hear a ticking clock upon the mantle over the cold stone fireplace of my chamber.

Ticktock. Ticktock.

Every option I have left fills me with dread. The kindly herb mistress who helps me disguise what I am has cautioned me that I cannot take the herbs forever. Now I am trapped in a corner, caught in my own web of fool deceptions, and I'm at a loss for how to escape.

"Dede!" I turn as my door is flung open to admit Mia, my one dear friend through the hellish last two years. "They have returned, and Killian stopped them at the gate. Please, you need to come!"

"Who?" I ask, frowning as I allow Mia to drag me from the room.

"Grady!" she says. "The Blighten have retreated. Grady and those who left for the war are back!"

૬•

Byron

"Grady is back!"

I grunt, shaking Barnaby off after he slams me against a wall in his enthusiasm to waylay me. He is built like a strip of wind and is a clumsy oaf who does not realize his strength.

Wait? Grady?

"What the fuck?" I mutter, my brain turning to mush as I try to process this news. Relief washes over me because Grady is a badass fucker who will finally knock Killian off his perch. Unfortunately for me, Killian won't be the only one displaced by the former commander's return. Gritting my teeth, I temper a growl. I'll not give Dede up. The bastard abandoned her and Langetta to the dogs. Although it aggrieved me at the time that I was considered too young to go to war, with hindsight, I'm glad because Dede was not alone with Killian. Now Grady rides back like a conquering hero after two fucking years? He can go fuck himself sideways, him and fucking Declan, who is doubtless at his side.

At least Dede knows I want her and not her title. I swear I would sell my soul to the devil for another moment buried inside her magical pussy that takes all of my cock, even if she is yet to be coaxed to take the knot... Some betas can take one, it just requires a little time and training. I am so patient, I should have a fucking award for how patient I've been. Now I wonder if I've been *too* fucking patient. I am convinced that on more than one occasion, her protest that I drive too deeply is accompanied by poorly disguised groans.

"You need to come," Barnaby says, jolting me from a well-scripted fantasy where Dede finally takes me to the root. Grabbing hold of my arm, he hauls me out of the shadows and into the bustling courtyard, where he stabs a finger in the direction of the battlements. "Dede has gone up there. You need to stop her before she gets hurt!"

Clarity crashes through the fog.

The locked gate, the men on sentry with arrows poised, Killian up on the battlements, lording over his small power.

He is impeding Grady's entry.

If Dede is up there, she will assuredly place herself in the crossfire of a confrontation of epic proportions. "Call any loyal guards," I say before taking off at a jog. Barnaby calls after me something about not getting myself killed.

I would ride into the jaws of hell for Dede and even challenge Killian, though I would probably fucking fail. I asked her to leave with me. There is nothing for her here, just a dying king and a decaying castle, and the path before us fraught with danger because I know I cannot best Killian.

Now Grady is back, and a different threat is before me, one I do not welcome.

But I'll take Grady over Killian any day. One would be the end of Dede, the other is the end of me.

Chapter Two

Grady

L angetta Castle is a whimsical reminder of a bygone era, set upon a low stone bluff overlooking the River Tyne. The main keep hosts six towers surrounded by a wall hosting a further dozen towers and the gate house. Moss and creepers have encroached upon the outer curtain wall in places, adding to its aging beauty.

Surrounding it are lush farmlands and villages under the care of seven lords. To the east, the walled port town of Tweed Head is the major source of commerce, with bountiful fishing and shipping routes across the Lumen Sea. Despite being a smaller kingdom, Langetta has weathered the ebbs and flows of power, far enough from the border to rarely suffer Blighten attacks and wealthy enough to afford its own small army to keep bandits and raiders away.

Most Hydornian kings and queens abandoned their old ancestral castles, building stately homes instead, but I fell in love with Langetta when I came here as a temporary replacement after the previous commander died.

Five years on, and it was more than the castle that captured my attention. Dede was only eighteen, barely a woman, when a messenger came from my brother, calling me away. I wanted to wed her, for a man knows when a woman is the one, but it felt selfish on my part to claim a young lass while there was a strong possibility that I might leave her a widow.

Besides, I intended to return swiftly.

That didn't work out to plan.

The gates are closed, I realize with a frown as we ride closer, although the drawbridge is down. Soldiers cluster around the battlements near the gatehouse, weapons at the ready.

"What the fuck?" I mutter. Myself and fifty former members of the castle guard pull to a stop outside, remaining mounted, waiting for whoever is in charge to come forward and tell us what is keeping them from opening the fucking gate. A pair of riders took off for the castle when we crossed the bridge at Redland, and I assumed—wrongly—they were intending to herald our arrival. I was not expecting them to ride back and close the fucking gate like we are raiders intent upon mischief.

"It would seem we are not welcome." Declan nudges his horse in beside mine.

I'm confused. I expected...what? What the hell did I expect? It was supposed to be for a few weeks, but weeks turned into seasons and seasons into two years. My brother mentioned troubles consuming the rest of Hydornia with so many deployed to the war, so what fucking choice did I have? My brother's estate is north of here, close to the border with the Blighten. Should his kingdom have fallen, the Blighten would have moved south unchecked, until even the beautiful Langetta fell.

I could no more ignore my brother's call than stand by while the Blighten attacked Langetta

"You're going to need to lie," Declan says.

I swivel on my horse to face him. With his shaggy dark hair and beard, Declan is a herculean alpha and one of the few men taller than me.

Grinning, he shrugs his big shoulders. "You're not fucking welcome." He gestures toward the battlement, where twitchy soldiers eyeball us. "My guess is your successor is comfortable and doesn't want you around fucking that up, so you lie. Say you are traveling south, stopping by each estate to give them the news of the war before returning north to your brother's home and where the threat of Blighten lingers. They will be obliged to offer you hospitality. To do anything else would be to declare war upon your brother."

I don't like that his words make sense, nor the unease churning in my gut.

What has fucking happened? I swallow past the lump in my throat, but it is not only worry that stokes me. No, it is also rage.

Dede?

"I concede to your excellent advice," I say. "Tell the men what I'm doing."

We wait another long while before a new cluster of men appear above the gate.

Killian? Tall for an alpha, with a thin face and scraggly beard, he's a former member of the guard, who was suspiciously absent when the alphas left with me. Proud of his prowess as a swordsman, and skilled, from what I remember, Killian was not command material and seemed more interested in lifting the lasses' skirts than applying himself to his duties.

"Please tell me the king has not put that useless bastard in charge of the castle's well-being," Declan mutters beside me.

The sickness roiling within me tells me he has.

"Hail, Killian!" I call, plastering on a bright smile that is all teeth. Hopefully, the small distance between us disguises the hostility in my eyes. "I bring news from Borne to relay to the king before I must move on. What prevents the gates from opening? Are they broken, that you would keep a messenger waiting?"

I can see the bastard gritting his teeth even from here. The soldiers beside him grow ever more twitchy, and a couple of them go so far as to aim arrows upon us.

"What madness is this? Open the gate at once!" The new voice is familiar to me, one that has whispered in my ear on the eve of battles and on rare quiet moments. One that has guided my hand in the brief respites from the fighting, when I take my cock in hand to find relief.

"These are Borne men seeking an audience with my father," she hisses, her voice carrying on the breeze. "It is not your place to decide on their passage, nor to bring war upon Langetta for breaking old traditions."

Then I see it all—the way Killian looks at her, the way he fists her arm after barking orders for the gate to be opened.

Fisting *her* fucking arm.

Every muscle in my body coils with tension. My hand is on the hilt of my sword, my knees squeezing my horse as I ready to charge, and the gates are not fucking open yet.

"Peace, brother," Declan says as he brings his horse to bear, putting it between me and my quarry, shielding my foolish actions from our watchers. "Let us gain entry and assess the situation. We cannot start a fucking war until we get the lay of the land."

All he says is right and sensible, but as the great wooden gate lumbers up, I battle the potency of my rage.

Is she his? There is familiarity in his touch, possessiveness, fucking *ownership*.

"We have been gone for two years." Declan's steady gaze holds mine. "They could be wedded and Dede may have pushed out a couple of whelps by now."

My nostrils flare. His attempts to cool my temper are a mile off the mark. I don't care if she is his, I realize. Before I leave, I will kill him and claim her regardless.

Declan grimaces, reading my thoughts upon my face. "Peace, brother," he repeats.

Behind me, I sense the readiness of my men. All are battle hardened alphas who will follow me without question, but I am not reckless and I will keep myself in check.

I nod, and Declan huffs out a breath before his lips tug up. "Hold that thought. Something tells me your quest for blood will come soon enough."

❧

We move forward, horses at a walk, under the portcullis to enter the inner bailey. A few of the soldiers give me a wary nod, but most stand on duty without meeting my eyes. The once well cared for leatherwear and armor of the guards has taken on a shabby edge. Obviously, they have not been oiled, cleaned, or conditioned in many months. The castle itself suffers similar disrepair, with weeds littering the pristine courtyard of my memories.

I do not recognize this prideless place.

As we dismount, Killian is waiting for me, flanked by whom I presume to be his high-ranking men.

Dede is not here.

I know some of the men with Killian, although an equal

number are new to me. To his right is Peter, an older alpha who showed me the ropes when I first arrived and a man I considered a friend. An old battle injury prevents him from riding a horse, which is the only reason he remained behind when I left.

He meets my eyes, and there is something there, a silent communication, but I look away first, letting my eyes skim over those gathered. I will find a way to talk to Peter directly...or maybe Declan would draw less attention.

"The king is busy," Killian says, a belligerent set to his jaw.

"Busy?" I keep my tone light, despite the urge to break every finger in his hand for touching Dede. "I will wait. This news is important."

"You are not riding on to other estates," he says. "Do not take me for a fool."

I raise a brow, sensing my men shift behind me in subtle readiness. Killian has just tossed an insult at my feet. "Are you calling me a liar?" I ask with a casual air I do not feel. The idiot cannot be making it that easy for me, can he?

His eyes lower, although he wears a cocky smirk that makes me want to knock every one of his teeth out as I ram my fist down his throat. "A poor choice of words. The king is not often well of a morning." He shrugs. "Or an afternoon, or an evening sometimes. I'll arrange some space for you and your men in the barn while you wait on an audience. Although it has been known to take him days or weeks to rouse himself."

So this is his game? To make us wait this out in the fucking barn eating food laced with rat droppings until our bellies revolt and we quit the estate of our own accord. What a fucking welcome this turned out to be. Two years of fighting the green-skinned bastards who do the Blighten's bidding, two fucking years of hell, mud, and blood, only to be treated worse than beggars. Meanwhile, Killian is touching Dede...

Declan's words of caution are the only things staying my

hand from reaching for my sword. I do not know this castle anymore. I do not recognize a single fucking thing, save a sweet woman who is every bit as fiery and beautiful as I remember.

She still has her fire.

"We will wait," I say with an incline of my head.

Chapter Three

Dede

"Take your hands off her, assholes," Byron rumbles, stalking toward us along the stone corridor, his face a picture of alpha savagery.

The two beta guards wilt under his censorious glare, coming to a grinding halt no more than a pace away from my quarters. With sandy brown hair, blue eyes, and a blond beard, Byron tops the two guards by head and shoulders. The guards' hands tremble where they grip my arms as they stand their ground. Byron may be an alpha, but he is a gentle giant and young enough that I feel bad for how much I lean upon his support and protection.

Thick fingers, that can drive me near delirious with pleasure, grasp the throat of the nearest beta when he does not immediately comply.

The guard wheezes and drops my arm, Byron smirking as he releases the man. He is still very much an alpha, for all he is overly concerned with harming me whenever we are together.

That would be my fault for letting him think I am a beta, although I do not believe any woman, omega or otherwise, would view his cock with anything but a measure of nervous trepidation and a challenge to be broached in stages. He is the first and only man I have lain with, yet I have it on good authority from Mia, who is more experienced in such things, that my improvised approximation of the length and girth using a rolled scarf is significantly larger than average, even for an alpha.

"We are to stand on watch," the guard says, before losing his nerve and taking a step back.

"Go ahead then," Byron says, scowling at the man before returning his attention to me. "Are you going to be okay?"

He is asking a deeper question, as evidenced by his sensitive eyes. Grady, who once held all my love and the whole of my heart, is back. I cannot lie, more than a lingering spark remains for the man who, through cruel circumstances, was forced to leave both Langetta and me. Although I try to school my features, the softening of Byron's face tells me he recognizes this too. "I don't know," I answer honestly.

"I need to check what the fuck is happening. Maybe I can speak to him for you," he says. Then he turns and strides down the corridor, leaving me with the guards who nervously indicate my room.

I don't argue, now is not the time, but once inside, I pace and reflect upon my woes. My whole body begins shaking as I move back and forth before the window. The sky is blue outside, but in this room, a storm is brewing. I am waiting, I realize, to be liberated from my ever darkening nightmare.

No call comes, no one beats upon the door, and no sounds of battle come from the courtyard far below. As Killian sent me inside with two of his loyal men fisting my arms, I heard the distinct sound of the gate lifting. Was it done to lure Grady and his men forward so they could be killed easier?

Pacing, I wring my hands, muttering under my breath. I need to talk to my father. I need to do a lot of things, and I can't do any of them because I'm locked in my damn room. Hopefully, Mia is not also incarcerated. Killian will not be pleased if he learns she forewarned me of Grady's return. Doubtless, his men will also be quick to report Byron for speaking to me.

The direction of my thoughts is not helpful. Now, it's not only Grady I worry about, but my dear friend Mia, who stood by me and kept me sane through the darkest parts of the last two years.

Tears of anger well in my eyes. So close, and yet Grady may as well be at the far reaches of Hydornia still. He looked different in that tiny glimpse, older, harder, battle weary, and scarred, yet when our eyes met, the same spark flared between us.

Declan is still at his side, and given that man takes nothing seriously, I found myself worrying about him too on occasion. There was a time when I thought the two of them might be more than friends, when I viewed Declan with a measure of jealousy because he was close to the man I'd worshiped from afar. But no, Declan has only been good humored if teasing with me, which never changed, even after Grady declared his feelings for me, so I must have been mistaken about a relationship between them.

Goddess, how I missed them both, hungering for Grady and his return. Poor fool that I am, I am ready to incur Killian's wrath for a fleeting glimpse of Grady, so I might fill up my memories of his face and my heart with giddy hope.

Yet the world has moved on, and I've changed as much as he likely has, perhaps more.

When he climbed into the saddle and rode out the gates

with fifty of the castle's best alphas, I was still innocent, but that is not the case anymore, and not only because of my decision to lay with Byron. Now I am broken down and weary from my own battles, ones so different and yet equally challenging to the ones Grady has endured.

So many emotions assault me, it's hard to decide which must take precedence. To see him after so long, only to find out he intends to move on, is a cruel blow. I still love him, I realize, just as fiercely as I loved him the day he left. Now I must consider Byron, my protector, who comforted me and acted as a safe place during the storm of the last two years. I cannot unmake my feelings toward Byron any more than I can turn off what I once felt for Grady.

But this is Hydornia, and in Hydornia, an omega mates with only one male.

I swallow. Across the Lumen Sea is a land belonging to the Imperium, where omegas are mated to three or more alphas, sometimes as many as five or six. I would not be averse to two men, were they Grady and Byron, even though that is not our way here.

Fearing Killian might force an unwelcome bonding upon me, I hid my nature. Byron is a huge alpha, but he is no match for Killian with a sword. It is reaching the stage where I am considering Byron's whispered urgings to leave the castle and my home behind.

Now, hope blooms, but it's a tenuous kind, given Grady is leaving once he speaks to my father, although goodness knows how long that might take. My father is not well, weak in mind and body, and he dwells in memories of better times, when my mother still lived. In this enduring state of grief, it does not matter to my father that his daughter, the product of their great love for one another, withers and dies a slow, ugly death of neglect. He was not always thus. Once, he was proud and noble and ruled his kingdom—small though it may be—with compassion, respect, and strength. I do not know if that version of him still exists, or whether he can be roused from his deep sleep. Sorrow rises inside me too, for my mother, for these circumstances beyond my control, and for the path laid out before me.

We all have choices. We can pick ourselves up in moments of strife and rise above, or we can wallow in loss and disappointment. I miss my mother and the joy she brought into our lives, and the stability that was present when she and my father ruled our lands.

Pacing over to the window, I fling it open and strain to see and hear as much as I possibly can. From here, I can only view a small portion of the courtyard, the rest hidden behind lower level roofs. The sounds are the normal ones of the everyday activities that go on within a castle and keep—the clatter of horses' hooves upon the cobbles, the occasional cry or call. Nothing is out of the ordinary.

The lost side of me craves the sounds of battle, but none come.

The sun is still high. It is a pleasant day, and were it not for this business, I might have walked the orchards in an echo of my past life, taking a few precious moments to forget about Killian and his plans to take over our kingdom.

Killian is a weak alpha. He is not weak like my father, but in a different kind of way. He would make a poor king—a poorer king than my father, which is saying something. Killian is the sort of man who can only realize his greatest potential while under the firm direction of a better man. No such men lingered here to keep Killian in check, and in the absence of a guiding hand, he has run amok.

Sounds of a disturbance come from beyond my chamber door, and my head swings to look back over my shoulder. My heart rate rises to an erratic tattoo as I wonder if my dream is finally about to come to fruition and Grady is about to break down the door.

When the door opens, it's not Grady but Mia who slips inside before shoving the door shut again. "Goddess! You would not believe the fuss those guards made, and all I'm asking is to speak to you!"

"Mia! What is it?" I demand. "What has happened?"

"I had to make promises to the guards outside so they would let me in." She rolls her eyes dramatically.

I bite my lip, surprised amusement can still rouse within me. Mia is renowned for making promises that are not always fulfilled. I'm relieved the guards are foolish enough to fall for her words...and her cleavage, which she undoubtedly put on display as she was wrapping them around her finger.

"Killian ordered them to be kept in the barn, and at this time of year! The nerve of the man when there is no hay to soften the ground for them after the raiders burned so many crops this year past. Ordered them to bed down there like they are peasants looking for work and not heroes who kept our lands safe from the Blighten."

"Did Killian inform my father?" I ask.

Mia shrugs. "Knowing Killian, I think it unlikely. Why would he? More likely, he's going to put something in their food tonight that will make them puke their guts up or empty their bowels in the most uncomfortable of ways."

I grimace, wondering if I can do aught about it, although Grady is surely intelligent enough to recognize the hostility in these thinly veiled insults.

"Killian is many things, but he is not a fool. He will make it difficult for Grady to meet with my father, even though it might start a war." I almost wish it would, although no one goes to war willingly, and certainly not a man like Grady's brother, who has spent two years battling Blighten orcs. No, Grady will move on.

They will stay until it becomes apparent that they will never speak to my father. Perhaps a servant or member of the castle guard will forewarn Grady that my father is not the man he was.

"You could leave with them," Mia suggests.

"Leave?" I frown, caught off guard by her suggestion that echoes the one Byron has made.

"You and Byron. Grady would take you, I'm sure of it."

I wish Mia would not put such thoughts into my broken mind nor fill my heart with hopes. I would go anywhere with Grady and Byron, even if it meant abandoning Langetta. Anywhere with anyone would be better than here.

I shake my head, stupid tears welling behind my eyes.

"Why not?" she asks. "Why would you not take this chance? You have no life here, and your father is a lost man. How long before his grief takes him completely? Then you would be wedded to Killian, and sweet Byron will die trying to save you. You know what lies before you, Dede, and what this is about. Killian wants to be the king. Goddess! Can you imagine him as king? He is useless now, and he is only the commander of the army and the chancellor. What is Killian? He is nothing, yet he lords his small power over everyone.

"No, there is only torment, anger, and pain for you here, more than you already suffered in losing your dear mother, and ever more bleakness consuming Langetta."

"It is not so simple. How can I abandon my home, my father, and my people to that man?"

"Are you prepared to risk your life, or Byron's? Better you try to leave with Grady now, than on your own later. I know you were waiting for his return, hoping for it, yet it's not only about you now, but also about Byron."

She is right, and her words cut through the indecision that has consumed many sleepless nights. I want to leave, I acknowledge, because desolation and homelessness would be better than the tyranny I endure.

"You cannot linger here," I say. "Killian is sure to check on me. Better he not know we have spoken, than for you to incur his wrath as a result. The guards will hold their tongue for your promise."

"Let me see what I can find out," she says. "I'll speak to Grady, at least to judge if he will help you to flee."

This is happening. I am really contemplating abandoning my familial home...and my father.

"He is not your father anymore," Mia says, like she can read my thoughts. "You need to protect yourself, lest Byron try to get himself killed."

Today has already been like a wild tumble down a steep hill, and the tumbling is not yet done with me. My lips tremble as my eyes meet those of my dear, best friend. I imagined a thousand scenarios of Grady returning, but none of them ended with him sleeping in the barn before quitting Langetta and us not speaking a single word.

Did I read my memories wrong? Did I presume greater feelings between us than truly exist?

"Stop it," she admonishes. "You have been strong this long, so you can be strong a little more. Maybe Grady will come to his senses and remember the promise he made you. You still love him. It's written all over your face."

"I was a child then," I say, emotional pain lancing me as effectively as a knife. "It is not so clear cut now."

The thought of leaving Byron is every bit as debilitating as the heartache I suffered when Grady left two years ago.

"You were a woman in every way save being claimed by a man," Mia says. "He left you, and you found something unexpected with another alpha. I do not blame Grady for leaving, any more than you are at fault for coming to love Byron. Grady is a noble man, and he thought he was doing what was best for all Hydornia, but he went and did not bother to check upon your well-being in all that time. I cannot easily forgive him for that. He owes you, Dede, at least to help you to escape. I can find some good will toward him should he give you that much."

Leaning in, she steals a swift hug before slipping through the door.

Mia barely leaves before Killian arrives. I have been dreading this moment. Truth be told, I suffer every time he is in my chamber, but today, I dread it more. One glance tells me Killian is a man still holding all the power within the castle, and in his eyes, I see my hopes being crushed and the wreckage coming for my life.

Chapter Four

Grady

The barn is fucking empty.

How can a barn be empty at this time of year? On one side, our horses are lined up and corralled, eating a few handfuls of silage and a miserly amount of hay. On the other side, we lay out our bedrolls over scattered scraps of straw.

Declan is chuckling. Declan is always fucking chuckling about some mischief or other and finds amusement in the darkest of moments. His dry humor, even in the worst of times, is nothing short of legendary and one of the reasons I got through the war.

We are not at war anymore, at least not the one familiar to me—the one against the Blighten. I can handle orcs, for I understand their ways, their weaknesses, and their strengths, but the slow, creeping death that consumes Langetta castle is as foreign to me as the Imperium lands across the sea, where the king is the king of all and not a small castle and surrounding estates.

This new silent enemy, this terrifying awakening approaching me is a thousand times worse than any club brandishing orc.

Dede?

As I stare broodingly out the open barn door into the courtyard, I worry about Dede, about what is happening here, and about a million and one other things when I look at the decay befalling this once vibrant castle.

"So, we're gonna sit around here with our hands up our asses for a few days, are we?"

Turning, I find Declan rolling out his bedroll beside mine. "You are the one who cautioned me to get the lay of the land," I point out with a scowl.

Big shoulders shrug, and after finishing with his task, he comes to join me. "Aye, I did, but now we've seen the place, so to speak. Reckon we should just go and skewer the bastard. Killian was always a whining whelp—now he's a whining whelp with power. Clearly, it has gone to his head."

I sigh heavily, surmising as much myself. Yet we are not close to understanding the situation here, despite Declan's determination otherwise. I doubt this will change while, as he so eloquently stated, we are all but prisoners in a barn with our hands up our asses, awaiting some mystical event that will indicate the king actually wants to speak.

Before we left, Ellis was fading after the death of his beloved wife, but he still retained his intellect and will for life, and he loved his daughter, Dede, the image of her mother and their cherished only child. I cannot believe what I am seeing, yet my eyes do not deceive me. The castle crumbles, with brick walls in need of repairs, broken cobbles, and rotting wood. A cloud lingers over the place and manifests in the way people walk around, shoulders slumped, eyes bleak.

They are barely surviving. At this time of year, the barn

should be brimming with hay, ready to feed livestock through the winter. There is fuck all here, making me wonder what the food stores are like. While raiding may cause some problems, the kingdom maintains its own army, with enough men for regular patrols, to protect the castle, towns, and villages.

How could this happen? How could it fall so far?

Now I'm here, witnessing the decline of this once grand family, I blame myself for not thinking beyond warring with the Blighten, who have besieged the northern kingdoms.

In those brief moments of respite when I might have lifted my head, we were busy shoring up defenses. I spent as much time with a workman's tool in my hand as a sword. Whatever needed doing, we soldiers labored beside the ordinary folk because the jobs needed to be fucking done, and we did so with humor and purpose. In times of war, that is what you fucking do.

Very little word came from beyond our lands and the neighboring estates. Most of the news went outward.

News of the battles and skirmishes.

News of whether we were winning or losing.

News of whether we thought this might ever fucking end.

There were occasional reports of infighting between duchies, disgruntlement, and even dishonesty. The lords, dukes, kings, and queens live untroubled lives. In the southernmost parts of Hydornia, and particularly the capital, they are still occupied with parties, grand balls, and whatnot, too far removed from Blighten raids to grant them much attention. To them, orcs and wars are fanciful tales they beguile guests with over dinner.

I would summon bitterness, but they have ever been this way. Short of tossing a rotting orc head upon the high king's table, I cannot see this changing, though I considered such an approach more than once while knee-deep in mud and blood, fighting for my life.

"We don't know what has happened," Declan says, for once serious. He does have occasional bouts of seriousness in between the humor. We are as different as night and day, me the second son of a king and to whom soldiering started as a game, while Declan is a former orphan street rat, with a coarse accent and rough manner. Yet the man is as noble as any lord in deeds and ways.

"No," I say. "I do not." I really wish I did.

"He was in a gloomy frame of mind when we left," Declan continues, talking of the king I presume.

"He is a king," I say, "and a king must move past personal grief to endure for the sake of his people. I see no evidence of a king."

"Killian could be drugging him?" Declan says. "Fuck knows. The place is rancid like a cancerous wound—open and festering. No joy resides here. We need to ask questions. The castle folks are sure to be nervous at first, maybe avoid us. I'm thinking Killian has put the word out that we are not to be spoken to and threatened a beating on anyone who does. Give it some time, and people will start to come to us."

Remembering Killian's hand upon Dede, and the familiarity of the gesture, makes me break out in a cold sweat. My fingers itch for my sword. "What about between now and then?"

"They're going to give us some half rotten food that will give us the fucking runs. Yep, going to be eating dry travel crackers until we can resolve this. It was only ever meant to be a small stint at your brother's estate." He gestures toward our men, who are similarly preparing their bedrolls and checking saddlebags for rations. "This is their home, as much as it is yours now. They would not have journeyed back here with you otherwise."

He does not mention it is *his* home, making me aware of changes between us that began when I first declared for Dede. She bloomed swiftly from a girl to a woman, and I was not alone in noticing. The lass was always tongue-tied around Declan, who is considered a devilish type of handsome and an abominable tease. She would not be the only lass confused about whether Declan's attention is terrifying, arousing, or both, but he also does not confine himself to only lasses, and at times, he looked at me much as he looked at Dede.

I always imagined Declan would be around until the end of my life. Only now, as I suspect he is considering moving on, do I acknowledge the void his absence would leave. I feel selfish in my presumptuousness and wonder about the man I have come to know in all ways save one.

Returning here is stirring up much sediment, and I'm yet to determine if this is a useful development. Langetta is my home now, where I intended to spend the remainder of my life with the young woman who is now older and who I don't recognize in many ways.

Declan is right—a day at a time, and we will get through this.

"We shall see," I say.

"Don't have any choice." Declan slaps me on the shoulder, grinning like a fucking madman.

A tentative knock upon the barn door beside us heralds the arrival of a young lad.

"Barnaby?" Declan's brows draw together briefly before his face splits in a grin.

I study the lad with the lanky build of one growing too fast for muscles to catch up.

Barnaby grins a familiar grin—Peter's son.

"You remember me!" Barnaby exclaims, beaming. "You are a sight for sore eyes. Ma said you would return, and we hoped for a good long while. Many gave up hope, but I never did."

"Barnaby!" a gruff voice calls from outside. He is a guard I do not recognize, a newcomer who joined after we departed. "Move away from the barn unless you want a whipping."

"I'll come by later, if I can." Barnaby winks. "The lazy bastards all fall asleep as soon as it goes dark."

Declan's grin widens as Barnaby hurries off.

"The lad will talk," Declan says, nodding approvingly.

"As long as somebody fucking talks," I say.

It is an opening, a small fucking opening, but I will grasp any opportunity under the circumstances. In the absence of anything else to do, I sit down on my bedroll, lie back, and put my hands behind my head. I think about the girl who stood upon the battlements, boldly calling out the man who later fisted her by the arm.

My fist clenches as I remember Killian touching Dede, even as I consider what else might have transpired during my absence.

I will deal with Killian, with Dede, and whatever else may come.

Chapter Five

Dede

"That bitch has been in here, hasn't she?" Killian eyes every corner of the room like he expects Mia to be hiding underneath the bed.

It's not actually so ridiculous, for I might have taken such an approach had he arrived a few minutes ago. I can't allow Mia to become caught up in this, and I worry she might incur Killian's wrath. Goddess, that sweet woman is fierce, loyal, and unwavering with her love, and I'm blessed a thousand times over to have her as a friend.

"I don't know what you're talking about," I say. "You sent me in here under guard, and don't pretend that was for my protection. How much lower can you possibly sink to call Mia a bitch and seek to prevent me from speaking to her."

His nostrils flare as my words tumble out of the desperate, bitter place inside me.

My outburst is not helpful. Nothing is. I need to be polite, to maintain the status quo until I can flee.

Flee? Am I really going to run away and leave my home? Can I abandon it to this man, this monster, this wannabe king? Killian doesn't even do his job anymore, hasn't in a long while. Rumors circle the castle, and Mia makes sure I'm kept informed about how the guards grow lazy, how they rarely patrol the outlying villages and farmsteads. Most nights, Killian can be found in the great hall, drinking beer and rutting, when he should do his damn job.

Tomorrow, I promise myself, things will change. Only I promised myself as much far too many times already, and still, it has not come to be.

"I know she was in here," Killian says as he grasps my shoulders. He has put his hands upon me in anger before, left bruises where he gripped too hard, and shaken me on occasion. Today, I am like a flag flapping in a storm. I'm petite, and once I revealed as an Omega, I understood why. Where Byron's gentle ways comfort me, Killian's strength and power cows me.

Suddenly, I am thrust away. I suffer a terrifying notion he's going to hit me...and he does. The sharp sound as his palm connects with my cheek is shocking and precedes pain that robs me of breath. He has never struck me before, though he threatened to. He's made all kinds of ridiculous threats and followed through on some of them, but tonight, a line is crossed, one which cannot be uncrossed. I am shocked by both my vulnerability and by how much it hurts. Perhaps I should be more surprised he held back this long.

He stabs a finger in my face. "Don't fucking test me."

We both shake—me with terror, Killian with rage.

His finger lowers, and he begins pacing. "The bastard will be gone soon. Once he is, things are going to change. I waited too fucking long. I've seen you scurrying off to your little herb mistress to rid yourself of Byron's whelps. I wasn't ready to push it before and turned a blind eye, but I'm willing to push matters now. You won't be seeing her or Byron again."

The dark gods walk over my grave, and coldness sweeps down my spine. How did we come to this? A year ago, I tolerated Killian, but now we are the deepest, most embittered enemies. In part, I am relieved by his presumption, even though the thought of harming Byron's unborn child sickens me, but it is not true. I go to her for a very different reason.

I tremble from the pain radiating from my cheek, but also with a potent mixture of emotions and outrage at how unjust this is. What right does Killian have to me, my title, or this castle? To the people who live here? None. He fails his one job in commanding our guards, and he is no chancellor either, unless you call his alliance with the cutthroat bandits to be a contribution to the crown. He should be put to the whipping post for his negligence alone. That is the truth of this—his right and entitlement are summarily less than none.

My fear and anger manifests in a shake that becomes so violent, I can barely stand.

"Don't look at me like that," he says, face twisting into a sneer, fingers curling into a fist. "Don't look at me like you're confused about how this happened and where this is going." Heaving a deep breath, he brings his pacing to a stop. "I want you fat with my whelp. Once you're with child, Langetta will be mine." His face turns a ruddy shade of red as vitriol he's never voiced before tumbles out. "Your father is as good as dead and has been for a long while now."

Words become knives stabbing into my belly, more painful than my throbbing cheek, more shocking than the fact he, an upstart, dared to slap me, the daughter of a king.

Yet I'm not safe, and until I am, I must bide my time, bite my tongue, and endure.

Endure? What does that mean? Am I enduring? Not very well. I'm failing, cracking, my skin breaking apart under the pressure of living every day.

"There will be no herb woman," he repeats, hands fisted at his side, his whole body seeming to thrum with the potency of his rage. "And Byron, you can be sure I will deal with him."

I swallow bile down. The young alpha is well liked within the castle, and I wonder what Killian can do without backlash. Could he hurt Byron, or discredit him? Perhaps order him banished? I don't know Killian anymore. He puts his hands upon me with violence and seeks to claim me for his wife. He has lost the Goddess' way. The whole castle weeps as our lives turn desolate when they do not need to be. Yet all this falls into insignificance beside the life of a young man I have placed into the path of danger. The urge for action is like ants under my skin. I cannot wait for Grady. I was foolish to delay this long. I am ready to flee, to quit my once vibrant home and go somewhere, anywhere, else. Anything is better than living under this tyranny and Byron suffering as a result.

Killian turns and strides from the room, slamming the door into the jamb.

My knees nearly give way in the absence of his suffocating presence. Guards are posted outside, but I still push myself into a stumbled run and throw open the door. I glare at the two men who dare to hold me prisoner. They both shift their stance and do not venture to meet my eyes, uncomfortable with their orders.

"I wish to visit my father," I say to the nearest man. Killian has not yet turned the corner, and his boots sound in the distance as he strides down the corridor toward the hall.

"You cannot leave your chamber," the guard says gruffly. His gaze lowers to my cheek, which throbs in an echo of the blow, before skittering away. I'm glad he is uncomfortable. He *should* be, given he abandoned his vows to protect Langetta and its people.

"I want to visit my father," I repeat, but the man is not looking at me anymore. He is staring straight ahead, as is his companion.

Should I try to step over the boundary? Recklessness invades me, charging me with the urge to take risks.

"I want to see my father," I say once again.

Nothing. They give me nothing, so I slam the door and go back inside.

Alone, I fall prey to the demons that consume my mind in the darkest hours of the night. I feel dizzy and a little sick. On the table is a water jug and I go to fill a cup, but I'm shaking so badly, I can't hold the cup against my lips. I spill a little, but I manage to gulp a few mouthfuls down.

Putting the cup aside, I tentatively touch my aching cheek. My eyes go to the window, beyond which is the courtyard, and although I cannot see from here, I orientate myself in the direction of the barn where Grady is, along with the fifty alphas he took two years ago, all returned miraculously whole.

No, not entirely whole. They will have seen horrors and monsters during the years they were away. On returning, they should have been welcomed with jubilation and cheers as they passed the threshold of the gate.

We should not house them in the barn. We should host a feast for them, but instead, they meet this dour, depressed environment.

So close. My hand reaches toward the barn as though I might be able to touch him.

Surely the Goddess will see how desperate things grow here?

But she is only one, and she has many to care for, many who suffer far more greatly than I.

And isn't that a pity?

꘎

Byron

I should have anticipated this was coming—Grady's return, Dede charging up the battlements and calling Killian out. The castle chancellor turned commander of the guard always hated me. I've been discreet about the intimate nature of my relationship with Dede, but it's fair to assume most castle residents know we are more than friends.

Not one but five betas corner me as I head for the barracks to talk to Barnaby. I fight, but these are not the local guards. They are the scum who joined us over the last year—raiders and cutthroats in the pocket of Killian. There is no discussion, and they don't hesitate to give me a beating. Sturdy batons are put to efficient use, and although I take two of the bastards out in the fray, they are vicious and relentless as they knock me to the flagstones. Afterward, I am dragged off to the cells and tossed inside.

As the door rattles shut, I stagger to my feet and spit out a gob of blood. The sound of their footsteps is fading into the distance by the time I reach the door and rattle it in fury. "I recognize you, fuckers!" I shout.

They don't bother to reply, and why would they? I am locked up and out of the way.

A deep growl bubbles up in my chest, one full of menace, one I do not give voice to often. Blood drips from my nose to the stone floor, and I feel like shit, ribs aching, head aching, and right shoulder throbbing where it copped a particularly savage blow. I watch my blood spattering against the stones as the enormity of what happened crashes through my pain addled mind.

Dede is alone and unprotected. I have failed her.

Chapter Six

Fifteen years earlier...

Declan

K noll is a nothing city full of filthy, thieving bastards... like me. For as far back as I can remember, my life has been about survival—doing whatever it takes to put food in my belly. I am bold, prepared to take risks and steal food, possessions, goods, a coin purse if I can...if I'm lucky. I've been caught a few times and gotten a beating for it, kicked to the gutter and left to consider my crime. So long as it isn't the city watch rounding me up, I roll with it, pick myself up, and get back in the game.

Going to the wealthy tavern district is a risk, one that doesn't always pay off, but the icy wind and pain gnawing my gut puts danger into a different perspective. The chance of a beating is higher here, but so are the rewards. I'm freezing my nuts off, the biting northerly wind making a mockery of my thin clothes, and considering retreating to my hole for the night when they show up.

A fine carriage pulled by horses rolls up, with personal guards that sweep on ahead, rousing the innkeeper who emerges and bows his head with the kind of exaggerated deference that brings a smirk to my cold, cracked lips. A lordly man dismounts his chestnut gelding, while his wife and daughter, at a guess, emerge from a carriage. Normally, I'm on the subject with the biggest payload, yet something about the young girl draws my eye. She's a tiny, frail little thing wrapped up against the cold in a fur-trimmed cloak with all the trappings you'd expect from lordly people, but there is a grace and poise to the child unexpected in one so young.

I am leaning in the shadow of the building, but her eyes find me with an unerring accuracy that traps the frigid air in my lungs. Most ordinary folks don't notice the street whelps until we steal from them, and then they see us and scream. There is neither horror nor revulsion in her steady gaze, only curiosity.

The innkeeper is still bobbing his head, arm out in a sweeping gesture, as he ushers the family toward the beckoning heat wafting from the tavern, probably rubbing his fat fingers together in anticipation of a full coin purse coming his way soon.

But my eyes are all for a pretty, high-born lass, who likewise must tear her gaze from mine. She's distracted as her mother draws an arm around her, and something drops from her hands. Fine leather gloves with fur-trimmed cuffs to match her cloak are left sitting in the dirt as they walk by.

I move in soundlessly, instinctual now in such situations, and collect the gloves, her gloves, in my filthy hands. At first, I have no notion beyond removing them from the dirty cobbles, and it is only afterward, when they're in my possession, that I realize my hands are not much cleaner than the ground. A part of my decision to snatch the gloves is a strong, almost compulsive urge to claim something of hers, then the street rat part of me kicks in. I could sell them perhaps, but I won't make very much. They are small, designed for a child, and most of the kids I know are street rats like me. In the back of my mind, experience says lordly people sometimes reward a good deed.

The desire to keep them is strong, but so is the hunger in my belly. I'm still weighing my options when the innkeeper turns, eyes narrowing on the beautiful gloves in my hands, and screams bloody murder. Given I've rifled a thing or two from him in the past, his reaction is understandable.

The guards close in, snatching the precious gloves away and administering a sound beating. I cry foul, not that it helps me.

"Rouse the city watch!" the innkeeper cries.

"Stay your hands!" another voice calls. I peer up from where I am balled up on the ground to see the lordly man glaring, not at me, but at his guards. He makes an impatient upward motion with his fingers, and I am dragged up by the scruff of my threadbare coat to my feet. My ear throbs, my lips are bloody, and a shiner is developing on my right eye. The rest of me is equally bruised and battered. The lord's wife is holding the young girl close, watching on with jaundiced eyes, but the daughter, the lass whose gloves I touched, sobs.

"Please, Papa," she says. "Do not let them hurt him anymore."

Her father turns to me, sizing me up, seeing me for what I am. "Speak up, lad."

This is a new development. People rarely stop to ask me anything at this point.

No sense in lying about who or what I am. The guard's grip is firm, but mayhap I could wrestle free, leaving him holding my coat. Better a lost coat than be handed to the city watch, but for once, I don't want to fight or lie. Shame is a new experience for me. Before, there was only hunger and a desire to survive, but as I stand before these people, I understand the wrongness of my life thus far and firmly decide there should be more. I'm no fool, I know most people live better, even though I've always been on the outside.

"It's true," I say boldly. "I am a thief. Not the gloves, for the young miss dropped them upon the ground. But I have stolen much. I take whatever I can get my hands on because if I don't, I will starve and die."

The girl gasps, and her mother tries to urge her away. "No, Mama," she says. "I want to hear what he has to say."

The guard's hand loosens a little. Perhaps he is not wholly bad either. Even the miserly innkeeper's face softens some. He never beat me for my mischief, only roared and chased me off. An innkeeper needs to make a living too, and thieving whelps take away from him and his family.

"Where are your parents?" the lord asks.

"I have no parents, my lord. My mother died of the pox, and I have been on the streets ever since. I thought about taking the gloves and running. I might have gotten coins for them, or scraps of food, but sometimes lordly people, such as yourself, reward them with money...and sometimes they instruct innkeepers to offer a bowl of stew. I was hoping for the stew." I am deep into the fantasy now. "Maybe a crusty chunk of bread to dunk in it. Mayhap it'd be the happiest day of my life."

The young lass' lips tremble with sorrow. I meant it in humor, but it is a pitiful tale, even to my own ears.

"Papa," she says. "May he have some food?"

The innkeeper mutters under his breath, though not loudly enough for the high-born miss to hear.

"The lad is brawny" —the lord narrows his eyes on me— "with the bearing of one who might reveal an alpha."

"He'll more likely hang," the innkeeper says. "The city watch doesn't tolerate thievery. If there is a chance he'll become an alpha, they'll most likely hang him at dawn. They don't want those types roaming the streets, turning violence upon common citizens. No, better the whelp be strung up now."

Only his words don't have the desired effect. The watch still has yet to arrive, and the girl begins to cry, not noisily, just a trickling of tears over her cheeks. Her eyes do not look away from me. Many turn their noses up, openly sneering much of the time. Yet she looks upon me with something rare in my life —compassion, empathy, sorrow, and pity.

Likely, I will hang on the morrow, but I do not want her pity, so I square my shoulders. For a street urchin, I have a fair measure of pride. I may pity myself, but no one else has the right.

"Papa," she says. "We return home tomorrow. Let him come with us. We may find honest work for him within the castle. He only needs a chance to labor for food and decent clothes upon his back."

My eyes dart between the young girl, her mother, and the lordly father, wondering what he will do. I know nothing of castles, save the occasional tall tale. The whole of my life experience is the city of Knoll and the streets where I live. I wonder what work they might employ me to do, but anything is better than hanging from the watch's noose.

"He is half wild," the lord says, which is a fair assessment. Mayhap I am more than half wild, holding but a hint of all the decent things a person might aspire to be.

"Please, Papa," she says, once again.

Her father sighs heavily—a king, for if he lives in a castle, he must indeed be a king. "Should he cause us a moment's trouble, he will hang as he would here. Now though, the lad must agree to this, swear upon his life, and submit to the service and protection of Langetta."

Langetta? I mull over the name, liking the sound of it. My gaze returns to the young miss, who indirectly presents me with hope, while the innkeeper huffs. He does not agree with the king's offer, yet he holds his tongue, understanding he is in the presence of a greater man.

A shiver passes down my spine as I realize these people, all of them higher than me, are waiting on my word. I don't offer prayers to the Goddess, thinking her a cruel deity who wreaks only horror and desperation. Yet today, I witness a softer side of the Goddess. "I will do all of that," I vow. "For the remainder of my life." The guard releases me, and I sink willingly to my knees, ready to embrace the opportunity.

I doubt I shall see the king nor his kindly daughter again. Once we arrive, he will order some bastard to whip me into shape and set me to drudgery, but I find I do not care. Being homeless, I have shivered and felt so hungry, my belly ached. I have nothing to lose, save an appointment with the watch's noose.

The city watchman arrives then, storming in and sizing up the situation of me on my knees before the king and his regal family. "What happened here?" the watchman demands. "Leave this to me, and I will ensure the ruffian hangs at dawn."

The king steps forward. There is a coin in his hand, which he passes to the watchman. A hand closes over it swiftly. I note the silver color and how thick the coin is. It's enough money to feed his family for a week.

"The lad pledged to us and will join us when we leave." The king turns to me. "Tonight, he will sleep in the stable. Should he leave, he will be at the mercy of the watch."

I don't speak, keeping my eyes lowered as I wait.

"By your will, my lord." The watchman bows his head before taking his leave.

I'm still kneeling, unsure what I should do.

"Come on up, lad," the king says. "The innkeeper will feed you, and tomorrow when we travel home to Langetta Castle, you will come with us. Make no mistake, I will not hesitate to hang a man or boy who steals when there is no reason to."

"I will repay you for your kindness, sire," I say, and that is exactly what I do.

Present day...

We are brought food and lanterns, which we take with a nod of thanks I do not fucking feel. As soon as the bastards leave us alone, we find a corner of the barn and dispose of the food, lest one of us, in hunger or desperation, be tempted to try it.

There was a time when I would have eaten it, rotten or not.

We console ourselves with travel rations and clean water from our skins. Night is falling, and it is cold here. I've slept in colder places and on worse surfaces many times in my life. As the sun fades, lights come on within the castle and around the battlements. In the absence of daylight, it's almost possible to forget the broken shambles and mess.

I owe Langetta and its people much, the king and his family, more. Unlike Grady, my passage into soldiering was not the coveted one of a lordly brother and all the advantages that goes with it. I was an orphan, a beggar, roaming the streets of the vast city of Knoll, stealing whatever I could to survive. I don't remember much of the time before that, just a hazy image of a mother dying of the pox, her cheeks pale, skin waxy, sores upon her face, weak fingers grasping mine before the cold of death. These memories are vague enough that I believe I was very young. Yet I remember the streets clearly, and the other children, and brawling over a scrap of bread. Being the smallest at first, if I wanted a full belly, I soon learned to fight.

"Thought I'd be eating roast pork by now," I say wistfully. "Spent many a night fantasizing about Langetta pork."

"I prefer to fantasize about a willing lass sucking on my cock," one man calls.

I chuckle, recognizing the voice of John, a young alpha who is always quick with his mischief. I admit, I walked into that. It gladdens me when Grady's laughter joins in.

Langetta pork is renowned throughout Hydornia, so I doubt I'm the only man dedicating thoughts to it on occasion. I also fantasize about lasses, one in particular, and the reason I returned, even though it will be the sharpest kind of pain to see her with someone else.

I was twelve when my life changed, brawny for my age, although I had yet to reveal as an alpha. My uncharacteristically good deed in picking up a young girl's gloves led to my capture...and my later salvation. I owe Langetta, its king, and Dede a debt. I pledged myself to them for life, only I wonder, as I look around, if they even remember or care about the pledge. I had a mind to see her one last time before moving south. To where, I don't fucking know, but anything is better staying here and watching Grady with the woman I love. The lass never paid me much interest afore we left, so there is no fucking hope, even were she not a princess and I a former thief. Besides, she's not the only person I harbor feelings for, and the other object of my lustful interest is even less fucking hopeful a cause. I can't have both, and having only one is somehow worse.

"Do you think he'll show?" another man calls.

"Aye," I say. "I reckon he will try. I'm surprised Killian hasn't been to check on us." No one has checked on us, save the man who brought the food, and he came with two guards—scruffy bastards I don't recognize, who eyeballed us the whole time. I wonder what the people here think of us, whether they are disgruntled we stayed away so long and blame us for what has befallen Langetta.

As true night falls and the lights within the castle dim one by one, there is a creak and crack on the other side of the barn. Having spent the last two years battling orcs, to a man, every one of us is braced with his sword drawn in readiness for an attack. A long lanky lad tumbles to the floor.

"Barnaby," I mutter, shoving my sword back into the sheath.

"Peace," the lad says, holding up both hands as he stares at us from his vantage upon the floor.

Grady grunts as he similarly sheaths his sword. "It is not wise to startle men so recently returned from war."

"Aye." Barnaby scratches the scruff on his jaw nervously as he gains his feet. He is nearly as tall as me, but all bone and no muscle. "I didn't rightly think it through."

"You are here now," I say, clasping him on the shoulder. "Any trouble getting over?"

"No," Barnaby says, shaking his head. "Pa saw to that."

"Tell us what has happened," Grady says, all business. "Tell us everything."

With two men taking up positions to watch for guards passing, we take seats on our bedrolls, keeping our voices to a hushed whisper and not risking a light.

"Not long after you left, the raiding started," Barnaby says. "Small scale at first, a goat here, a few sheep there, grain from the stores. Not only here, the villages and farms suffered the same. The farmers complained, but they often whine—too much rain, not enough rain, too much sun, not enough sun. You know how it is with those folks. Nobody paid much attention."

"Then the villains began to band together, and with half the number of men here, it wasn't easy to patrol. The king...he never leaves his chambers, so that's all very odd. The attacks increased, and the raiders became bolder... We needed a leader. The king had no interest, falling ever deeper into his grieving. I think you leaving tipped him over the edge."

Barnaby's eyes flash to meet Grady's through the gloom. "I understand why you left, being called by your family and blood. Most folks understood, although some whined. But fuck, I don't want any Blighten bastards rampaging around here. Everybody understands when orcs begin warring, men must go to aid those who call northern Hydornia home."

Barnaby sucks in a deep breath. "So the raiding got worse —crops burned, farms were attacked, and in some cases, farmers and villagers got killed. More often, the bastards just took what they wanted and left them with nothing. Then the farmers came here, begging for help to restore order, but they got none. Some moved south to where there is less trouble, places with stronger kings. Many soldiers weren't happy either, wanting to do more for the farms and villages they were born in before taking up service to the king, but some also wanted to do less. Folks don't mind taking on a couple of ruffians who are up to mischief. Twenty cutthroats are a different matter."

"Twenty?" I ask.

"Yeah," he says, nodding slowly. "Some gangs are sizable and well organized, and they have gotten bolder over time."

This news is every bit as painful as the news of Blighten attacking Grady's familial home. It is like lifting the bandage on a festering wound and hoping for a miraculous recovery.

"Killian took the role of chancellor shortly after you left, old Denton having passed away suddenly. Next thing, he's being appointed commander. My Pa would have been a better choice, but the king hadn't been seen for many weeks and the only person talking to him was the new chancellor, Killian."

Grady growls, and the same tension coils in my body.

"Which is when he started" —Barnaby clears his throat— "pursuing Dede."

My fists clench. I cautioned Grady to learn the lay of the land, because while he is a level-headed commander, he is a doting whelp for Dede and inclined toward recklessness, but I am similarly feeling reckless now. So this is Killian's game? Snatching a kingdom from a weak king and preying upon a vulnerable woman without anyone to protect her.

"Go on," Grady says. "Tell me all of it."

The lad fidgets in a way that sets the blood thudding through my veins. "He does...odd things. She needed protection, and well, Byron stepped up. He's about the only one in the castle who's got enough alpha to stand up to Killian. He's no swordsman, though, and if Killian pushes it, Byron is going to be dead."

"Byron?" Grady spits out like the name is a bad taste in his mouth. "The lad wasn't an alpha when we left."

"Better Byron than Killian," I say, although my mind is whirling. I don't have a fucking clue how to make sense of this.

Barnaby shrugs. "He is now, late reveal and a big bastard. He was on poppy milk for weeks when he transitioned. Never seen a reveal like it before. Dede helped his Ma tend him through it, and...well, that's how they met. He's a good man and would die for Dede. The princess loves him as well, from what Mia tells me. What with Killian rutting lasses in Dede's room like some dog marking his turf..."

"The fuck he does," I snarl, just as Grady surges to his feet.

I eye him warily, still reeling myself, worried about Grady, Dede, and now the whelp, Byron, who has placed himself in the crosshairs of Grady's wrath right beside Killian. Byron was a scrawny kid when we left, so I'm struggling with the knowledge that he is now an alpha and the biggest bastard in the castle.

"Well, so Mia says, and Mia is Dede's best friend. She's also my best friend, and I get all the details from her."

Mia? Sweet girl, as I recall, with a feisty disposition. I'm glad Dede has Mia, if nothing else, and that Byron is a buffer between her and Killian, although it burns my blood to think of anyone bedding her. If the lad is sensible, it will have been innocent thus far.

"Mia has been encouraging Dede to flee with Byron afore he ends up getting killed. Killian is becoming ever bolder, making noises like he's about to wed Dede, even as he ruts every lass in the castle. Most of them encourage his attention, seeing themselves as getting preferential treatment because he ruts them in a dark, shadowy corner."

"Fuck," Grady snarls. "The fuck they will fucking wed."

"Hold it," I say, but Goddess stay me, I want to snatch up my sword and strike now at the castle and everyone in it.

"Is Byron with her now?" Grady demands through gritted teeth.

"We need to hear everything the lad says before we go on a fucking rampage," I caution, although I'm cautioning myself more than Grady. "Also, we need to remember Byron has protected the lass from Killian."

"Aye," Barnaby says. "He did. Then he disappeared, and no one's seen him since this morning when you first arrived. Without him, Dede is unprotected."

I curse under my breath, wondering where the fuck Byron is and what this means. Did he flee upon hearing of Grady's return? Yet that doesn't fit with Barnaby's declaration that the lad stands up to Killian. I hate the thought of Dede being vulnerable and wish we'd acted earlier. Now it is dark and the worst possible time to attack. We will not get fucking in, not without slaughtering half our numbers, maybe all of us, and then where will Dede be? Likely, the doors are already barred and they're waiting to cut us down under a hail of arrows.

We need to be smart, but the thought of Killian being with her, touching her...

Fuck!

"Mia is beside herself with worry," Barnaby continues, like Grady and I are not about to lose our shit. "Thank the Goddess Killian has left. Mounted up not long after you arrived. There are rumors he's in with the raiders, buying them off. Half the guards who enlisted over the last few months are raider scum, from what I can tell. They don't boast about it, but they don't try to hide it either."

I growl. I am not the only alpha growling.

"Aye, you get the idea..." Barnaby trails off.

At least Killian is not here threatening Dede tonight. I would take up arms, even if it got me fucking killed, but I need to be fucking calm because Grady is less rational than me. We must take the bastard Killian down, for if we fail, Dede will be deprived of all hope.

And take him down, we will.

"Do you know how far he travels?" I ask. "Or when he is expected to return?"

"Pa thinks a few days. He only took a couple of men with him. The rest have orders to keep you locked up tight. Arrows trained on the entrance to the barn. Poke your head out, and you will die," he says ominously. "The crack at the back I used leads to a passage between the wall and the outbuildings, but it will not take men of your build."

"Do you think we can speak to the king?" Grady asks.

The lad shakes his head. "The king is well guarded, and besides, he does not take visitors. Killian was not lying about that. The few maids who tend to his quarters all say he is a shell."

"Fuck," Grady hisses between his teeth.

"Is he witless?" I ask.

"Aye, witless with grief, and has been that way a long time now. Mia does the best she can for Dede. No other men touch her, given she's with..." He trails off, sending a shifty look Grady's way.

I blink as his words penetrate. Is he saying Byron is rutting Dede? Grady will skin the lad after he deals with Killian. My thoughts are interrupted by a deep, menacing growl emanating from Grady. It's the vicious kind of growl reserved for the direst enemies and when piercing the throat of Blighten bastards.

I rise, placing my hand upon his shoulder, stirring him from the potency of his thoughts. I want to comfort him. It feels fucking good to touch him any way I can. I feel like a bastard knowing Dede is not safe here, and I should be focusing all my attention on that. Dede, who is with another man. In all the time we have been fighting, how did we never consider this possibility?

"The bastard is not here," I say. "Let us take the time to plan."

Grady nods, seeming to come back to himself. We fall into quiet conversation as Barnaby takes us through events within the keep. We talk for many hours, until we are stiff from the cold.

"I best be going." Barnaby rises. "Pa said he would come back afore dawn to make sure I had a clear path out. Don't want the shady bastards Killian brought in to notice what we're up to."

"Are there any other than Pete who would side with us?" Grady asks.

"Aye," he says. "Some will. A few are tentative, while yet

others don't know what the fuck to do. Pa says as they need their heads bashing together. But you know how my pa is. Plain talking, dodgy leg and all. Limp is pronounced now. He'd never have lasted the battle, although he moans about how we wanted to go."

At least Peter is on our side.

"Thank you, lad," I say. "Talk to Peter and any others you trust about what we have said, but be careful about it. I don't want to see any of you on the whipping post. Come back to us tomorrow if you can."

Grady growls again.

"What?" I demand, turning to Grady. "We need to make plans. Killian leaving gives us some breathing space. Let's not kill any good men. We'll need them to deal with the fucking raiders after."

Grady nods. I've watched his back these last five years. It's going to fucking kill me to leave once this is cleared up, but it would cut me twice as deeply to stay. Besides, it's gotten much more complicated now.

Chapter Seven

Dede

Evening falls, and Killian still has not returned. I have been alone ever since he locked me in here after our spectacular confrontation. I've heard nothing from Mia either, and I can only hope she is safe. Byron is also notable in his absence, and so my unease grows.

My vulnerability and the concerns I have for the people I love draws my nerves toward a breaking point. With every passing second, the inevitable arrival of someone looms while I wait, dreading Killian yet hoping for Mia or Byron.

As the sun sets, I rise from my chair to light a lamp when a knock sounds upon the door. Mia and Byron would simply walk in, as would Killian. It has been a long time since he offered me courtesy of any kind. At my call to enter, Anna bustles in with a tray. I indicate the table, and she places it there without a word. After a swift glance and a curtsy, she scurries out the room. I was unkind to her the last time we met, although my reaction was understandable.

I'm not in the mood for food, but there is a goblet of wine and I'm more inclined toward that. Killian's words haunt me. After our altercation, there are no more pretenses between us. I fully expect him to bed and rut me the moment he returns.

My stomach churns, and I give serious consideration to barricading the door. It will only piss Killian off if he's the one seeking entry, and besides, I'm still hoping for Byron or Mia.

My eyes alight on the cutlery resting upon the table. The knife is sure to be blunt, but it is still a knife. A part of me recoils, even as another sits up and listens. Can I kill a man? Do I possess the necessary conviction? If he puts his hands upon me in anger again, I think that I would be willing to do anything to make him stop. What if I take it and hide it? Would Anna mention it? Would she take the tray away without a word? Or worse, run to Killian with the tale?

Swallowing thickly, I take the wine with me as I sit on the long couch. I'm not one for the oblivion of alcohol, but I wish I had a whole jug. The light fades further, the lamp becoming the only source of illumination, and still, I'm alone. The wine goblet, now empty, is returned to the table beside the tray that awaits collection. With no food in my belly, the wine leaves me unsettled and a little queasy. My cheek still aches where Killian struck me, a constant reminder that I need to act. I want to beg Byron to flee before it's too late, only I fear it already is.

I pace a little, eyeing the knife, wondering if I should take it or not. There are no lights outside now, and the clock ticking over the mantle of my unlit fire confirms the late hour. Mine is perhaps the only lamp against the night. Restless, and in want of something to do, I go through the motions of undressing and cleaning myself before slipping into my nightgown.

I go to bed. I worry.

Finally, after the hours have ticked by and Byron still has not returned, I fall into a fitful sleep.

❦

Byron

Night falls, and still, I'm imprisoned in the cells. I haven't had any food or water, and my throat is parched. My body aches from the beating, but the center of my chest hurts more as I fear for what is happening to Dede while I am stuck in here. I berate myself for taking the stupid shortcut to the courtyard, for not acting swiftly, for not anticipating that Killian might take this approach. His interest in Dede is nothing new, but now more than ever, I sense our time is running out. What can I do? This is her home, where her father yet lives. I feel like a monster for even suggesting that she leave.

Only I can't protect her. *Grady could*, my inner voice taunts. He's an experienced man and soldier, good with a sword. Is he as skilled as Killian? I'm familiar with Killian, having witnessed him fight in both the practice pit and against men in a real skirmish. My knowledge of Grady is mostly anecdotal, although I've seen him sparring occasionally when I would sneak in and watch as a younger lad. Still, he has a better chance than I do, and fifty alphas at his back. Maybe he's already freed Dede?

I can hope.

Yet instinct tells me that he has not, and if he hasn't, she is vulnerable to whatever Killian decides.

A loud thud and distant gruff cry comes from beyond my cell door, rousing me from my thoughts. I stand, grimacing at the pain, and hasten for the wooden door, fingers grasping the bars of the small window as I strain to peer out.

"What the fuck..." The next words are muffled, but that is Pete's voice, I am sure.

"...Killian..." someone answers. A hefty bang is followed by a wheezed groan. I grin. Someone just got their ears boxed by Peter. His hands are the size of shovels, so you don't want to get clocked by him. Nobody's too big or too old for it.

I dare to hope, straining to hear, although I can only see half the corridor from here and can make out no more than the odd word and tone.

"...orders..."

"Fuck the orders," Pete roars loud enough for me to clearly hear. I smirk, cursing when it cracks my parched lips and opens up a cut. Fuck!

Another grunt is followed by the scraping of the wood across stone. The rumble of voices and heavy footsteps draw near, mumbled complaints, the occasional curse, and then they enter my view.

"Open the fucking door," Pete says. "I've a mind to kick you out of the bloody castle."

My heart thuds wildly in my chest, making my head and the bruises pound. I step back as keys rattle into the slot before the sturdy door swings open with a creak.

"Fuck!" Pete mutters gruffly, lips narrowing as he motions me out. Turning, he snatches the keys from the guard before cuffing him again for good measure.

I step forward, eyeballing the guard. He was one of those who put me in here, and I don't hesitate to slam my fist into his face. He crumples to the floor. I have a decent right hook, or so those on the receiving end tell me.

Peter's lip curls as he stares down at the fallen man before returning his attention to me. "I came as soon as I found out. Everyone was wondering where the fuck you were."

"Dede?" I ask.

"Her chamber, under lock and key like yourself." Peter thumbs at the downed guard and then toward the cell. I pick the fucker up and toss him inside before turning the key. Peter takes the key from me and motions me to follow him. Barnaby waits by the guard station, shifting from foot to foot.

"Fuck!" Barnaby says. "What did they do to you?"

"Beat me," I say dryly. Barnaby hands me a waterskin, and I take it from him with a grateful nod, tipping it up and draining it. I swipe my hand across my mouth and heave out a sigh. "I was heading for the courtyard when I caught a couple of guards marching Dede to her room. The bastards had their hands on her, so I set them straight. When I came back out, five of the bastards jumped me. They beat me with clubs and then tossed me in the cell. What's been happening?"

"Killian left," Barnaby says. "This morning, not long after Grady arrived. Probably shitting himself. Took a horse and fled. Expect he is threatened by Grady being here and is rounding more raiders up. We'll need to move fast."

"What are we going to do?" I ask.

"We need Grady to talk to the king," Peter says. "... and maybe you should spend some time with a healer."

"No," I say, shaking my head, which sets everything pounding and makes a mockery of my words. "I need to see Dede."

Peter huffs out a breath. "I'll replace the guards outside her room. With Killian gone, they're all a bit twitchy at the moment. A bunch of new alphas turn up, then their lord and master runs for the hills? Yeah, they're rattled, and that's fine by me. We've reached a point of no return. I intend to take Grady to meet with the king in the morning."

"What good will that do?" I ask. "The king is gone."

"Don't know until we try," Pete says. "Grady asked to speak to him, so I'm going to help. Killian has enough outlaws inside the castle that it's going to be a challenge, either way."

We come to a stop at the back of the cell block. "I'll let your ma and pa know you're okay after I clear the way to Dede's room."

"Thank you kindly."

Pete heads inside to deal with the guards. There is a water barrel near the cell block entry, and I pause to dunk my head and shoulders. Winter is approaching and the water is fucking freezing, but I feel better for washing the grime and blood from me, plus the cold soothes the aches and pains.

"I spoke to Grady," Barnaby says. "I told him everything."

My head swings toward him, heart thudding in my chest. "Everything?"

"Aye." Barnaby's eyes turn shifty in the gloom. "He needed to know about you and Dede. I told him you looked after her. Can't be sure what he wants or why he's here, but I reckon he won't just disappear again. Why would he? Mayhap that was a lie he told Killian so that he could get in the gates."

Things are moving, shifting, and we can't go back. This future that we're rushing toward is far too uncertain for me, where Dede's safety is concerned. "How did he take it?"

"He swore." Barnaby shrugs. "Started pacing and growling up a storm, and not just him. Declan did as well."

"The fuck has this to do with Declan?" I mutter, shivering as the cold makes my clothing stick against my skin. Bad enough I am on Grady's hit list without the other alpha wading in. At least Grady has the pretense of a lord. Declan is a crazy bastard who makes no attempt to fake being civilized.

"Declan will do whatever Grady tells him. Half the lads in the castle moon over Dede, so I can't read much into it." A low growl bubbles up in my chest, but Barnaby is into his flow. "She sees the herb woman every month. Then today, Killian ordered the herb mistress be tossed outside the castle to the mercy of raiders. Pa had her picked up and taken to Little Meade."

My eyes shift to the doorway leading inside, and to Dede, but I'm now thinking about the damn herb woman. "Herb woman? Why the fuck would Dede go to a herb woman?"

Barnaby shrugs, making me realize that I've asked that out loud. "It must be important that she does. Is she getting rid of your whelps?"

"No." Heat creeps up my cheeks. "I've not knotted her yet. I told you this when we discussed my problem, and everyone says an alpha can't breed a lass unless he knots her."

"How would I know? I've never gotten a lass with child."

"You know more than I do."

"That's not hard," Barnaby says. "You've only ever been with one lass."

He doesn't need to make me sound so fucking inadequate. Dede never complained. Then I realize she's never been with anyone but me. Fuck! I could be fucking useless at rutting. "Dede wouldn't do that." Only I can't think of a good reason for her to visit a herb woman, and I'm now worried she's unwell.

My gut tightens. "I'm going to her."

"Aye, mayhap Pa will have cleared the guards by now. Killian won't be back tonight, but still best not linger in her room come morning."

I nod. "Thank you, to you and Peter for freeing me. You took a risk to do so."

"You would do the same for me," he says. "Pa was livid when he found out. We'd been looking for you all day. I went to speak to Grady, and when I came out, a lad said he'd noticed a light on in the cell block, even though the bastard was sleeping when we arrived."

"I'm glad you did," I say.

We split up and I head inside, taking the stone steps to the back of the castle, thoughts full of Dede, wanting to see her and assure myself that she is well. I hasten along the corridor, up the stairs for the kitchen, and into the great hall. There are a few men and lasses sleeping on benches and on the floor, or huddled in corners. None of them rouse as I walk past. I take the stairway, then the corridor to the east wing, where her room is.

I stop when I reach the top, checking the corridor. There are no guards. My boots ring against the stone, and I slow, becoming tentative as I grasp her handle and turn. It's unlocked and creaks as I push it open, revealing a shadow filled dayroom. Another creak follows as I shut the door and slip the bolt across.

The floorboards groan under my weight as I move through to her bedroom. There I stop, for she is lying on her side, golden brown hair cascading in waves, her white nightgown mostly hidden behind the lilac embroidered bedding. My fingers itch to touch her. Moonlight falls over me where I stand, but the bed is all shadows and I can only make out the faintest outline of her shape.

"Dede?"

"Byron?" Her voice is slurred with sleep and a little confused before she jolts up suddenly.

"I'm here." I want to touch her, and yet I am sullied by what has happened and where I have been.

She blinks up at me. "Goddess! What happened to you?" The moonlight, I realize, illuminates the evidence. She pushes the covers back and hurries to me, stopping a step away, fingers to her lips like she is fighting a sob.

Then I see it, for she's standing beside me in the moonlight. "What the fuck, Dede?" My hand shakes as I tentatively lift it to cup her cheek, brushing my thumb over the bruise, hoping it might be a trick of the light. My nostrils flare when she winces, and I growl. I do not often growl in her presence, conscious always of tempering my alpha ways, for she is a gentle beta.

Claimed by Three

Everyone says that an alpha must temper his beastly side, and I would do anything for Dede. "Who did this, Dede?"

"I could ask you the same thing," she counters.

"Don't deflect, Dede. Who the fuck did this?"

Chapter Eight

Byron

"Killian," she whispers. "Please, I don't want to talk about what happened. I don't want to talk at all, I just want you to hold me."

Another growl escapes my chest, and a shudder ripples through her body in response. I frown, but my mind is too much at sea to understand the nuances of her reaction. She has responded to my call before, but today, it almost seems to arouse her.

I don't hesitate. She has to be held, and there is only one way that I might hold her that will satisfy the alpha part of me. I kick off my boots and rip my wet shirt over my head, poorly stifling a grunt of pain.

A hiss passes through her teeth, and I still, allowing my shirt to drop to the floor. Gentle fingertips trace over the bruises that litter my body. I gather her dainty fingers inside my huge, clumsy ones, struck, as I often am, by the great difference in our size. I swallow. "They are not so bad," I say. "I've had worse from training sessions."

She makes a cute little harrumphing noise.

"Maybe not a training session, but there was this one time when raiders cornered me, and—"

A single finger is pressed to my lips, halting my words. "Don't make light of this, Byron. I want you to hold me, so long as it will not hurt you to do so."

I would hold her, even if it killed me, and die happily. My fingers are on my belt, yanking it open, before I push my pants down. The faintest hint of a scent—no, her mere presence has a predictable effect upon me, and my cock is already hard.

Her eyes dart down, and I smirk. "I can't help myself, just ignore it. Now take your nightgown off, please. I want to feel your skin next to mine. I will do naught else."

She nods, fingers clumsy as she pulls the little ribbons at her throat, tugging impatiently until they come free. The nightgown is lifted up and off, tossed to join my clothes upon the floor. She asked to be held, but somehow, my hand is tangled in her hair and my mouth slants over hers.

She whimpers. Am I being too rough? No, I do not think so, not when her hands cling to my shoulders and neck, pulling me into her. Bracing an arm under her ass, I lift her up before taking her down on the bed, mouth moving hungrily over hers. The cuts on my lip sting like a bastard, but I don't give a damn. My tongue plunders her mouth, tangling with hers, my dick stone hard and desperate to get inside her. I have words with it, although it does not often listen to reason where Dede is concerned.

Dede groans, her small hands clenching in my hair. Her impatience is an infection crawling under my skin, driving me feverish with a need to connect and a primal urge to claim. Desperation to finally knot her makes me break out in a cold sweat, while pre-cum begins leaking all over the bed and Dede.

She parts her slim thighs, encouraging me to settle between. Her legs curl around me, ankles crossed around my lower back like she's trying to draw me in, nails scraping over my back. My growl is ragged, and she moans in answer. I love this savage side that she displays on rare occasions, the tempered aggression evidenced in the scratches and nip of teeth that create an echoing wildness in me. Usually, I fight to control my darkness, ever mindful that she is a gentle beta and I am an alpha beast. Tonight, I find restraint difficult when she arches up into me, pushing her breasts against my hair rough-ened chest, rubbing pebble hard nipples against me, dragging my attention from the plundering of her lips.

I rip my mouth from hers, sucking gusty breaths as I stare down at her.

"Please," she says. "I need you inside me."

No need to ask me twice. My hand shakes as I cup her cheek, lips lowering as I kiss her with all the reverence and love that I possess. I adore Dede with every part of my being, and I want to show her.

"Don't hold back, Byron, not tonight."

My chest rattles with another growl. I cannot fucking stop myself.

"Goddess," she whispers. One hand clamps over her tummy, and she presses her open palm against it.

"What is it?" I demand. "Are you gushing again?"

She shakes her head, but I know that she is. I am as obsessed with her wet pussy as I am with the woman it belongs to. Sometimes, when she is very aroused, she will flood a little slick. She doesn't like the sensation, gets embarrassed and tries to hide it from me. I've no idea why, since my dick gets stone hard whenever it happens.

"Dede?" I say, a warning in my voice. "Is your pussy making a mess?"

Another swift head shake of denial. She can be naughty about admitting it, even though I can smell the sweet scent. My eyes lower to where her tummy ripples.

"Oh!"

Fuck, she just gushed again, and my mouth waters in anticipation of her sweetness. How is it possible for a pussy to taste so good? Maybe it's because I love her? I don't know, and don't fucking care. I pluck her hand away and place it against the pillow beside her head. Then my mouth lowers to her throat, and she groans, hips lifting, rocking her pussy against my stomach. She's so needy and so fucking wet.

Dede

I am gushing so much, it saturates the bedding beneath me, making the worst mess. It doesn't help that Byron likes it so well, almost like my body wants to offer him even more.

His lips move with slow intent down the column of my throat before he pauses at the crook, teeth grazing the skin, not quite biting, just teasing me with the possibility. I want him to bite me, suffering from a deep-rooted imperative to be marked, for him to sink his teeth in until it stings.

He doesn't, though. Instead, he takes my lips in another heated kiss, our tongues tangling, sending my libido spiraling.

I have hidden what I am from the world, but I cannot hide it from myself. There are no omegas here for me to talk to. The kindly herb mistress is my only source of knowledge. The herbs help with my scent and prevent me from going into heat, but that is all. I still have the urge to nest, one I am forced to suppress. When I'm near Byron, his scent and his growl trigger a delectable kind of thrill, making my pussy weep slick and filling my mind with lusty thoughts.

My heart breaks at seeing the bruises and cuts upon his beautiful face and body, yet he is somehow also resplendent in all his broken glory. He conquers my mouth, and I open to the kiss, wanting to worship him, to show him my love. Yet tonight, he is intent upon tempering me, pinning my smaller body beneath his—the best feeling ever. Teeth nip and tug at my lower lip, and I groan with joy. He is rarely rough with me, thinking me a gentle beta, yet my omega nature craves and desires things no beta man could give me and no beta maiden would want.

For so long, I have smothered my reactions for fear of giving myself away, but with all the potent emotions crashing through me, I find it impossible tonight.

My heat is inevitable, and every time we come together, I sense the herbs' potency breaking down. When I do, the alpha who ruts and marks me will claim me as his mate. For so long, I have concealed my omega side, fearing Killian might force a bond upon me.

I want to join with Byron, but I cannot mate with him tonight. This is not my heat, it is merely my sorrow and stress manifesting a greater depth to emotions. I'm seeking a connection through touch, that I might lose myself in this man. I still fear at any moment that this joy we have with one another might be snatched away.

His lips move on to my breasts, sucking against the plump flesh, more brutish than he normally is, and I beg, with no thought to hold myself in check, intent only to offer encouragement.

My cries of pleasure and the constantly weeping slick all seem to drive him on. His fingertips circle my nipple, drawing it to a taut, hardened peak, before swiping back and forth, back and forth.

My fingers sink into his thick hair, trying to coax him to go where I want. Finally, he takes my nipple inside his mouth and lashes it with his tongue. Goddess, the sensations make my toes curl and my tummy clench. He sucks hard, and the ache is like a shot of arousal rushing all the way to my womb. I cry out in pleasure, and he sucks harder still. Then he moves on to the other side to administer the same sorcery, playing with the nipple, flicking, licking, running his wet tongue around the peak before sucking it deeply into his mouth. He squeezes my breast like an offering to himself before his lips move off to the side, where he sucks love bites against my skin, making me near dizzy with desire.

I am desperate for his cock, but I also want his knot, despite how much it terrifies me. "Please," I whisper. "Let me taste you."

He stirs, head lifting abruptly.

I rise, taking advantage of his momentary confusion, and push him onto his back. I hate his hiss of pain, and I pause. "I want to taste you."

"Fuck," he mutters gruffly. "I'm so fucking close. I'm not going to fucking last."

"Good," I say decisively. "I don't want you to last. I want you on my tongue, down my throat, and deep in my belly."

His growl turns rumbly as I close my fingers around his cock.

"Come here," he says. "Feed me your sweet pussy, and you may suck my cock all you like."

Understanding dawns upon me, and I bite my bottom lips as heat creeps over my cheeks. If I do this, I will be *exposed*.

Stilling, he stares up at me. "You don't have to do this if you don't want to, Dede."

In my hand is my prize—hot flesh I want to lick and suck until he gifts me his cum. A dark flush spreads across his face, and I understand that he needs to do this to me as much as I need to do this to him.

I hesitate for only a moment before I slip my leg over his body and shuffle backward, squeaking when he grasps my hips and yanks me back. My mouth hovers over his jerking cock, even as my wet pussy is over his mouth.

He growls, a sound of pleasure. "You are absolutely drenched," he says, and I don't even care. His hiss accompanies my small hand enclosing his thick shaft. My scent might be tempered, but his is not for me. Here, his pheromones are heady, driving me to the point of nearly coming from that alone.

As my lips enclose the tip and I lash it with my tongue, he jerks, pulling my ass back and placing me right in the path of his wet tongue. The first lap, and I'm humming around his cock. His wicked tongue lashes my clit before taking a broad sweeping lick all the way down, then poking into my drenched pussy. He groans, dragging me right onto him, his beard tickling me in the best kind of way. He eats me out, using his tongue, lips, and nibbling with his teeth. Nowhere escapes him, and all the while, I try desperately to take him deeper. My throat and jaw ache, my fingers turn slippery. I can't get enough of him, head bobbing up and down, fingers working down his shaft to the ridge of his knot. I always imagined an alpha's knot would only bloom once inside, but Byron's is always swollen. His growl deepens against my pussy in the most delightful way as I run my fingertips over the thick ridge. I lap, lick, and suck, as he does to me. Pleasure is soaring, his growls and grunts echoing around the room, his hot length filling my mouth, all conspiring to take me ever higher.

Then he thrusts one thick finger into my ass, and I clamp

down over it, tumbling into bliss, my fingers lowering to his balls just as they draw tight and the first gush of his cum fills my mouth and throat, even as my pussy and ass spasm. A great flood gushes out of me, and he growls, fingers tightening over my hips, holding me close as he laps up every little drop. All the while, I am swallowing down his offering, frustrated when a little escapes.

I twitch as I come down, lapping the length of his cock, getting all of the stickiness up. I become sleepy and boneless, yet my body still buzzes and the wicked torment of his tongue coaxes me into wanting more.

Suddenly, I'm lifted up and tossed onto my back the wrong way around in bed. A predator is here with me, one who crawls over me. The moonlight bathes this side of the bed, casting the terrible damage into relief.

His mouth crashes over mine. I taste myself, and he tastes himself on me. The kiss is wet and lusty, tongues tangling and teeth nipping as we clash together. I want to meld with him, to feel him inside me. Seeming to sense my urgency, his body shifts between my open thighs, his cock jerking and nudging as he lines up before it snags my entrance. Heaven, there is no more blissful sensation in the world than this, as he oh so slowly penetrates me.

"Fuck," he says roughly. "Your pussy is so fucking good. Hot, wet, welcoming. Whenever I'm inside you, I lose my fucking mind."

My arms and legs wrap around him, drawing him as close as I possibly can, squeezing his powerful body, sucking him all the way in, clenching, relaxing, and clenching again as I accept his thick cock into me. I don't want to let him go, I want to stay like this, holding this moment of impossible perfection, when he's buried inside me. Only he is not fully inside me, for his knot butts up against my pussy entrance, and we are not yet complete.

"I want your knot," I say.

"Dede." His voice carries a warning, and he shifts like he's about to pull out.

I cling tighter. "Please, give me your knot tonight."

"No," he says. "I'm not giving you the fucking knot. A beta cannot take a knot without training, and I haven't even begun to train you."

I don't like the word 'training,' given I am an omega and have no need for it. Yet he doesn't know that, and I'm not ready to tell him. "Fuck me," I demand. "I want you to fuck me."

He nips at my throat, arm shifting, sliding under my ass, clamping around my waist to hold me still. Then he moves, pulling out and slamming back in. Wet slaps accompany our rough rutting, driving the air from my lungs with every deep thrust.

"More," I urge, impatient.

He pulls out and slams back in again, my pussy gripping, trying to suck in the knot. I could take it, I'm sure. He ruts me with hard, deep strokes and a barely tempered edge of violence that makes my omega heart sing. I come swiftly, convulsing around him, but he doesn't, powering through, slamming into me over and over.

I love everything about this. I score his back with my nails, nip the strong column of his throat, beg him, and speak all manner of nonsense as I tumble into the delirium of other-worldly bliss.

His growl is constant. He cannot temper himself tonight, and I like that he is unhinged. I want him to be.

"Mark me."

"I will not fucking mark you," he says, his hips snapping as he slams his cock in and out. "Don't fucking ask me that."

"Mark me," I repeat. "I want you to. I need you to."

His groan holds frustration and longing. I am being unfair, and he doesn't even realize what he's doing or how it impacts me. He thinks I am a beta, but the omega side of me craves his mark. His heavy rutting increases in pace, making me flutter on the edge of another peak that I know will sweep me up and spit a dry husk back out. I fight to stave off the climax, wanting this moment to last, then hold the blissful tide at bay until he relents. His lips find my throat, he is weakening, and I moan, groan, and sob with joy, so close to the rapture I sense will be mine if only he will bite, marking me as his.

Then his teeth sink into me, and I convulse around his iron hard length as finally, he claims me as his. My body rejoices, pussy locking tightly upon his cock, desperate for the knot. I feel him squeezing his knot with his fingers as he comes with a groan, and a hot flood fills me. He strains, his knot pressing against my entrance, threatening to slip in. If it did, he would be so much deeper. I want more, even as the pain terrifies me, and I come again in great rolling waves of pleasure that skitter all over my body.

His teeth dislodge, and gusty breaths are breathed against my throat. He eases out, sending a gush splattering and leaving me empty, even as he gathers me close.

The emotions I've been holding back escape, and I sob. He draws my cheek against his chest and makes that deep rumbly sound—an alpha purr. This is the first time he has purred for me. Why would he? He doesn't know how I crave it. I hold tighter.

"What a beautiful sound. Why have you never done this before?"

The rumble deepens, becoming a rattle with a different timbre on the way in to the way out as he breathes, one lighter, one deeper. The vibration under my cheek soothes me, and I cling, sticky legs tangling with his. Here, in the safety of his arms, is where I want to be, but the heady glow does not last. He is injured, as am I, and somewhere beyond the door of my room, along corridors and outside, Grady, Declan, and the alphas who left for the war are locked up in a barn.

Chapter Nine

Grady

It's a long restless night as I lie on the cold barn floor, contemplating the choices I have made in my life. Somewhere inside the castle, Dede is sleeping alone. I wish I could go to her and this trouble was already over, that Killian was dead and Dede was mine. Yet there are many steps to take before that can happen...and another man who has laid claim to her. Now I want to rip my heart out and offer it to her for leaving her to this fate.

She could be with child now. The rage that grips me thinking about her bearing another man's whelp is near debilitating. I'm struggling to picture Byron as a credible threat, and yet I have to accept he might be. Barnaby certainly implied so, and while the lad is new to being an alpha, he is plain talking and clearly bright, if a little unorthodox.

As the dark of night gives way to the light of dawn, I'm still no closer to a plan beyond taking up my sword and slaying everyone in sight. It is only Declan—who, for all his humor, is ever a steady influence when I need it the most—that stays my recklessness. We need men who are yet loyal to King Ellis on our side, and I don't want them injured or killed through infighting. These are men I have fought beside against raiders and other vermin who roam the lands, and they are like brothers to me. That they did not travel with me to the war is as much testament to the fact they have loyalty to the castle and that some needed to stay.

Against this hopeless backdrop of frustration, I'm surprised, when the guards come to change posts, that Peter is one of them. The man accompanying him is the tallest beta I have seen, and the reason for this choice becomes apparent when they slip inside the barn and the younger man hands his cloak over to me. I am going somewhere, it would seem.

There is more gray in Peter's hair than I remember, a few more lines around his eyes, and as per Barnaby's description, his limp is more pronounced. "You're looking old," he says, bestowing me with an up and down look.

Declan emits a deep guffaw beside me, and I shoot the bastard a scowl. When I turn back, Peter is likewise grinning, but it fades swiftly. His armor, I note, is maintained and clean. The guard next to him, and whose cloak I now hold, wears armor that is similarly well-kept compared to the previous guards.

"Heard you wanted to speak to the king?" Peter says.

"I do." I want to talk to Dede too, but with limited time, her father is the priority.

Peter nods. "Not going to be simple. Everything Barnaby told you last night is true and more. Half the guards are former raiders—some are not so former, in my opinion—and constantly pilfering from the stores to keep their associates away."

The beta beside Peter shuffles from foot to foot.

"It's not your fault, lad," Peter says, eyeing him. "Makes decent soldiers uncomfortable when stocks go missing. Killian has always been a whelp, and he's still a fucking whelp."

"Killian is a whelp who knows how to use a sword," the younger guard says.

"Aye, he's a skilled swordsman, but he should be, given he practices every fucking day."

"I couldn't give a fuck how skilled he thinks he is," I say, and I really don't.

"What are you going to say to Ellis?" Peter asks, nodding his head at me.

"That depends on how much he can be reasoned with, how much of him is still there."

"Well, I wish you luck. Afterward, you're going to need to make decisions and make them fast."

"Fair enough. How many men might be with me?"

"A few," Peter says. "People are disgruntled you were away so long. Some think Killian is better. Not everyone realizes he's handing goods over to raider scum. He should have skewered the bastards long before they started banding together, but he's a lazy bastard, too busy rutting and practicing his fucking sword swings. So yeah, there's a few as would come to you, others will need a bit of persuasion. Get through to the king, and it'll be easier. Without him, well, you're no better than Killian."

His words unsettle me. I don't want to be another Killian, but fuck, I'm not going to let this pass. I won't leave Dede here unprotected, where that bastard can put his hands on her.

"Take me," I say. "I'm ready."

Declan and I share a look, and he nods once. I trust Declan implicitly, and I know he will be prepared for whatever comes next.

Throwing on the cloak, I follow Pete, skirting the edge of

the courtyard until we arrive at the back entrance, where the kitchens meet the stores. It is strange how the worn steps offer a familiarity, bringing a bittersweet longing to reclaim what was once mine. Not the castle, but the woman who is destined to be the queen. She would make a fine ruler, possessing both a keen mind and sense of fairness essential in such a role.

"Do you know how Dede fared last night?"

"The lass is well. Byron went to her last eve. We liberated him from the cells after Barnaby left you. Turns out Killian had five betas put a beating on him before tossing him out of the way."

My emotions swing like a pendulum, horror that Killian ordered an innocent lad beaten, followed by jealous rage that said lad subsequently went to Dede.

"He's a good lad and alpha." Peter stops to pin me with a look. "Afore you left, you had a claim to her affection. The important word is *had*. Byron would walk through a fire for the lass. He was beaten black and blue, and the first thing he asked when we released him was whether Dede was well."

I feel like the lowest form of scum because I want to beat the bastard all over again for touching her, for putting his fucking cock in her, because I am certain he has. "Are you saying I should walk away?" The words turn to grit in my mouth, but they need to be said.

"I'm saying you should right the mess you left. It's not a simple matter of wading in and claiming Dede. However this plays out, someone is going to be hurt."

Point made, he begins walking again. My gut churns as we ascend the stairs of the east wing, where the family suites are found. I am ever an alpha with his sights set upon a mate. Can I bow out gracefully should she tell me she wants another?

"Will the guard on his door give us any trouble?" I ask, forcing myself back to the matter at hand.

"Killian has whipped the useless bastards more than once for supping too liberally of the beer. The newcomers are poor quality guards, many of them raiders sent to watch developments here, but they do Killian's bidding. I'm going to play on that."

When we arrive on the highest floor, we find a pair of guards standing outside the king's chamber. I visited him here on many occasions, yet I sense the passage of time and the changes wrought, seeing the unfamiliar faces at his door.

"I've come to take over duty," Peter says, walking boldly up to them.

"You?" the guard asks, eyeballing Peter before giving me an appraising once-over. "You're not the usual men."

"Well, the usual men spent too much time in the ale last eve, and nobody has seen hide nor hair of them since."

"Were supposed to hand over to Band and Eddy," the left-hand man says, eyes narrowing in suspicion.

"Aye, we've covered this already," Peter says in the manner of a man bored with the conversation. "Want to stay here another day? That's fine by me. I'm just offering to take over."

The two guards fidget.

"I need to fucking go," the man on the right says. "My dodgy back is giving me grief standing in this drafty corridor, and I need some fucking food and sleep. Band is a lazy cretin and always supping more than he should. Mayhap Killian will thump the worthless whelps when he returns."

The other guard sighs and spends long moments wrestling with the decision. Clearly, he doesn't want to spend another day on guard duty, either.

"Maybe Killian will return soon," Peter says. "Maybe he won't..."

"Fine then," the left guard says, and without further comment, both of them walk off.

"That was easy," I say. "Easier than I expected."

"Aye," Peter says. "Well, you've not gotten in there yet. Mayhap you might not achieve much either way."

"I won't know until I try," I say, and turning the handle, I slip inside.

Chapter Ten

Dede

After a night of wild rutting with Byron, I'm roused by banging. Is someone knocking on my door?

Pushing the covers back, I sit up, ears straining as I wait for another knock.

Nothing.

Dawn has arrived, casting the room in shades of gray. Byron is gone, the bed beside me cold, indicating he left some time ago, though the pillow bears a faint indentation. His scent calls to me, and I want to bury my face against the cool cotton and pretend the real world and all the troubles within it no longer exist. I miss him, and that brings a little tightening in my chest, even as I welcome the soreness in my pussy.

My fingers go to my throat, feeling the sting as I pass over the mark.

Mark. I wanted him to claim me, encouraged, begged, and pleaded. Now, in the light of day, I worry it might trigger a reaction when Killian finally returns.

I feel crumpled and out of sorts. My hair is a knotty mess because I never tied it back, my eyes puffy from tears, and my stomach is empty because all I had last night was a glass of wine.

Another round of knocking rouses me from my contemplation of my woes. Few people knock on my door anymore, except the guards or maid occasionally, but it is far too early for that.

Yet another pounding rattles my outer door.

I'm exhausted, still tired and groggy. I just want more of the oblivion of sleep, but I'm awake now and it would seem I'm not going to get more rest. Swinging my feet over the side of the bed and into slippers, I rise, gather my dressing gown from where it lays over the chair, slip it on, tie the sash, and make my way to the door.

When I open it, I find Mia. "Good! You are up," she says.

I peer around her through the doorway, but she swiftly darts inside and slams the door shut. "Why did you knock? Are the guards outside?" I ask, frowning. When Byron arrived last night, I didn't dedicate time to wondering how he got in.

"It was early, and I wondered if Byron might be here. I was just slipping past to check if they were guards I might be able to charm when I noticed they'd already gone. Some are getting wise to me now, but I figured it was worth a try, and—" Stopping abruptly, her eyes settle on my cheek, then she takes my shoulders in her hands and all but drags me over to the window, where the weak dawn light is pouring through.

"Did he... No." She shakes her head. "Tell me he didn't."

My hand goes to my cheek, and subconsciously, I draw the collar of my dressing gown higher over the bite mark on my throat. My cheek is sore and a little achy, but the pain is overwritten by what happened with Byron.

Her fingers tremble where they grasp my shoulders. "Did Killian do that?"

I nod slowly, tears threatening to spill.

"He has stepped over the line."

"He stepped over it a long time ago," I say sadly.

Her hands drop to her sides. "Perhaps not for much longer. That's what I was coming to tell you."

"Tell me what?" Goddess, I need a cup of tea laced with fifteen spoonfuls of honey.

"He's in with your father."

"He?" I frown. Is she talking about Killian? "Killian?"

"Forget Killian," she says. "Well, forget him for now. Grady is inside the castle, poorly disguised in a cloak. As if putting a cloak on an alpha would make him look like anything else."

"He is?" My eyes immediately shift to the door, like the man in question might burst through. "What is he doing with my father?"

She shrugs. "Talking to him, I would guess."

"Are you...are you sure he's with my father?"

She nods. "Barnaby told me."

Barnaby? "Who is Barnaby?"

"Barnaby, the lad I was telling you about. He sneaks me apples if I show him my breasts. I told you I had a friend."

"Goodness! Mia...why would you do such a thing?" My hand goes to my mouth.

"What?" she says with a fake innocent expression. "I like apples, and he has full access to the stores."

My chuckle bubbles out, which surprises me, given the chaos consuming my life, but the lass is outrageous at times and it's good to laugh. "So who is Barnaby? And how does he know these things?"

"He's Peter's lad."

"Peter, the old guard who didn't leave for the war on account of an injury?"

"Exactly! Barnaby is his son. Looks nothing like his pa, but he's a decent sort and I trust him. He tells me all his gossip, and I tell him all mine."

I'm assaulted by a sudden fear that she talks to Barnaby about me, all the while showing him her assets and demanding an apple in payment.

"I don't mind showing him my breasts, to be honest. Seeing the look of reverence on his face is enough of a reward. We often talk. I like him, it's uncomplicated, and there is something about an uncomplicated lad that appeals to me."

"Are you doing anything else with him?"

Her face flushes, and she smirks. "Maybe. I do like the lad. He's very entertaining."

"I can see why if you're getting all this gossip and apples from him," I say dryly.

My mind rolls back to her earliest statement. "What do you think Grady and my father are talking about?"

"No idea, but it's got to be a positive sign. Goddess knows we need someone to stir things up around here. Anything is better than what we—no, what you suffer now. Perhaps he took the opportunity, given whatever is happening with the guards leaving their posts. Maybe you could go to your father now, while Grady is there and Killian is away? It may be your only chance."

"I didn't realize Killian had left."

"Gone to call on his raider buddies, most likely. He won't be gone for long, and he wouldn't want Grady unattended, even with his men watching."

"I need to go to my father," I say, but I'm not only thinking about my father. I'm also thinking about seeing Grady without distance and people between us, without Killian twisting my arm cruelly because I dared to speak up. "We argued, Killian and I. He admitted he wants the castle and intends to see me with child as soon as possible."

Tears pool in her eyes as she takes my hand and squeezes it gently, and in that touch is a lifetime of shared love. "The man has lost the Goddess' way. He was not always wicked. At first, he was just hapless and suffered burgeoning delusions, but now he is wicked and cruel."

"He has gathered too much power in the time since he came to command. There are many men here who are loyal to him. Grady has far fewer with him."

"They are alphas," she points out.

"Alphas are not invincible," I counter. "They are still men. They still bleed if you cut them." I'm worried about Byron, how I should be hunting him down and begging him to take me from this terrible place, lest he suffer harm again. I'm similarly concerned Grady is about to be reckless. Now he is talking to my father, and he doesn't have enough men to counter all those loyal to Killian. Why is it only now that I realized this? "I don't want him to die over me."

"Him? Byron or Grady?"

"Both of them," I admit.

"Fool lass. You finally have some hope that does not involve fleeing your home, and a future where Byron is not beaten and tossed into a cell. Yes, I heard about that." Her face softens. "Grady owes it to both Langetta and you after he took our men with him for a war that lasted two years."

I want to hope, but I've been without it for too long. My thoughts turn to the sweet herb mistress guilty of nothing more than helping me over the last two years. "Do you know what happened to Lyra? Killian found out I was visiting her and said he'd had her thrown out."

"She went to Willowbark farm," Mia says. "No one knew

why he booted her out. Peter saw to it that she was picked up and taken to safety. We will sorely miss her skills. Did he realize why you were seeing her?"

I shake my head, relieved Lyra is well. "No, he thinks I'm ridding myself of Byron's whelps, as he put it." It makes me want to empty my stomach even thinking of killing Byron's child.

"Better than the truth," she says before nodding her head at me. "Best you dress, my lady, and be ready in case the path is clear."

As she slips out of the door, I hurry to my dresser, throw off my dressing gown, and then toss on a gown, fumbling with the buttons. Impatient, I slip into my shoes before drawing a scarf around my throat. A part of me rebels at the thought of covering up Byron's mark. The omega side of me wants nothing more than to display it with pride, but now is not the time, and the cautious side is nervous enough about seeing Grady in person. Throwing another man's mark into the mix would be a bad idea.

Did he expect me to wait for him? I intended to, wanted to, yet my love for Byron was unexpected and the consequence of treacherous circumstances driving us together. I cannot regret what I share with Byron, but I still experience a delayed guilt. After two years without a word from Grady, how was I to know?

By the time I returned to my dayroom, Mia is slipping back inside. "It's clear," she says. Together, we leave and hasten for my father's chamber.

Chapter Eleven

Grady

As I enter the king's chamber and quietly shut the door behind me, I find King Ellis sitting at a grand dining table upon a plump carver chair. Before him is a dome topped plate, knife and fork, and goblet. He stares vacantly out a wide window that offers views across the meadows. As he turns slowly to face me, my first thought is that he has aged. The man I knew is long gone, and what remains is a shadowy reflection.

Confusion clouds his face, and it only grows as I throw back the hood of my cloak. Does he even recognize me?

"My lord," I say, lowering my head briefly in deference.

He swallows, eyes darting to the door before returning to me. "Grady?"

"Yes, my lord. It is I, Grady."

Trembling fingers rub back and forth across his brow. "You have been absent for a long time."

"I have, my lord. The war with the Blighten took both time and effort, but finally, they are in retreat."

"Is...is Killian dead?"

"No, lord," I say. "He has merely left the castle for a short while. Were you notified of my arrival?"

"No. Did you arrive just now?"

"I arrived yesterday. We spent the night in the barn."

His fingers worry a little faster at his brow. "How did you get in? He... Killian usually places guards at the door."

Does he even wish me to be here? Does he want me to leave? "Do you understand what is happening to your kingdom?" I ask. Ellis appears both distant and disconnected. Peter's words taunt me, reminding me that without the king, I am no better than Killian.

He sighs heavily, fingers dropping from his brow. "I do... some of it. Lately, not so much... You were gone so long. The raiding started soon after you left, affecting the villages and farms. Then they grew bold enough to attack the castle. We didn't have enough men, and Killian threatened to leave if I didn't give him the position. What could I do? Someone needed to protect the castle while you were supporting your brother."

I was fighting the fucking orcs so this castle would be kept safe, I think, but I do not voice this opinion.

"I gave him the command," the king continues. "That's how it started."

"You unleashed a fucking monster," I rumble, losing all pretense of civility. "You left Dede, the daughter you share with your beloved late wife, alone. How could you abandon her like that?"

"Don't talk about abandonment." His eyes flash with a little of his former spirit. "Not when you left, taking fifty of my soldiers with you. Nearly all the alphas went with you, save the few who were injured or too old or young to help. What was I supposed to do? I had to pick someone. He said he wanted to step up."

"He stepped up all right—stepped up and readied himself to take both your daughter and your kingdom!"

"Dede was never part of this," he says, eyes fogging with confusion.

I want to grab the old fool and shake him for being so fucking naïve. "When was the last time you left your chambers?"

"Months," he says, lips trembling and eyes glistening as understanding sinks in. "Many months."

The king still possesses his wits, although he appears not to have used them in a while. My time here is too limited for anything but blunt words. "He wants Dede. He's scenting her fucking room."

He shakes his head.

"Yes," I counter. "He similarly told her he would leave unless she showed him favor."

He flinches as though my words are a physical blow.

"Your daughter is a prisoner of this man and relying on a lad, barely an alpha to protect her, while you sit in this room, abstaining from life." Finally, a spark of gratitude and empathy rouses within me for Byron, although I'm yet to be convinced I can tolerate him in any capacity.

"What was I to do? How was I to keep us safe when no one was here?" His eyes turn toward the window. "We could have been overrun."

"You could have put a fucking dog in charge, and they would have done a better job than Killian," I say.

"I'll give it to you," he says. "Now you're back. You are here to stay, aren't you?"

I nod. It would take the Goddess herself appearing to drag

me from this castle. "I intend to stay, but you cannot simply give me the command."

He frowns. "Why not?"

"Because it is not so simple anymore. Killian has made deals with the raiders and replaced half the guards with their men, and so many of those who wear your colors are loyal to neither you nor Langetta. From what I understand, he has gone to fetch further villainous support. Were you to make such an announcement, it would likely trigger a bloody internal battle. I have fifty alphas with me and a few others I know I can count on. The rest are raiders or confused and could swing support in either direction should it come to conflict. If Killian has done this much, it is not only the guards you need to consider but potentially other castle inhabitants who stand to lose if he is displaced. He makes false promises and gifts your goods and wealth to the raiders to keep them in his pocket. So now we must deal with that."

"What am I to do?" he says. "How can I fix this?"

I spent much time last night contemplating the best approach to wresting back control of a corrupt castle. "You will organize a feast tonight in my honor and to celebrate the Blighten retreat. You will invite me into the castle, which will give me an opening. You must also announce that I am leaving within a few days. That way when Killian returns, he has no reason to go to war with me. Once I have access, I can better plan how to overthrow him. Let us hope he does not bring more raiders here, for I only have fifty men."

"Your brother would help?"

"He would," I reply. "But seeking my brother's aid would take weeks, and then we would need to find a way inside. We are here now, and we need to act."

"I have not spoken to my advisors in some time and heard nothing from Tweed Head or the other parts of my kingdom. I have no visitors, save the maids who come to clean my room and bring me food."

"You are a prisoner in your own castle," I say. "By any means necessary, he would have wedded your daughter, and once that was done, killed you."

Tired eyes hold mine. "I care little for my own life, but I care greatly for my daughter."

I want to flail him where he sits, for his words are made lies by his actions thus far. Only I believe he does care for her, but he has failed her regardless. "I will see that your advisors are sent here while Killian is still away. Make the announcement and invite us in, but say that we will be leaving shortly. I will remove Killian from power."

He nods swiftly. "Thank you."

"Do not thank me, not yet, for this is not over. Nor should you delude yourself that I do this for duty. You will give me your daughter's hand in marriage. You will grant us your blessing."

"Agreed," he says, and I hate the spineless bastard again for folding so easily. "She would have wed you anyway," he continues, thawing some of my hostility.

"That was two years ago," I say, thinking about Byron. "I know nothing of Dede now, save that she must have been changed."

Chapter Twelve

Dede

Although Mia checked ahead, I am still shocked to find the guards gone from his door. Well, the usual ones, who dress slovenly and don't wash for weeks, if the reek coming off them is any indication, are missing. Instead, only one guard is present, and that man is Peter.

I have not seen Peter often, but of all the people within this castle, I trust Peter second only to Byron. He would have made a better choice than Killian to command the castle. His hazel eyes widen as he notes our approach, then his nostrils flare as he takes in the bruise upon my face.

"I need to go in," I say.

A myriad of emotion crosses his face, but above all is a heaviness that makes me think of regret.

"The bastard will be strung up," he says.

Not once has he voiced a negative opinion of Killian in my presence in all the time he has reported to the younger man's command. Today, his animosity is vocal and blunt.

I sense hidden agendas and change.

"When was the last time you saw your father, lass?" he asks.

He has always called me lass, and it brings a warmth to my chest. Few men would dare to do so. I'm always *your lady* or *Lady Dee*, never lass. I'm comforted that this gruff, older alpha still calls me by such a simple term. This is the same man who, on occasion, dusted off my knees as a child when I scraped them in a fall. He is a good man, I decide.

"A year, a little more, maybe. Is...is Grady inside?" I ask tentatively.

Peter nods. "Discussing matters with your father."

His eyes lower again, and I know he is looking at my bruised cheek. "He also has matters to discuss with you, lass, I dare say, but we have little time. I have men watching who will give warning if Killian returns."

I nod. Unexpectedly, and although I've never once done this in my life, I lean up on my tiptoes and press a kiss to his rough, weathered, prickly cheek.

"Goddess, lass! You can't go around kissing a man like that!" He steps back, a faint flush to his cheeks, drawing my smile. "Go in if you're gonna," he says gruffly. "But be warned, I've heard terse words coming from inside."

Mia remains outside with Peter as I slip into my father's chamber for the first time in a year. I had mentally prepared myself, but now that I do see him closely, it is nothing short of a shock. The emotions that assault me are every bit as turbulent as the great Lumen Sea I witnessed as a child.

My mother held my right hand while my father stood to the side as we braced against the gusting wind, watching waves crash against the white cliffs. We had been traveling by carriage to see the high king at the capital. I peered out of the carriage window as we crested a rise, and had been enraptured by my first view of the sea and the wildness of it.

"*Is it always like this?*" I asked.

"*No,*" my mother said, smiling. "*Usually, it is much calmer, but sometimes, the sea gods are angry or playful or even sorrowful, and they let us know.*"

"*I think they are playful, today,*" I announced with a little whoop.

My parents had laughed at my enthusiasm. It is only now, as I revisit the memories of these events, that I realize how very loved I was, how they always showed patience in the face of my curiosity.

Today, it feels like the sea gods are sorrowful, that they are making a storm out of all I feel, one of tumultuous churning seas with frothy white swells, crushing and breaking so violently until no gentleness is left.

Two men are present in the room, and both hold a claim to my heart.

My father, my dear father... Goddess, I could weep as I look at him. The man who stares back at me, face stark and white with shock, has aged much while we have been apart.

Then I look at Grady, and oh how I have dreamed of his face. A few more lines crease the corners of his eyes, but his hair is still a rich, dark brown, although a little gray is sprinkled through his beard, lending new maturity. Distinguished is the word that comes to mind. A powerful alpha, he towers over me and my father. *Safe.* That is what I think when I look at Grady —how safe I will be. Me, a small unremarkable woman, and yet we fit perfectly together.

Fit, as in past tense, for that part for us is over now.

He does not yet know what I am, for I have told no one save Mia and Lyra.

His eyes lower to the scarf, and his nostrils flare. It takes every bit of will not to lift my hand and adjust it, even though I know I placed it securely over the mark. My cheeks flush. I tossed my clothes on without taking time to wash. While he is unlikely to scent my omega pheromones yet, he will assuredly scent Byron on me. Why did I not consider this?

His gaze does not linger there, for it is now locked upon the bruise on my cheek. His jaw tightens, as do his fists at his side. I have not thought any of this through. Does he believe that Byron struck me?

We are at an impasse, all three of us caught in the shock and impotency of my arrival in what was clearly a tense discussion.

"My love!" My father takes a step toward me, opens his arms, and draws me in. "What have I done? My precious child, what have I done?!"

I weep, there is no hope to avoid it. The roiling emotions are inescapable as they pick me up and toss me around, breaking me down to grit and sand. For so long, I have been angry at his abstinence, but now I am in his arms again, I see him as merely a man, one who made choices, as we all do, and who did not always get them right. That swiftly, I forgive him with all my heart. He couldn't have known how Killian would turn out. None of us could predict events, nor how another person might behave.

"I am so sorry, my sweet child," he sobs, lips against my hair.

We both tremble as this emotional storm ravages us. Yet he is not the only man present, and I feel the weight of the tall alpha's stare as he watches us from the other side of the room.

I was so unsure about Grady and anticipated his indifference, but even in such a brief exchange, there was no indifference. Gently, I push away from my father, rubbing my cheeks before throwing a glance over my shoulder to where Grady stands, immobile.

Like the Goddess is sending a sign, a shaft of brilliant morning sunlight pierces the room, streaming through the window, casting the bruise upon my cheek into stark relief.

Drawing a shaky breath, I slowly turn around to face him.

"Byron?" A tic thumps in his jaw.

I shake my head swiftly.

"Killian." His eyes darken. There is no question this time. I swallow past a lump in my throat and scrub fresh tears from my cheeks.

I want to go to him.

I want to touch him so badly.

I want him to put his arms around me and tell me this will end.

My lips tremble as I realize he cares as truly and deeply as he did before he left.

"Killian?" This time, he uses a little of the power all alphas possess.

I shake, teetering like I am being pulled toward him by an invisible thread. Alphas only hold such domination over other alphas...and omegas.

"Tell me who." There is no uncertainty in his tone. This is a demand, one I must respond to.

"Killian." The word is ejected from my lips, ripped from the depths of my guts. "We quarreled last evening. He said things he has never said before."

Today, I am terrified of Killian. While I have been mindful of his unspoken intentions, now all is revealed. I do not tell Grady this. The pulsing tic in his jaw tells me he sees and understands much.

"Come here," he says.

The thread pulls me. I can no more deny my need to go to him and his request than I can starve my lungs of their right to air. Yet the steps are slow and tentative. He is impossibly broader than my memories, and I sense the body beneath the plain but well-kept leather armor is firm and taut with muscle.

He is a man in his prime.

He is an alpha.

He is deadly, yet he has only ever been gentle with me. Where I fear Killian, I welcome everything Grady might give.

As I stop before him, becoming aware of our great disparity of size, his left hand gently cups my cheek. I wince a little, although I am desperate for the touch.

"He will pay," Grady says, and never has a statement pleased me more in my life. Then his hand lowers, and my breath stutters as his strong fingers collar my throat. I can feel their power and my vulnerability in a way I never do with Byron. They are different men and alphas. Where Byron is a gentle protector, Grady is a mature, dominant male. His fingers keep sinking down until they reach my scarf. My breathing turns choppy, our eyes locked until he carefully pulls it aside, exposing the column of my throat. Then his eyes lower, and he *sees*.

I whimper as his thumb presses into the welt left by Byron's teeth, and a little cruelty enters Grady's eyes. Lips lowering to my ear, he snarls, "I want to obliterate this fucking mark. I want to wash his stink off you and replace it with my scent. I don't fucking share."

"You're going to have to." I'm shocked as the words tumble from my mouth. Where this boldness comes from, I cannot say, but I'm suddenly certain this will be so. I can no more give up Byron than I can quash my love for Grady. Both reckless and fearless in the face of this powerful male, I expect harsh denial, but what I get is a lazy smirk that sets off a slow clench in my womb.

"First, Killian needs to die."

"How?" I ask. I don't want his touch to leave, yet his hand drops away and he takes a step back.

My heart is ripped from my chest by the small separation.

"This will not be easy," he says. "It will take some time."

I shake my head. I do not want to wait. I want it to happen now.

A series of heavy thuds sound upon the chamber door, and a gruff voice calls, "Killian is sighted. We need to leave."

Grady growls at the interruption before turning to me, his hand cupping my face once again. This time, he lowers his head and captures my lips in a brief kiss. I sway into him, wanting to suck his rich scent into my lungs. The herbs I take mute little while I am in the presence of such a powerful alpha.

"Stay strong for me, Dede, just for a little longer." Then he is leaving, turning, and striding from the room.

The door opens and closes. A gut-wrenching sob escapes my throat as I crash to my knees. My father kneels beside me, gathering me into his arms and rocking me, but the door is flung open again to admit Mia.

"Dede, we need to go, now," she says, urgently grasping my hand. "I'm sorry, Dede. I'm so sorry. You can't stay here, not when Killian is on his way."

Her words make sense. I understand she is looking out for me and I must do this, but it is the hardest thing to tear myself away from my father, for we have barely spoken more than a few words.

"Go," my father urges. "Go, my sweet daughter. Soon, I pray we can talk to each other as much as we should like."

I remember nothing of the return journey to my room. Steps are lost through the tears. My heart is wrenched, pulled in different directions. One toward my father, who has made so many mistakes. One toward Byron, who is now at risk with Killian back. And finally, toward Grady, the man who first claimed my heart and who I have been separated from for longer than I thought I could endure.

I fall upon my bed, where I sob.

"Calm yourself, my lady, please. You must be calm, and you must find strength for whatever will come next." She presses a cup into my hand, and I take it, gulping down some water. "Be brave for a little while more. It will be over soon."

Finally, I find the control she entreats of me. My lips still tingle where Grady pressed a kiss, as does Byron's claiming mark.

"I will," I say. "But you must go now too."

"I will be back later," she says before taking my hand in hers for a gentle squeeze.

Alone, I lie down on my bed, where Byron's scent lingers. Last night was different between us, wilder and more satisfying to my omega side. Then Grady's kiss, his aggression when he saw Byron's mark...me telling him boldly that he would need to learn to share, stimulates my buried nature.

I fall into a dark erotic dream, one where my sweetly wicked Byron coaxes me to open and accept his knot, even as Grady's teeth sink deeply into my skin, obliterating Byron's claiming mark.

"Possessive bastard, isn't he?" Byron rumbles, lips close to my ear, burgeoning knot slipping in and out as he ruts me from behind, burning me, stretching me so good. *"Don't worry, I'll mark you up later, again and again. I'll put marks all over your lush, little omega body, so many that he won't know which are his and which are mine."*

His teeth find the other side of my throat just as his knot sinks and holds. Inside, I feel the hot flood of his cum bathing the entrance to my womb. He growls, then Grady growls in answer, and my body convulses in a phantom climax that eclipses all others. Caught between the two dominant males, I ride wave after wave of bliss.

But they are not the only alphas in my salacious dreamscape, for another male, darker, brooding, watches what we do.

Chapter Thirteen

Grady

We hasten along corridors in silence, alert to the danger but also ruminating over what just transpired. If anything, the king proved even weaker than I expected. In the back of my mind, I wondered if he'd been forced down this route, but that wasn't the case. No, he bumbled into it like a fool.

"He offered it to me," Peter says, dragging me from my thoughts.

Stunned by his words, I come to a halt. We are between a couple of outbuildings, thank fuck, because I am not seeing straight.

His eyes turn flinty. "What the fuck was I to do? An old alpha with a gammy leg. Can't lift my sword arm properly anymore, can't ride a fucking horse for more than a mile and not be half crippled at the other end. I'm no fucking commander!"

"Take the fucking position was what you were supposed to do. I told him to put you in charge, said you would be best. You don't need to lift your fucking sword arm to command, you just need to make sound decisions and tell the whelp underlings to do their fucking job. Thump the lazy fuckers among them now and then, and place someone you trust as your second to watch them while on patrol."

He swipes a hand down his face. "Aye, I figured that out after Killian took charge."

I growl under my breath, thinking about the different scenario that might have greeted us had Peter taken the position. Farms and villages still safe, certainly safer than they are now. Dede still fucking pure and untouched and waiting for me. Any time I think about Dede, I want to go on a fucking rampage. How is it possible for the lass to be even more beautiful? There was always something about her that drew me. An alpha is predisposed to find the smaller, sweeter ones attractive.

She is not so sweet anymore, and her pretty hazel eyes hold both fire and sorrow. I fucking hate that circumstance put them there, hate myself for abandoning her, and am utterly livid at seeing those marks upon her. The bruise on her cheek brings out a cold, deadly rage in me, but the claiming mark is every bit as potent, just in other ways. I cannot believe her fucking boldness in telling me that I am going to need to share.

I cannot believe I am considering it.

People will think I have lost my fucking mind, but her raw vulnerability is near enough to send me over the edge. I hold myself together by a thread, only the firm belief that caution is needed to see her freed safely keeps me in check. I don't have any fucking weapons and, so far, only a handful of trustworthy castle guards to call on.

"We'll need to move swiftly," I say. "We'll need our weapons. I won't leave Killian a threat to her for another night."

Peter nods. "We will. I'll ask Barnaby to locate your weapons. The lad has access to the stores where they likely put them. But Killian is returning, and we cannot linger here."

We continue on to the barn where Declan waits with the other men. At the entrance, I hand my cloak to the younger guard with a nod of thanks, and we slip inside. Here, I lay out my plan, and the men hasten to gather their things.

I feel Declan's eyes on me. "Are you sure you're going to be able to do this?" he asks.

I give him a look. "Do what?"

"See her with him. You were ready to charge the fucking castle last eve."

"I don't know how I'm going to handle that yet, but I will."

Chapter Fourteen

Byron

"I don't think this is a good idea," Barnaby says, shifting from foot to foot. Two years younger than me, he is new to being an alpha and almost as tall as me. Castle folks often joke he is built like a flagpole. Even so, he is a strange alpha, for his personality is much like a beta.

"No point in beating about the bush," I say. "Grady has spoken to the king, which is more than anybody else managed during the last year. Dede belonged to him before he left, and he might have expected her to wait for him, although there was no official agreement between them. Better I just get this over with. I'm not prepared to give her up unless she asks me to."

"He is going to thump you for poaching his woman," Barnaby says bluntly.

"We are not fucking savages," I say, while admitting privately that I feel savage whenever I think about Dede being taken away and can't rightly fault Grady for wanting to thump me.

Grady is not Killian, and that gives me hope that he will do right by Dede. I remember little of him before we left, for I was but a lad. My father is a baker, and I mostly helped him there. Then I revealed as an alpha, and alphas are invariably conscripted into the guard. We don't have the disposition for jobs like baking... Well, except Barnaby, who is yet an odd sort of alpha. While I don't know Grady well, I know of him, given people speak about him so often.

"I'm going anyway," I say. "Better the air is cleared, so I know where I stand."

"The decision is not up to either of you," Barnaby points out. "Everyone knows omegas are the ones who choose."

"Dede has not had a lot of choice of late..." I trail off, frowning, noting how Barnaby turns crimson. "Barnaby? What the fuck did you just say?"

"Nothing." He shakes his head vigorously. "Nothing at all... Except, she looks a bit like an omega, if you think about it."

"She is not an omega," I say, trying to shrug off the burgeoning awareness. Thoughts are clamoring in my head, seeking precedence over each over. The herb woman? Her wildness when rutting? The way she groans every time my knot presses against the entrance of her pussy? Then last night, when she begged me to knot her, told me she wanted it, scratched my back and bit me. She also begged me to bite her, to mark her—her words, not mine. Can she be an omega? Can she be disguising what she is?

Barnaby gives me a shifty look before shrugging.

"Fuck!" I mutter gruffly, grasping my hair in my fists as I pace back and forth. "What the fuck does this mean?"

Barnaby shrugs again.

"How long have you known?" I demand, rounding on him.

"When she started going to Lyra, I put two and two together and questioned Mia. She swore me to secrecy. I don't talk about my feelings much, but I love Mia and intend to wed her...well, mate her, when she is ready. So I keep Mia's confidence. Mayhap I'll be in trouble for slipping this much."

"Fuck! Do you really think Grady will give her a choice?"

Barnaby shrugs yet again. "He is our best hope to be rid of Killian, and for certain, Killian must go. Grady is a lord, a good man, and noble in deed, but an omega's scent can turn weak alphas into beasts, driving them into a frenzy, where they will rut and claim them without care. Mayhap that is one of the reasons Dede went to Lyra. Killian is not a strong alpha. A man like yourself, and Grady, would not fall to their beast side because of a change in scent...but while Killian is around, revealing her nature would have been a risk."

I feel betrayed. Why would she not tell me? I'm now certain, deep in my gut, she is indeed an omega. All the signs have been there, her slick pussy for one. I have heard tales of omega's slick and of how sweet it is, how men turn crazed for the taste. Little wonder I've spent half our precious time together with my head buried between her slim thighs.

"Are you still going to Grady?"

"Aye, I am."

"Are you going to tell him she's an omega?"

"No, that is her secret to tell."

"You are a braver man than me," he says. "It is the right thing to do. Better now before the feast."

The feast! I cannot believe there is a fucking feast tonight. Killian is back and on the rampage, from what I have heard. Should he find out I'm no longer in the cells, he'll be pissed about that too. I'm hoping he is too distracted to come after me.

"You need to keep a low profile," Barnaby says. "Killian is going to be an angry bastard. Not that I think it will take that long for...um...Grady to act."

"Something is happening? I'm about to declare myself before Grady. Tell me what you know."

"The feast is a front. I've pilfered the key to the store where their weapons are being kept. I think it would be better for you to talk to him now before anything goes down. You don't want to be on the wrong side of him. They're putting the word out through Pa and me to loyal soldiers, so we can be ready to act."

"I'd choose anyone over Killian."

"Goes without saying." He nods his head at me. "So what are you going to say?"

"I'm going to be honest with him. Tell him how I feel about Dede. If she truly wants him, it will fucking kill me, but I will leave."

❧

I part ways with Barnaby, heading along corridors and stepping into shadows more than once as guards loyal to Killian stomp past. I'm a big man and an alpha, and if any of them see me, they are sure to accost me. Killian brought half a dozen additional men with him, with more due tomorrow, so it's little surprise that Grady is intending to act swiftly.

I don't expect men to be outside the room where Grady now resides, yet nevertheless, there are two soldiers standing outside. Two alphas...and one of them is the infamous Declan.

He does a double take as he sees me approaching. I remember Declan as a giant when I was a lad working in the bakery with my pa. We are on eye level now, and my shoulders square as I note I am broader in the chest. He may have many years' experience over me, but I am not cowed by the man.

One brow lifts in question before his lips tug up on one side. "Byron?" His eyes say it is a statement, even though it sounded like a question. "Quite the mountain you turned out to be."

"I want to speak to Grady."

Declan's grin grows until it nearly splits his face. "Aye, lad, mayhap he wants to speak to you too." He throws open the door, holding out his arm, and performs a dramatic, sweeping gesture that encourages me to step within.

I glare at him. He is an odd bastard, that much is for sure. Inside, I find Grady talking to another man. They stand at the table in a pleasant dayroom not unlike the one belonging to Dede. A great scroll is spread out, which I note shows the castle plans.

Their conversation stops abruptly as the door clicks shut behind me, with Declan on the inside. Declan motions to the man beside Grady, and the other man leaves, the door opening and closing again.

Grady straightens slowly, staring at me with a telling tic thumping in his jaw. I feel trapped between these two dominant males.

Alphas are very much about hierarchy. We understand our place. Sometimes, when the men are close or aggressive, they might fight to establish a place. Other times, our ways and manners establish our place without a single blow being traded. Betas naturally fall below us. An alpha like Barnaby is below me, while I might respect older alphas like Peter, who is higher than me, I believe I could win if it came to a fight, but it is not always about brute strength.

As I study Grady, I note he holds neither my height nor brawn, yet he is powerful in ways beyond his physical capability over me. Instantly, I understand he is the more dominant male, maybe more so than Declan, who is renowned as a ferocious fighter.

I allow none of this to intimidate me. Keeping my shoulder squared, I meet his steady gaze.

"Byron," Grady says, much in the way Declan did.

"Aye, my lord. It is."

He gives me an up and down look, sizing me up. I don't mind it, since I suppose I just sized him up similarly.

"I owe you my gratitude," Grady says, surprising me.

"Fuck your gratitude," I say, my temper charging, all thoughts of maintaining a civil tongue flying out the fucking window. "Do not fucking insult me by thanking me."

Declan chuckles. "Mayhap I like the lad and his boldness."

Grady directs a brief, narrow-eyed glare at the other man.

"I love Dede," I say. I'm not a man shy of my emotions. I suffer no shame, but I do not care for their ridicule. To me, weak men—be they alphas or betas—have trouble declaring their love. A strong man proudly states his intentions.

Dede owns all my heart. It began when I first met her, when she tended me through my change. I remember well her worried face and gentle hands, pressing a cool cloth against my forehead. The pain was excruciating. Several weeks it went on before the transformation was done. Most men take months and years to fully transition to an alpha, often starting when they are young. For me, it was swift and sudden and the catalyst for a bond between us. I've heard omegas are naturally gentle in their ways, caring and empathetic. Dede is all that and more.

"She is mine, and if you try to take her from me and she does not wish it, I will fight you, even if I die. But if she chooses you" —these next words must be forced past tightness in my throat— "then I shall leave."

I expect Declan to laugh. He does not, and neither does Grady.

"You would let her choose?" Grady asks.

"Aye. I am no fool. She was yours, but for circumstances that gifted her to me. You have been gone two fucking years, and in that time, danger has overtaken her life. Killian is a bastard through and through. If I were a stronger alpha, I would have challenged him already. I am mindful of my capabilities. To throw my life away offers no service to Dede, not unless there is no other choice. Killian doesn't want to challenge me openly, for my death would not be easy and would stir unease in the castle, but he grows ever bolder. He has the power of position, and I am but one alpha who lacks experience." My lips tremble. I do not like to admit I am not the best man. Yet I must, for I alone have failed to protect her. If I were older, if I had fifty alphas with me, it would be a different matter. "I do not want to fucking go."

"I am not asking you to," Grady says, surprising me once again.

Is he saying he has no interest in Dede? Or that he will accept her decision?

"The lass indicated how she might decide," he says, tone dry.

I can't work out how to read him and instantly fear the worst.

"You have spoken to her?" Sickness roils in my gut. I told myself I would be strong, yet now this path opens before me, it stings worse than any wound.

"This morning, briefly, when she was covered in your fucking scent and barely hiding your mark behind a poorly placed scarf."

My nostrils flare, chest rising with pride at knowing he saw her thus, hot little cunt full of my cum and my mark at her throat. He doesn't realize she is an omega, and I gloat a little at having that knowledge over him. I wonder what she said...

"And what did she indicate?" I ask, impatient, not liking the way Declan begins to chuckle again.

"The lass ever had a mind of her own," Declan says. "It's good the two of you are open to letting the woman decide. Saves me from beating the pair of you."

Grady's eyes narrow on the other man before returning to me. "A discussion for tomorrow, not today. You and I will have business to finish once matters are resolved."

"What matters?" I ask. "If you're going after Killian, I want to be part of it, although I do not know what fucking use I'm going to be, given he is on the warpath for me. If he finds me out, he'll order his raider bastards to beat me again and toss me in a cell."

"Well," Grady says dryly, and I can read his amusement this time, "though they gave you a thorough beating the first time around, it appears it hasn't dampened your fire yet, but let us endeavor to keep you out of the cells. Are you willing to help?"

"In any fucking way I can. Killian's death cannot come too soon for me. I have watched him put his fucking hands on Dede one time too many. Only knowing I would likely die and leave Dede without any protection at all stayed my hand thus far. Many times, I have been ready to challenge the bastard, even though it would get me killed. I am only one man, and he has many at his call. He is a weak alpha, and I will gladly help you in any way I can."

"Excellent," Grady says decisively, curling fingers in an upward motion at Declan. "Call John back in."

As Declan moves to obey, Grady looks at me and then at the plans spread out on the table. "Come on over, lad. Your insights will be useful."

Declan

"For what it's worth, I like the cocky bastard," I say as Byron and John leave the room. Plans are underway, simple ones—the best kind, in my opinion.

Grady sends me a withering look.

I grin. I might be gloating a little now that Grady is in my position... Payback and all that. He is still fucking clueless about the depth of my feelings. I should be more bitter, but I find I lack the energy for such feelings. Byron is not the only lad who covets Dede, but he has had his cock inside her, and that's one up on Grady and me.

I can't believe Dede boldly told Grady he must share her. Ever since he dropped this little revelation, it is all I can think about.

"There was always something about Dede, even before we left, yet it is different again now," Grady says.

"How so?" I ask. The lass is no longer innocent, which will account for much. "The fact she enjoys rutting? Plenty of lasses enjoy rutting. Just because she is a princess does not mean a man should judge."

"I am not fucking judging her." Grady scowls at me. "And I am hardly pure myself. No, I can't put my finger on it. It wasn't only his scent smothering her this morning. There was something underneath it."

I shrug. "He also marked her," I point out, because I enjoy winding Grady up.

His growl is territorial. She has offered him something, told him he may share her. He is already closer to her than me. What I don't know is how Grady feels about that, because he was ever skilled at keeping his cards close to his chest. He was civil with the lad, but I'm not buying into that. I admit, I enjoyed the verbal sparring between him and Byron. The younger lad is both ballsy and fiercely protective of his mate—and she is his mate, because he marked Dede while rutting her, and there is no escaping what that means.

I sense a period of heavy adjustment coming for my friend.

And I'm about to toss another load upon his shoulders. Grady is a dominant man, and I like that about him. He is no match for me physically, but an alpha naturally understands his place in the hierarchy. I defer to Grady, yet latent desires still clamor in the darkness of the night, when I fantasize about forcing him to submit to me in the carnal way, just as I submit to him in all other matters.

There's no shame or weakness in giving yourself to another in such a way. Not all men want this, but I do. It is a hunger that has long consumed me.

"If the lad goes, I'll likely go with him," I say casually, despite there being nothing casual about this. His eyes meet mine. Sometimes I think I see understanding, and then I think I'm fooling myself and decide he understands little. How can two men be so close and yet one not see? Perhaps he sees and chooses not to acknowledge it. I am approaching the stage of recklessness, of not caring how he takes my opinions. "Why would I stay?"

There is pain in the tightening around his eyes and lips. A tic begins jumping in his jaw—his little tell.

"You would fucking leave me now?" Raw emotion colors his voice, but it is not only about him, and for once, I want an equal say.

"Don't fucking ask me to stay," I counter.

"Declan." A soft growl, a warning.

"What? Not now? Is this not a good time for us to talk about things between us?" I point my finger between the two of us, emboldened and a little reckless. If a young whelp can stand up to him, why have I taken so fucking long?

He shakes his head in another warning—another one I do not heed.

"You know how I feel about you...and her."

Growl turning feral, he takes me by the throat and slams me against the wall. My cock is thudding and challenging my leather pants that quickly. My smile is smug, and his eyes lower, fixing with unerring accuracy upon the bulge.

With a hiss, he releases me.

"What of it? I cannot fucking help myself, although it is not your subjugation of me I want."

"I am not that way," he says.

"And that is why I will leave."

He paces, glaring at me. "We need to deal with Killian, and I need to fucking focus on that."

"We will," I say. "More than half the men have declared for you. Word is spreading. One way or another, Killian will be ousted before the end of the night. Then after? If you still won't fucking talk to me about what is going on between us, then I *will* fucking leave."

He growls. He doesn't want me to go.

"You cannot have it all ways, Grady." This time, bitterness bubbles up. "You have had me as a friend for the last five years, but I do not want to be only your friend any-fucking-more. I want you under me, groaning with pleasure as I force you to submit, as I fill you with my cock. I want you sweaty, grunting, accepting your base side, but I do not only want you. I also want her."

Fire sparks in his eyes, and his nostrils flare. "She is a fucking princess!"

"She is also a woman who has been with an alpha—an alpha, I might add, who does not strike me as the sort to force matters against a woman's will. He has marked her, so we must presume she asked him to. What kind of woman would do that?" I muse.

"No right-minded woman," Grady says through gritted teeth, "would ever ask an alpha to mark her. Likely, it was the stress."

"Hmm," I say, rubbing my chin.

His eyes narrow, and he shakes his head.

"Hmm," I repeat, enjoying this moment more than is healthy, still fixed on how she told Grady he must share. "A woman with not one, but two, and now three alphas all circling, made reckless by her tantalizing scent... Like Byron, I'm prepared to accept her decision. Dede might want the lad and the lad alone. Maybe you'll go back to your brother, while I travel elsewhere. I've reached the stage of acceptance. Maybe she does want both you and Byron, and I'll leave for that reason instead. I cannot live this way anymore."

His chest heaves. He has feelings for me, and in his own way, I believe he loves me.

"You want us both?" he questions. "Would you accept all three of us, if that was what Dede wanted?"

"For sure." I have opened up to him, confident he suspected some of it, but equally confident he did not suspect it all.

"So," I say, prepared to let it drop, "how are you going to play tonight?"

Chapter Fifteen

Dede

I am dragged from my woes when Mia arrives at my room. "There is a feast tonight in honor of the Blighten's defeat. Nothing Killian says or does can stop it, given it was announced before he returned. The cooks are a flutter."

Yet during none of this statement does Mia appear happy.

"What else?" I demand.

"Grady is leaving in a few days."

My heart feels like it's being grasped in a tiny, vicious little fist. "What does this mean?"

She wrings her hands. "Perhaps he intends to take you with him."

Have I been duped? *Be strong*, he said, and yet now I become weak. I need to trust him, which would be easier if I knew his plans.

"Byron?" I ask.

"I haven't seen him. Given Killian is back, he will need to keep a low profile, which is not easy for such a strapping alpha." She throws a glance over her shoulder before turning back and squeezing my hand. "I need to go, I'm to help with the preparation of the hall."

She leaves, and I drag myself from my self-pity long enough to take a bath and order the bed be stripped and cleaned. Killian is an alpha and ever aware of scent. I have been foolish in delaying this long before dealing with both.

I am finished and belting up my gown as Anna clears up when Killian arrives.

"So, your father roused himself from his slumber by inviting everybody to a fucking feast," he announces as he barges into the room. "A feast! We don't have enough to feed ourselves for the winter, never mind a feast."

I want to point out the reason we don't have any food is because he hasn't done his job, but I hold my tongue. Memories of him slapping my face are yet fresh in my mind. Grady told me to be strong, so I'm going to be, and I'm not going to antagonize Killian.

"A feast?" I ask, like this is new to me.

"Aye, a fucking feast. The only good news is that Grady will soon leave. Now he has updated your father, there is no reason for him to linger, other than this fucking feast. Two days, and then the alpha bastard and his men will go, and life can go back to normal. I hear the servants whispering about things, thinking the weak bastard will resume command. He won't. He abandoned you once. What's to say he won't get a message from his lordly brother and abandon you again?"

His wild eyes narrow on me. "I was the only thing stopping raiders from tearing this castle apart. The people of Langetta are all ungrateful bastards with poor memories."

I have no response that won't prove inflammatory, so I say nothing.

His lips curl up in a sneer. "Do you think he could have done better?"

I am certain Grady could. A blind rat could have done a better job than Killian. Incompetence is his middle name.

"You kept us safe," I say, "and we are all grateful to you." It is a strain to push the words out past my lips, when all I want to do is rail and set my fists against his body until he bleeds. This urge for violence is new to me. I have never struck a person in my life, yet I wish to strike Killian. There was never friendship between us, but tolerance existed once. Now even that is gone, and I just want this monster removed from my life.

He steps up to me, and I fight the urge to recoil. He smirks as he curls his fingers around a lock of my hair, giving a gentle, playful tug.

I want neither his gentleness, nor his playfulness. I want nothing from this man. His very touch repulses me.

"Wear something pretty. I want to be sure Grady and the whole castle knows you are now mine. I'll have you bred before the month is out."

And with those parting words, he pivots, then strides from the room.

Despite Mia's determination that Grady will not abandon me, doubts and fears remain. He kissed me and put his hands upon me in a way that bridges the gap of the last two years, yet the whole day has left me unsettled, and now there is the feast.

When my mother was still alive, a feast would be viewed with joyful anticipation. I had been still a girl then, and as the night would draw on and the revelry become raucous, I would be sent to my room. Barely had I entered womanhood when my mother went to the Goddess' side, and afterward there were no more feasts. Then, only a year later, Blighten began attacking the northern borders, and many men left. I was just escaping the depression of my mother's passing, and suddenly, my world was once more ripped apart.

Clouds have lingered over this castle for too long, while Killian's incompetence manifests ever darker days. To add further insult, he wishes me to dress in something 'pretty' so he may parade me around. He doesn't even want me, he just wants the castle. I'm merely a means to an end. His treatment of me is sure to take on a bleaker turn should he claim the kingdom.

"*Stay strong for me, Dede, just for a little longer,*" Grady said. I will, but it is far harder now that I have glimpsed hope.

My capacity to endure is waning, and I am tired of being brave.

"The blue one, my lady?" my maid asks, holding up a whimsical creation I last wore three years ago before my mother passed away. The fabric came from the Imperium lands across the sea, and it shimmers under the lamplight. That it will still fit is testament to how little I have changed over time.

I nod, despite my personal feelings, because Killian has given me his orders and his orders must be obeyed. My maid places it over the bottom of the bed, along with shoes and undergarments, before hastening to me, where she sets about curling my hair. The old mirror on the table before me is worn by time and a little foggy. The woman who looks back at me might as well be a stranger, for I do not know her. Surely the last three years should be imprinted upon her? Yet the face shows no sign of all the trauma, heartache, and pain.

Plain is the word that comes to mind when I look upon myself. I am small and unremarkable, with hair neither blonde nor brown, and my eyes are neither brown nor green nor blue, but a combination of them all. I admit they appear long lashed and luminous in the lamplight, and perhaps even pretty.

Done with my hair, the maid selects a pot from the collection she placed on my dressing table earlier. "My lady, if I may?"

Inside is a creamy powder. When I look at her in confusion, she gestures toward my cheek.

"It will cover the mark," she says matter-of-factly, like covering a mark upon a woman's face is an entirely ordinary occurrence. Such acts are not ordinary to me, and I hate that the readiness of such creams suggests it is I who is ignorant.

I nod once, and she goes to work masking the purple mark. The slight swelling cannot be disguised, but the color blends seamlessly into my skin, hiding the bruise from all but the most critical inspection. Then I direct her toward the mark at my throat. She frowns, perhaps thinking it odd that I would cover Killian's claiming mark. After a brief pause, she dabs the powder over it before fussing over my hair and dabbing a little color on my pale cheeks.

The quiet attention of the maid is brought to an end when Killian returns. Dismissing her, he comes to stand behind me. His hair is wet. He has bathed and donned a clean leather jerkin and pants. Killian is putting on a show, and tonight, I am his unwitting star. As our eyes meet the mirror, I'm relieved I thought to cover Byron's mark with the powder.

Gaze lowering, he plays with a tendril of my hair artfully coiled against my neck. He is a handsome man, but what lies inside his heart is black. Had our lives played out differently, had the Blighten not attacked and he not become so monstrously fixated on power, we might even have been friends. There is no way back to that now, nor of undoing tragic events.

"You will settle once you are with child," he says. "All

women do. Few marriages are based on love and desire. Most are arrangements. If you give me a child, I will treat you fairly. I will not hurt you again. I was angry. Can you forgive me?"

No, is the answer that explodes within my mind. I do not want to forgive him. "Yes," I say, forcing a smile past my tight lips. My confidence is crushed. Inside, I am trembling, frail and shattered, with him so close. I do not trust him. Tolerance is gone, and now his very proximity produces deep, dark fear.

As his lips lift in a smirk, I understand it is different from his side. For him, the matter is over and closed, and we can move past what transpired.

He holds out his hand, and it takes strength of will to place my hand within his and allow him to escort me from the room.

෯

My belly tightens as we enter the hall, where a lively tune is playing. Laughter and the din of conversation envelop me as I skim the crowd, and when I do not find either Grady or Byron, disappointment crashes through me. Is this a sick ruse? Has Killian slain them? Is he about to present me with their heads?

I stumble.

Killian catches my elbow to steady me. "Careful, my love."

I want to snatch my elbow from his grasp, but he is already guiding me across the room to the high table. We take a seat, and he calls over a servant, who is swift to pour us both a drink. Snatching up the goblet, I gulp down half of it. Killian chuckles, raises his beer to his men, and calls out to them that his woman is 'limbering up.' The soldiers guffaw and cheer at my expense.

It is not for Killian's benefit that I drink, it is merely a desire for oblivion.

A guard comes over to talk to Killian, and they engage in a

conversation of no interest to me. I busy myself skimming the crowd filling the castle hall. Faces, both familiar and less so, jumble together. Some of those people were once loyal supporters of my father but have turned toward Killian of late. They are only hedging their bets, as people are wont to do, but it still hurts.

The castle is my home, and the hall is comfortingly familiar. The walls are whitewashed between the dark wooden pillars and bracing, with two stone fireplaces centering either side. Evenings can be chilly at this time of year, and both hearths are ablaze. Six long, wooden tables sit to each side of a central corridor leading to the dais, where the high table is. Lamps, intermixed with candelabras, hang from thick age blackened chains in the high vaulted ceiling.

A few people are seated, while many others stand. Among the crowds, I recognize some of the returning alphas and I take this as a positive sign, although I still cannot see Grady. Declan is not here yet either, I notice with a frown. Declan is hard to miss.

Then the far hall door opens, and Grady enters. At his side is Declan, one of the few men taller than he is. They have a presence. My stomach starts to flutter, and my heart wants to beat out of my chest. I bury my nose in my goblet while sending a surreptitious glance their way. Goddess, I come alive, simply that the two of them are here and near. I love Grady, I realize. My feelings never diminished in all the while we were apart.

I didn't fully appreciate Grady's presence earlier in my father's chamber. Tall, broad, and handsome, and yet he is also a formidable warrior. Then there is the darkly brooding Declan, who always tied my tongue in knots. Grady wears tan leather pants and a lighter shirt under a matching leather jerkin. Declan wears black leather pants and full-sleeved armor jerkin. They draw the interest of the room, from women and

men alike, and heads turn—women with undisguised appreciation, and men with appraisal, perhaps jealousy, even respect,
maybe all those things. They are captivating, like a flame on a
dark night. Instinctively, people seek to be near to them,
wanting to engage and hear what they have to say. Within no
more than a few steps, they are swallowed by the crowd.

A man leans in to say something to Grady. It must amuse
him, for he throws his head back and laughs. A length of the
hall separates us, yet I can hear him over the raucous merriment
and lively tune on drum and fiddle that weaves between.

Goddess, I have been starved for that sound.

My eyes skim the crowd, searching for signs of Byron. I will
find no measure of relief until I see him as well. Doubt raises its
ugly head out of nowhere, threatening to crush my burgeoning
hope. Realizing my goblet is empty, I put it down on the table.

Killian calls a server to fill it. "My lover is amorous tonight."
He winks at the servant, who blushes prettily before scurrying
off.

The man beside Killian roars with laughter and pats Killian
on the back like he has already bred me. "Won't be long till you
get your first whelp."

"Aye," Killian agrees. Smirking, he glances at me. He thinks
himself clever to banish Lyra. I want to tell him that his inadequate cock could never get me with child.

On the far side of the room, I spot Mia weaving through the
crowd on a course for Grady. She slips her arm through his and
says something to him. I snatch up the goblet again to take
another sip, just as the great doors open and a procession of
servants enter, carrying food and more drinks. Guests hasten to
take seats at long tables filling the hall as platters and jugs of ale
and wine are distributed around the room.

The gaiety feels stifling, and my father is notable in his

absence. I had a strange and misplaced notion he might enter and denounce Killian before the room.

He doesn't, and the man I have come to hate gathers my hand and lifts it to his lips. Carefully, I retrieve my hand, my eyes locked with Killian's.

"Tonight," he says ominously, "we will begin a new chapter of our lives."

I raise my goblet to his tankard. *Touch me again, and I will stab you with the blunt knife I tucked under my pillow.* "To a new chapter," I agree.

Chapter Sixteen

Grady

How is it possible for her to look so beautiful and yet painfully vulnerable all at once? She is tiny in the shadow of Killian, her gown a whimsical creation in blue silk, while her golden-brown hair has been curled and catches the light. I told myself I could handle this, but as Killian raises Dede's hand to his lips, I decide that I cannot.

I growl.

"My lord?" A small hand grips my arm fiercely and rouses me from a fantasy where I beat Killian's smug face into the table until it turns to bloody pulp. It takes a supreme effort, but I drag my attention from the bastard touching what is mine and redirect it to the tiny beta woman standing at my side. "Your growl was extremely loud!"

When I survey those closest to me, I see wary expressions. No more than ten paces away, Declan is only half listening to the man beside him, for he is staring at me in the way of someone who expects to imminently intervene. He also smirks, amused by my slip.

Our tense conversation earlier is another worry on my mind. I've always known he had feelings toward me, for the man is not subtle about anything. What I did not suspect was how polarizing the situation was.

My focus returns to Mia, and I place my hand over hers, just as the double doors open and a procession of servants carrying food, drinks, and platters of every kind and shape move into the room to the cheers of the crowd. We take a seat, Declan to one side of me, Mia to the other, while the remainder of my alphas are distributed around the room.

I go through the motions of faking enjoyment, but inside, I am a mess of conflict and pissed with Declan for bringing an ultimatum to my door. I try telling myself he was just taunting me, yet for once, he was serious. I cannot imagine a life without Declan, nor one without Dede. Then there is Byron boldly announcing he loves Dede. I think it might be the fucking lad that has set Declan off.

I don't know how to share, nor how to submit, which is what Declan wants. I'm an alpha who would naturally rise to the top of any hierarchy. That is not boastful on my part, but simply an understanding of facts. I have looked at Declan on occasion and appreciated the value of the man. From humble and challenging beginnings, he has risen up and somehow still retains a sense of humor. He is also a powerful alpha and pleasing to the eye.

"Do you want me to test it?" Mia gestures toward the wine I am yet to pick up.

I raise a brow. "Do you need to?"

Her lips tug up. "No, lord. The serving lass who came over to us is my friend. Given Killian has tried to rut her a time or two, she will help anyone to be rid of him. You need not fear any food she brings.

Snatching up the goblet, I take a drink. I need something to take the edge off the rage building inside me. I can't look at the high fucking table, for seeing Dede sitting beside Killian is enough to throw all my caution to the wind.

"Will you act tonight?" Mia asks, smiling sweetly like we are talking about the weather.

"I will. For now, I want Killian to think I'm truly intending to leave and merely here to enjoy a feast."

"Good," she says decisively.

Dede

The night is long and painful, but this time, it is not the physical kind.

I have seen nothing of Byron, and I'm forced to endure hours of revelry that grows ever more raucous. Beside me, Killian is talking to another man, but his hand often strays to gather mine. I cannot abide his touch. It makes me want to vomit all over the table. All the while, my eyes feast on Grady... and Declan.

The two men sit together. Mia is beside Grady, and I take comfort in that until she rises and slips out the door. No sooner does she leave then another woman enters and approaches Grady, leaning right in with her breasts in his face! My temper rises further when she dares to put her hand on his shoulder.

He is not mine, I remind myself, then I realize where he is staring, the way his lips rise in a smirk... The lass climbs onto his lap, then he picks up his tankard and offers it to her.

My heart thuds erratically, and my palms turn clammy. Thank the Goddess Killian is busy talking and does not notice me. The lass sups the beer before passing it back to Grady with a grin. He takes another drink and leans back into the seat, while my thoughts collapse into chaos. There she is, where I want to be, a sweet little beta nestled on his lap and gazing up at him as she plays with the ties at the collar of his leather jerkin.

Declan laughs and slaps Grady on the shoulder as he rises gracefully from his seat. My eyes dart between the two men. Declan does not appear concerned that Grady has some floozy upon his lap. I am betrayed by Grady, by Mia, by my own heart, and yet how can I be, when earlier, I was the one telling him he must share.

Now I feel sick. What if he won't share? Why would he? This is not the Imperium lands, where omegas are claimed by several mates. This is Hydornia, and here, omegas are bound to only one man. He doesn't even know I'm an omega. He thinks me a beta, as does Byron. Does this make me selfish? I think it does. I think the fact that I am enraged by this hussy on his lap makes me the worst kind of hypocrite. The tankard is slammed against the table before he fists her long blonde hair, head lowering with intent.

My chest heaves, and I cannot bear another moment. I swallow as a hand closes over mine and turn to my right. I have been so focused on Grady, I did not realize Killian had finished his conversation and was studying me.

"It seems I read him wrong," Killian says.

I smooth out my expression, but his broad grin tells me I fail.

"My poor love." Killian smirks. "Did you still think he was coming to save you? You did, didn't you?" He throws back his head and roars with laughter.

I cannot stay here suffering the raucous merriment saturating the room. I rise, but as I do, his harsh fingers grasp my wrist, holding me in place. "Best you prepare yourself. I will join you shortly." He nods his head to two guards as he releases me.

Shaking, I can barely stumble from the room. As though on cue, the revelry rises another notch, wild laughter and singing rising, while a fight breaks out to a great cheer. The men are dragged apart and handed beers with a slap on the back. They chink tankards, and the fight is forgotten. Suddenly, the castle is a strange and dangerous place as I hasten for my room. My two jailers follow close behind. I can tell the difference between the genuine men of the castle and those who are Killian's raider scum.

The urge to run grips me, but I keep my steps steady, all the while I'm thinking about the knife tucked under my pillow. My backup plan is now my only plan. I won't let him touch me. If he tries to again, I will stab him in any way I can.

Lost in my thoughts, I belatedly realize we are nearing my chamber. The corridor appears unnaturally dark with several lamps out. Out of the darkness, two shapes loom toward us, men approaching, and the nearer they draw, the more obvious their great size becomes. Alphas? They must be. There are only a few alphas within our castle—Killian Peter, Barnaby, and Byron. That is it. The rest all belong to Grady.

My heart races as I try to work out what this means. Their faces are hidden behind helmets. Who would wear helmets inside?

Behind me, the guards are busy muttering complaints about being called from the festivities to babysit me. The lack of beer and rutting is the extent of their attention—a petty conversation for petty men. My breath catches in my chest as I cross paths with the two towering alphas. They pass, then the sounds of a scuffle ensue, thuds and grunts, and I turn to find them over-powering my guards.

"Open the door," one man rumbles. "Quickly, lass."

Lass? Why does the voice sound familiar? Is that...Declan? I gape, stupefied, as they continue grappling with the guards, grunting, thrashing, and flailing arms and legs.

"Open the fucking door!" the man barks, putting his alpha will behind it and startling me from my stupor.

I dash forward, clumsy fingers finding the handle of my door before I throw it open.

My two guards are now silent, dead or unconscious, I'm not sure which, and their bodies are dragged into my room.

"Shut the door," Declan barks. I am now confident this is indeed him.

I do as I'm asked, my vision becoming a tunnel that accepts only snatches. Declan is here. Does this mean...

One of the jailers rouses again, and Declan—I know it is Declan, even though he still wears a helmet—punches him in the face.

Silence follows, then Declan turns, ripping his helmet off.

Our eyes lock. I've always been intimidated by Declan. He is playful, and besides Byron, he is the largest alpha I have ever met. Unlike Byron, who is sweet and wicked when he does the things he does to me, Declan's playfulness hides a darker side that makes the omega in me shudder, forcing me to acknowledge the full potency of a man and alpha.

When he left, I was still a beta and didn't understand the emotions he stirred within me. Now I realize why the omega side of me cannot help but respond. He terrifies me, did and still does, but now, it is a sensual kind of fear that brings a sweet clench to my pussy, making my gown feel tight across my chest.

His eyes lower to where my breasts heave. Both of us

remain caught in an impasse until the other soldier thumps him on the shoulder.

"Stop ogling her, fucker!" he snarls as he yanks off his helmet. Byron?

"I can't help myself—the lass is comely." Declan turns back to me, smirking. "For the record, your mark doesn't bother me."

"The fuck?" Byron says, facing off with Declan, who only shrugs. They are of height, Byron slightly broader in the shoulder, but he is young and does not have the wildness nor the darkness I sense within Declan. The two men are like day and night, their different journeys through life producing very different men.

My body goes up in flames. Goddess, this is the worst time to have this kind of response. Declan's comment about the mark captures all my mental capacity. How does he know about it? It must mean Grady told him. I wish I knew what was said.

A cry comes beyond the door.

"We can't linger here," Declan says. "The guards will not rouse again."

It's only now that I notice the blood pooling on the floor around the two downed men.

"It'll be okay, Dede," Byron says, and I wrench my gaze from the bodies to look at him. "We'll be back later. Lock the door, bolt it, and block it as best you can."

Then they are leaving, and I do exactly as he said, wedging a chair under the handle before throwing the bolt across.

Chapter Seventeen

Grady

Minutes turn into hours as I wait for everything to fall into place. The thought of Killian using Dede as a hostage or shield was too high a risk. I wanted her out of the room, and a lass by the name of Marie, now sitting on my lap, was Mia's answer to this problem, one that leaves much to be desired. It did get the job done, though, and Dede fled the room. What I didn't expect was the pain that lanced my body in doing this to her.

I trust Declan and Byron to look after her. They will have her safe in her room by now and her guards will be out of the way—two less for us to deal with. The night is yet young, and there is still much to do.

"You're tense, my lord," Marie says.

"Aye," I say.

"Barnaby will not fail you," she says. "He is the kindest, most amazing man I know."

It seems Mia is not the only one besotted with the unassuming alpha lad. Marie has talked nonstop about Barnaby. I don't know if the lad is with both women, or if it is merely hopefulness on Marie's part. It is not unusual for an alpha to claim more than one mate...but Barnaby?

A fight breaks out on the other side of the room between two of my men—a fake altercation to give the impression of alphas supping liberally of beer. Better Killian thinks of us as drunken slobs making the most of the feast. I watch him chatting to his men where he sits on the high table, like the castle is already his.

The sudden clanging of the castle bell takes a few moments to penetrate the fog of revelry gripping the room.

My heart rate surges. Over on the dais, Killian staggers to his feet.

On cue, Barnaby charges the room. "Raiders!"

I rise from my seat as the room dissolves into chaos. Marie darts under the table out of the way. "Here," she says.

I reach my hand under, finding the sword ready and waiting, strapped to the underside of the table. I'm not the only man similarly retrieving hidden weapons, and my cry is echoed around the room. People scatter, and Killian's brows draw together in confusion. The raider bell still rings, so perhaps he assumes I hold a sword because I intend to help him.

Assuredly, I am armed because I intend to slice the bastard from crotch to throat.

His eyes shift to the door to his right, the one Dede went through, before returning to the double doors Barnaby burst through. Fighting is already breaking out as I leap over the table and charge for him. His eyes swing toward me and he draws his sword, but it is not my challenge he comes to meet. No, he shouts to his men, telling them to cut me off before taking off for the door.

"Fuck," I mutter as I lock swords with the first man. I slash, parry, and punch past those in my way, all the while counting the seconds Killian has on me. Men fall under my savage assault as I kick, punch, elbow, and stab. I have battled the Blighten the last two years, and before that, soldiered both here and for my brother, so I am well practiced with the rough skills of raiders.

The good people of the castle flee the room around the fighting. I've gotten word out, and many left subtly throughout the night. If Killian had paid any attention, he would have noticed no women were present, save the one now hidden under the table, who Barnaby swore to take to safety.

Killian brought more raiders when he returned from his travels, and more are due tomorrow. I need to end Killian tonight, but there are people between the bastard and me. Keeping the plan simple was always my intention, but I expected Killian, enamored with his own prowess, to come straight for me, not slink off like a dog.

I stab, piercing the chest of the next man who attacks before planting my boot to aid yanking my blade free. He slumps to the floor, dead, as I swing to counter the next strike. John sees what I'm about and charges into the group blocking my path. Together, we cleave our way through, leaving me clear to take a familiar route to Dede's room. Killian could be fleeing, it would be a sensible thing for him to do, but something tells me the bastard is not ready to give up Langetta Castle, and further, would use Dede in any way he can to claim it.

The alarm continues to sound, while screams, cries, and the clash of weapons rings from every direction. There is no easy way to take back a castle infiltrated by raiders.

My boots clatter across the stone floor as I race for her room. As I round the corner, a single high scream rents the air, and I skitter to a stop outside the door.

My heart lodges in my throat as I find Killian fisting Dede's hair, his sword against her throat.

Killian is renowned for his skills, full of flair, always wanting to lord his prowess over others. He ever did like to play, but I won't let him toy with Dede.

"Let her go." I don't look at Dede. If I do, I will fail.

"I don't think so," Killian says. "I think that would be a very bad idea."

"Are you admitting that you're a lesser swordsman?" I taunt.

He laughs and tightens his fingers, drawing a whimper from Dede and a low growl from me. "I know I hold skill over you, but this is not about whether I'm better, is it?" He sneers. The blade is too close to her flawless skin.

Beyond the room, the bell is still clanging and the tumult of battle peaks, but inside this room, we are at an impasse. Although my eyes are locked on Killian's, my awareness is on the way Dede trembles. My hand, by comparison, is rock steady, for I am indifferent to everything save removing this man and threat.

I don't expect what comes next. Neither does Killian.

I catch a glint of metal as her hand swings down. A dagger?

He howls, sword wavering long enough for her to slip from his grasp. She staggers forward, throwing herself at me, and I clasp her to me with my free arm. For a too brief moment, I revel in the rightness of her being so close.

Killian reaches down and rips the blade out with a grunt before tossing it to the floor. "Stupid bitch," he says, spittle spraying from his lips. It is not a deep wound, which is a pity. The bloody knife upon the floor is a...dinner knife? My sweet, brave Dede has stabbed him with a kitchen knife.

"Out of the way, lass." I consider telling her to flee the room, but the truth is I need her close. Anything could be happening in the corridors as the battle continues. "Under the table and don't come out."

She clings. She doesn't want to let go.

"Now, Dede," I say, putting a bit of force behind it. She jerks away before scurrying for cover. Killian makes a dive for her. I cut him off, and our weapons clang together.

He dared to touch what is mine, sought to take her castle and birthright from her, this upstart, this weak man. Skilled with the sword he may be, but my determination will see this done.

Our swords clash as we slash, parry, cleave, and strike, coming together then drawing apart over again. His blade finds my flesh, cutting through my shirt at my shoulder, drawing the first blood, then second blood. Our blades clash, fists punch, and blood sprays, knocking over furniture as we punch and fight for our lives, while under the table, I hear Dede's whimpers.

Our swords clang and hold. My fist swings in an uppercut, and he staggers back, crashing against the table Dede is hiding underneath. He rolls off, toppling a chair before surging to his feet, his blade slashing out. I counter, metal clanging loudly in the room. Then he charges, another clash of swords, and I'm flying backward. He comes down over me, but I roll just in time as his sword smashes into the floor to the right of my head... I roll back the other way, narrowly missing the next strike.

A dull thud accompanies Dede smashing him over the head with a base of a thick candelabra. Her face is the image of rage as she goes to strike him again. "Get back!" I roar, kicking his legs out from under him before staggering to my feet. He tumbles to the floor, but he is not down for long and his sword glances my thigh.

Dede squeals. The lass is still holding her weapon like she is ready to wade fucking in. I need to end this! The Goddess is with me, though. I feel her guide my arm, and my blade comes up, my strike skewering Killian in the gut.

His expression is one of shock, mouth opening, blade swinging but losing momentum. The wound is mortal, his mind yet to catch up with this fact. Snarling, I rip my sword free, and with the next blow, slice through his throat.

"Grady!" Her improvised weapon drops with a thud as Dede scrambles for me, crashing into me. I stagger from the impact of such a tiny little thing.

"I'm fine. Are you fine? Tell me there is not a mark on you?" Breathing heavily, I try to peel her off so that I might check her thoroughly. My cuts sting, blood trickling over my eye where a blow caught my temple, but I don't care about any of this.

Finally, it is over.

Chapter Eighteen

Dede

A man I do not recognize charges into the room, but he does not register as a threat as I'm feverish, trying to check Grady for damage. There is so much, I can't decide what should take precedence. The fight was vicious and ultimately deadly for Killian. I'm in shock. I cannot assimilate that the man who tormented me for the last two years of my life is finally dead.

"What news?" Grady asks.

"It's over," the newcomer says. "Only a few stragglers left that we are rounding up. Do you want to keep any for questioning?"

"Aye," Grady says. "Put them in the cells with a guard on them. If they give you any trouble, kill the bastards and toss their bodies over the wall."

The man nods, but before he leaves, there comes the drum of rapid footsteps. Byron barrels into the room, and close behind him is Declan. Byron's face goes from me to Grady, who I'm clinging to still...then to the floor, where Killian lies dead.

"Dede!" Byron's voice is ripe with emotion. I want to go to him, but I can't release Grady either. I am utterly conflicted.

A deep growl emanates from Grady's chest, the aggressive kind that sets hairs raising on the back of my neck. I'm focused on Byron, about to disentangle myself, when Declan steps up, places an arm around Byron's throat, another around his waist, and begins to choke him out.

"What? No!" I squeal, horrified by the garbled, gasping sounds and the desperateness in Byron's eyes. Then nothing, and the alpha I love is lowered to the floor. "What are you doing?" I fight for freedom, but Grady clamps an arm around my waist, preventing me from going to my beloved Byron.

"Sorry, little lamb," Declan says calmly. "Grady has issues to work through, and they'll progress quicker with Byron out of the way." He turns around and calls, "John, help me carry the heavy bastard out."

I sob and plead as they carry a lifeless Byron from the room. Inconsolable, I rage at Grady, once my savior, but now I hate him. I cry, fight, and rail at him with all my small strength, but the disparity between us is so vast, it may as well be absolute. Grady simply tosses me over his shoulder and strides from the room.

"I want Byron! Take me to him now. I want Byron!" A moment ago, I loved Grady. Now I despise him for allowing hurt to come to my sweet Byron, and Declan for his part of this.

"I will stab you in your heart," I vow. "Put me down this instant."

"You can try," Grady says. "I'll be making sure there is no cutlery with your food, for sure."

I beat at his back, kick and thrash, wondering where he is taking me. It does me no good. We enter a plain room, furnished with a wooden bed, no covers, just a thin mattress and a high window with bars. Not quite a cell, but bare and unfamiliar to me, it fills me with dread. A white gown hangs behind the door.

"How can you do this after my father granted you access to our home! You are a monster," I hiss. "A monster!"

I'm dropped to land sprawling upon the bed. He stands over me, chest heaving, eyes a little wild. I do not recognize this cold version of Grady. My lips tremble, my chest rising and falling unsteadily with all the potency of my fury.

"I want Byron."

"When I'm ready," Grady says. "Strip."

"What?" I screech. "I will not take my clothes off for you."

"Take them off, or I'll cut them fucking off."

"I'll do nothing to help you," I spit out.

A wicked glint enters his eyes as he draws his dagger from the sheath, and coming down over me, proceeds to slice my pretty gown away. I beat at him, kick, and rake him with my nails. He pays me no heed, and having stripped me, he gathers up the tatters and tosses them out of the room. The white gown is taken from the hook beside the door and presented to me.

"You can put that on, or you can stay naked."

I thought him a noble man. How did I read him so wrong? "Why?" I demand, snatching the gown and dropping it pointedly to the floor. "Why would you do this to me?"

"You will not leave this room until you bleed. The only person who will tend to you until that happens is me."

I laugh. This is ludicrous. This is the most ridiculous thing I've ever heard. I kick the white gown away and laugh louder.

"You think this is fucking funny?"

My laughter dies as quickly as it arrives. "What would you do if I were with child?" My voice is barely above a whisper.

His chest rises on a ragged breath, before he slowly lets it out. "I don't fucking know," he says, and with those parting words, he strides from the room, slamming the door shut on me. The sound of the lock turning is like a splash of cold water on my manic state.

I wonder at how this night has turned out. I want my gentle Byron to hold me, and tell me this will be okay. But my last image of him is him being choked out by Declan. If I hate Grady, I hate Declan too.

Alone, the tears begin to spill. I reason they are not intending to kill Byron, for they could have easily done so already. No, they are merely keeping him from me, and I will not forgive them for that.

Curling up on the bed, I draw my knees in tight, not bothering with the white gown he gave me.

"You will not leave this room until you bleed," he said.

Given I am not a beta, I will never bleed for him, but soon, the lack of herbs will change me. My pussy aches, feeling strangely empty. Grady's scent is all over me, and my traitorous body can think of nothing else.

I weep for the lives lost tonight, for my father, for the hole left when my mother passed, for Byron, and for myself. There is no more raider bell, the sound stopped, and I didn't even notice. Now the deafening silence pulls me under.

Beyond the door, it is quiet, but my head is filled with the sounds of battling, screaming, and horror.

One day soon, Grady will realize what I am, only I will not submit to him easily then. I may not submit at all.

❧

Declan

"Well, that could have gone better," I say dryly. Grady sits on a chair, naked, being stitched up by a stick-like beta who is so painfully slow at sewing, I want to snatch the fucking thing from him and do it myself. My stitching is not the best. I'm literally the last person anyone would come to with a gaping wound, but fuck it, I reckon I could do a better job of it than this senile old goat. Not that I blame the man when Grady is issuing a deep rattling growl the whole fucking time.

"And it could have gone a lot worse," Grady counters.

I admit, he looks fucking divine sitting there, muscles pumped from the battle past, bleeding, with a thin sheen of sweat over his body, full of growly rage. I want to take his mind off all the trauma he's just tossed over our lives...and thump the dumb bastard up the side of the head for his handling of this.

"You're staring," Grady says.

I drag my gaze away from his cock. It's been semi hard the whole time, but he's had Dede plastered all over him, so it's not surprising.

"You didn't really think through your plans for Dede, did you?" I'm confident she's not a beta. I'm also confident Grady is utterly blind to reason at this point. He'll find out soon enough. Mayhap we all will. Life is already complex, and it's going to become a thousand times worse once she reveals.

Grady winces, and the fossil tending to him stammers an apology. Grady waves him to carry on. "She just laughed."

Goddess, the poor lass is hysterical. I feel a growl bubble up, ready to thump the chump now and storm the castle, searching for wherever the idiot has sequestered her. "When?"

"When I told her she was not leaving the room until she bled. Do you think she's with child?"

I huff out a breath. It would seem our little lamb has the measure of Grady.

Grady resumes his growling, and the man stitching him begins to shake so badly, it's a miracle he can get the fucking needle in.

I sigh heavily and approach the two, motioning the fossil to hand over the needle.

"No." Grady shakes his head. "Fucking no."

"It's me or no one. What with you spouting bullshit from your mouth, it's little wonder the man is ready to shit himself." I motion the man out, draw up a chair, and get on with stitching him up. It's not deep and needs no expertise.

"I'll look like a butcher has been at me," he grumbles.

"A stitch is meant to hold the flesh together. Anything else is a bonus, as far as I'm concerned."

"Fuck!" Grady hisses when I stab a little deep.

"You're acting like an ass. You can't lock the lass up."

"And choking Byron out in front of her was better?"

"I didn't have any choice, did I? He wanted to hold her. If he'd touched her, what would you have done?"

We both know the answer. The next couple of stitches come out fairly neat.

"You make a valid point," he finally admits.

"A very valid fucking point. I know you." The next stitch is too large and at a bit of an angle. I persevere, and the last few turn out fine. "You would have carved the poor lad up in front of Dede."

"I could have tempered it," he says.

"You're like a bull getting a whiff of a fertile cow." He doesn't argue. I've seen farmers trying to ward off a bull when he set his sights on a plump little heifer for breeding. Not a fucking chance. "Figured I would remove the lad from the

162

room until you calmed the fuck down. I wasn't expecting you to lock her up like some kind of fucking barbarian."

I'm done with his arm. There is a final wound on his thigh. He gives me a shifty look before nodding his head. His cock is hard, but that is what happens when a sweet, secret little omega descends upon your life. My own cock is hard, and it is not all Dede. I can smell him, the scent of pre-cum leaking from the tip. Mayhap he might feel a bit calmer if I sorted it out.

I stitch the gash up, and he remains stoic the whole time.

"I did what I needed to do to stop you from doing something you'll regret for the rest of your life."

"Thank you," he says.

"Now you're under a measure of control, I'll leave you to deal with this mess you've created."

He frowns as I set the needle on the table behind him and rise.

"What do you mean?" he says

"I'm leaving on the morrow."

"You're not fucking leaving," he says, and he's right, I'm not, but he needs some hard truths.

"You need to find a way to share with the lad."

"I don't know how to fucking share!"

"I dare say most men don't until they have to, and then they do. You can't punish him and you can't kill him. There will be enough damage, given I choked him out, but that's on me not you, so hopefully, she'll forgive you for what happened after."

I'm guessing she has been suppressing what she is, and if that's the case, sooner or later, Grady is going to have a whole other problem on his hands. I wanted her before, when she was a funny, mousy little beta with arresting hazel eyes and pouty lips designed by the Goddess herself to worship a man's cock. I have no doubt the rest of her—and I've seen only hints hidden behind clothing—is similarly lush, with a hot little pussy that will be able to take the whole of an alpha's cock and his knot. We've seen evidence of her passion and lust.

They share omegas in the Imperium, at least two, more often three or four, sometimes as many as five or six. I've seen such omegas, and they look happy, cherished by their mates. It's not the way here, where omegas mate with one, but rare omegas occasionally need more than one or their scent does not change. They call them throwbacks, reminding us of a time when we were savages living in caves. Alphas are descended from shifters, but somewhere along the line, we lost the ability to shift. Other changes happened over time. We still form a connection with omegas. All alphas are taught the lore after we change so we might be ready. Most bond with a beta, and they are happy. Betas can be trained to satisfy an alpha and his ways, but they are rarely shared in the way omegas are. The sweet hazel-eyed little goddess who befuddles Grady's mind is assuredly going to be a test.

"You're not leaving," Grady repeats.

"I'm not leaving, *yet*," I counter. "You're going to need to speak to the lad. You know that, don't you?"

He sighs. "Yes, but not today."

He could be balls deep in Dede now. I'm sure her first good rutting from an experienced alpha would bring her status as an omega to the fore. Once he had rutted her and claimed her, he would calm the fuck down and mend bridges with Byron. Only he's acting like a prize whelp. I want to reason with him, but I have known him too long. The shake in his hands, the discordant rattle in his purr, both speak of a man on the edge. I would need to beat him bloody to hope to counter that, and I don't have it in me, nor do I trust myself not to end up rutting him into submission.

I leave but miss him the moment the door closes, wishing I could go to Dede, or talk to Byron, even. But a great moat surrounds me. They are part of something, although mayhap they don't understand it yet, and I, the former street rat, am an unwelcome cog and outsider.

Chapter Nineteen

Grady

"How was the king?" Declan asks as he joins me on the battlements. Today is a drizzly autumn day, and the visibility is poor. The forest has been cut back in every direction from the castle. It's about a mile to the nearest tree line, and as we watch, a patrol of six riders emerges and approaches. Normality is starting to return. We've executed the last of the raiders and tossed their bodies in the woods as a warning to the others. We're going to need to deal with the bastards who still harry the villages and farms, but for now, we are reinstating patrols and gathering what information we can on where they are holed up.

"He ventured out briefly," I say. "We took a walk to the hall, where he met with his newly appointed chancellor. He asked to see Dede."

"Awkward," Declan says with a grimace.

Declan thinks I'm irrational. I probably am, but I need to

know whether she's with child. If she is, I don't have a fucking clue what I'll do for sure, but I'm hoping I can do the right thing and let her be with Byron.

"Have you been to see her yet today?" Declan is full of fucking questions this morning.

I shake my head. It has only been one week, yet it has been the worst week of my life. Every day, I go in there to find her naked, staring back at me and boldly telling me she wants Byron.

"You need to let the lad out. You need to let Dede out."

"Not until she fucking bleeds."

He chuckles.

"Why are you still here?"

"On this battlement, or in your life?" he says. Dark shaggy hair is sent whipping by the wind. He is a handsome man and a fiercely dominant alpha. Laughter lines crinkled the corners of his dark eyes a moment ago, but now he holds an air of deadly calm. Matters are not yet resolved with Dede, nor are they resolved between Declan and me.

And I wish I could snatch my fool words back. "I don't want you to leave." I am on my last chance with Declan—he is judging my behavior and deciding whether to leave based on it.

"You need to let them both out. You need to let them be together," he says, all reasonable now.

I snarl. What the fuck is wrong with me? I'm ready to snap. I want her. Her scent gets in my nose, and my cock is hard all the fucking time. Declan can't take his fucking eyes off it. I think one of the reasons he's decided to stay is to watch me fucking suffer and squirm.

"Stop thrusting the food at her and then running out the fucking door. You need to spend time with her."

He's talking sense. I know I need to mend bridges. I've set myself upon a course, and I cannot back out. The brat taunts me with her pussy, daring me to touch her, telling me in her imperious voice that she wants Byron and not me.

"I did not take you for a coward," Declan says, eyes narrowing before he stalks off, leaving me alone.

Dede

One week has passed since Grady sliced my clothes away, tossed me into this tiny room, and left me alone. True to his word, he is the only man who visits me. When he does, I explain to him in terms that idiots could understand how I despise him with every fiber of my being. He doesn't care. He's deep into whatever hole he's digging for himself. My anger blazes under the surface whenever he is around, yet the moment he leaves the room, a great well of sadness crashes over me.

Today, I am waiting for him with yesterday's uneaten dinner, and as he enters the room, I toss the plate at him.

I miss. It hits the wall, bounces off, and clatters to the floor, the plate miraculously whole. Given I've been plotting this all day, it is inconceivable to me that I have failed.

He growls, staring at the splatter on his boots.

I smirk. Not a complete failure then. "What do they say about practice makes perfect?"

Growl deepening to a rattle, he wades into the room and dumps today's offering on the table beside my bed before grabbing me by the arm. His growl goes straight to my wayward pussy, and I feel the first splat against the bed.

Nostrils flared, he glares down at me. How can he not notice what I am? We are engaged in a battle of wills. I'm at a disadvantage, given his scent is fully potent to me, but I'm determined not to lose. Maybe the herbs are taking longer than I presumed to wear off? I've never abstained this long, and already, I am changing, *craving*.

Brows drawing together in a frown, he releases me and lets me drop back to the bed.

My eyes immediately lower to where his cock strains the leather of his pants.

"I don't want you. I want Byron," I say cruelly, despite my mouth watering for a taste of his cock. Yet even that is not as cruel as what he is doing to me.

He is on me a moment later, hand shackling my throat, pushing me back, and I am shameless, legs falling open, panting, hips lifting, because all this is so deliciously right. Sinking to his knees, he spears two thick fingers into me.

Finally, he touches me intimately, and my libido rockets. I groan, pussy clamping down over him in joy.

"I won't rut you," he says as he slowly pumps in and out. "No matter how sweetly you beg."

"I am not the one begging," I taunt. The sticky wet noises his fingers make are absolutely filthy and belie my words. The rattle in his growl tells me I'm pushing him to his limit, but I am reckless. My pussy aches for a cock, and his touch only makes the ache worse. "I hate you, and I want Byron to tend to me."

"Not begging?" His voice drops to a seductive purr. "Should I stop then, Dede? Should I take my fingers away from this filthy, needy pussy?"

My squeal is ragged as he removes his fingers and stuffs them into his mouth. I lie there panting, watching his eyes roll back into his head with pleasure and so close to coming, I think his scent alone might take me over the edge.

"Beg me," he commands, fingertips returning to hover over my pussy.

"I'll never beg," I hiss, although I'm perilously close to

doing exactly that. A whimper escapes my lips as he oh so gently traces around the entrance of my pussy before sliding up until he is a breath away from my clit. I sob when he glides all the way back down. This time, he is achingly gentle as his fingers sink into me, catching the little rough patch that Byron plays so well. The faintest hint of confusion creeps into his face as he runs his fingertips back and forth over the ridge of my slick gland.

"Goddess!" I grab his wrist, trying to push him away, to pull him deeper, but he's as strong as an ox and does as he pleases. My legs twitch and kick as I wriggle and groan. It's too intense, and I cannot bear it. Then I am coming, riding his hand without a care, wild sounds of pleasure pouring from my lips as I gush around his fingers.

The hand around my throat disappears, as does the one petting my slick gland. I blink, disorientated, trying to work out what is happening.

"Oh!" The first lap of his tongue punches the air from my lungs. Hands clamp over my thighs, pinning me to the rough mattress as he noisily eats me out. Tongue, teeth, and lips move all over my pussy, lapping up the offering, probing my entrance for more, and lavishing my clit until my toes curl and my eyes cross with pleasure. Fingers spear into my pussy, finding that spot again, the one that sets me convulsing straight into glorious climactic waves.

I'm drunk on pleasure by the time he lifts his head, seeming as dazed as me as he looks down, dark hair disheveled, blue eyes stormy. I hate him, and I want him. This ruse has gone on long enough, yet I am wounded by his actions and I'm not ready to relent. "I want to see my Byron," I say quietly, even knowing the words will provoke his rage.

But there is no anger, only sadness in his blue eyes.

"The lad is well." His touch gentles, becoming soothing as

his hands brush over my bruised hips. "It was not Declan's fault. He was worried I would harm the lad if he tried to touch you."

"Would you have?" I ask.

"I don't know. I'd like to think not, but in truth, I was high on the fight with Killian and likely would have attacked anyone trying to touch you."

"Would you still?"

"I am not rational around you." He turns away.

Cupping his cheek, I pull him back to face me, full of sorrow that I cannot love only one or the other. "That is not an answer."

"It is the only one I have." He rises, eyes going to my bed. No attempt is made to disguise what I do there, yet he only now regards it with curiosity. The first day, when he brought me food, I refused to wear the dress, complaining how the material was scratchy. He took off his shirt and gave it to me. Now every day, he gives me another.

Without hesitation, he pulls his shirt free of his pants, brings a hand to the back of his collar, and draws it over his head. My eyes greedily roam over his beautiful body. Even while hating him, I can admit that he is a resplendent male and alpha. I take his shirt with a little nod, not meeting his eyes anymore, fighting the urge to lift it to my nose and inhale his delicious scent.

Then he is leaving, and as the door clicks shut behind him, I don't fight the pull. Burying my nose in the shirt full of his heady pheromones, I draw in a deep breath. His scent calms me, and I hate that it holds such power over me. I ache for his understanding as much as I ache for the gentle touch of my sweet Byron.

Placing the shirt with the others, I pat it into place, admiring the way the space is building around me.

How is it possible for an intelligent male to be so utterly clueless?

"The lad is well," he said. That was the first time he has mentioned Byron, and strangely, although I have no reason to, I believe him.

۶۵

Grady

I make it to the end of the corridor before it hits me. Swaying on my feet, I brace my hand to the nearby wall.

"What the fuck?"

How could I have been so stupid? Suddenly, everything makes sense—Declan's taunting, Dede's wild behavior, even Byron.

The sweet beta I left two years ago is not a beta. No, she's an omega.

Chapter Twenty

Byron

"What the fuck do you want, asshole? We've already had training today."

Declan raises an eyebrow as he swings the door to my cell wide.

I look from him to the open door and back again. Is this some kind of trap?

"It's not a trap, lad," he says. Smug bastard is always grinning like he knows some secret. "Our illustrious first has finally pulled his head out of his ass and is busy rutting the lass."

I blink a few times before my nostrils flare. "The fuck?! Have you come here to taunt me? Get the fuck back out again."

He frowns, appearing genuinely confused. "I thought you'd be happy things are progressing. The lass has been steadily building a nest all week. I don't know why it took him so fucking long to figure it out."

"Are you saying he knows?" I hedge. Declan is not stupid,

for all his accent is coarse. He's a mean bastard when he takes me outside for daily sparring, or as I prefer to think of it, beat the shit out of Byron and then kick him back in the cell with food when he's too weakened to cause trouble.

"He does," he replies, not giving a damn thing away. "And you are free to leave. Grady has spent enough time acting like a whelp with his favorite toy. I trust you not to do something stupid and get yourself tossed back in here. I've told Barnaby to aid you in drowning your sorrows...and to keep an eye on you. By the time you rouse from your drunken stupor, mayhap Grady will have roused himself from a certain lass' magic pussy."

I growl as I surge from the thin cot that has been my only comfort this past week. "Your pep talk is not fucking helping, asshole," I say as I draw level with him.

Barnaby is hopping from foot to foot beyond the door. He's built like a flagpole but freakishly strong, so I guess Declan is assuming he'll keep me from rampaging the castle to find Dede.

Fuck! I can't think about her with Grady. I told myself I could handle it, but after he locked her up and then locked me up, he has burned that fucking bridge. "I need a beer," I tell Barnaby. "A lot of fucking beers."

Grady

I need to get Dede somewhere safe. As I storm back into the room, door crashing against the wall, I find her curled up on the bed, still naked. Her eyes flash to meet mine as her head pops up from where she is tucked in a nest, one created from my shirts.

A nest. A fucking nest! How did I not see it?

It dawns upon me that what I have done to her and forced upon her is the highest travesty. I want to sink to my knees and beg her to forgive me, yet the imperative to address her safety takes precedence. She doesn't question me as I scoop her up into my arms. No, she clings to me, sobbing. She knows I know. Small arms and legs wrap around me as she buries her nose against the crook of my throat, making little snuffling noises as she sucks my scent in.

"I'm so sorry, Dede," I say, hands trembling as I try to hold her everywhere at once, to meld her smaller, fragile body to mine. Her skin feels cool against my warmer body. I have been a cruel bastard keeping her here. "I'm going to take you somewhere better now."

Bending, I gather a nearby shirt and draw it over her. I can't bear the thought of anyone seeing her nakedness while I take her to my room. The brief journey along the corridors is an exercise in restraint, though I snarl at anybody who comes near us. One man goes so far as to call out a greeting, and I thrust my arm out, sending him crashing into the wall. I am being an asshole, and I don't care. I just need to take her somewhere safe, close the door upon us, and assuage the rampant desires thrumming through me.

My room is empty when we enter. Thank fuck Declan is not in here. Using my foot, I kick the door shut with a thud, slam the bolt, and stride straight through to the bedroom, where I take my sweet little goddess down on the bed.

Brushing tears from her cheeks, she blinks up at me. "It's my room?"

"Aye," I say, swiping a hand down my face, compulsions tempered for a moment. My cock strains against my pants, and my ability to remain rational is limited. "I needed to be close to you...to your things. Why didn't you tell me?"

Only I know why she didn't tell me—I was acting like a savage.

"You weren't ready to listen," she says. "And I did not lie about the other things."

She's talking about Byron, although she is careful not to say his name. I have teetered close to my limit all week, but am perilously closer now. "I need to have you, to claim you. You understand this, don't you Dede?"

She nods. "I want you to. That is all I need."

I kick off my boots, fingers fumbling at my belt, my movements made clumsy with haste. I rip it off with a growl, shuck trousers down my thighs, and kick them away.

My cock is harder than ever, wanting nothing more than to serve his new mistress, this Goddess blessed revelation, my omega, my princess, who is lying upon a bed. "I can't be gentle."

"I don't want you to. I need you, Grady, need you to take this ache away."

Then I see her dilated pupils and the thin sheen glistening over her body. She is feverish, an omega who has been suppressing her nature for too long, and whatever she has taken is clearing from her system.

I come down over her, tracing my fingertip over her collarbone, and she shudders. I stick the finger into my mouth and suck. She tastes like heaven, spicy, a little sweet, a little salty, seeming to fizz on my tongue. Leaning down, I lick her skin. Her arms and legs wrap around me, holding me closer, drawing me in.

"Goddess, yes!" she hisses.

I can smell her. How did I not scent her before? Have my actions today in touching her finally tipped me over the edge? If only I had not acted like a fool by locking her up, I would not have wasted a week. I had my reasons, telling myself I could do the right thing if she was with child, let her be with Byron after leaving the castle in a state of safety, maybe encourage Declan to assume the role of commander. Yet there is a rightness about this. We are here now, despite the perilous path that led us to this point.

My lips trail over her satiny skin, drawing her heady scent into my lungs, letting it fill me, soothe me, consume my body and mind. I feel dizzy, a little *woozy*. I'm high as a fucking kite. My lips find the junction of her shoulder and throat, the place bearing a slight mark. I can't think of that whelp's name, nor how he marked her. I want to obliterate it, to fill her with me until I am the center of her world. My inner voice tells me I'm delusional, yet I brush aside the concerns for tomorrow and of others, because now, there is only her and me.

"I cannot be fucking gentle," I say again. "My need is too great."

"Please don't wait. I can't wait, either. I'm so empty, please fill me up."

I trail kisses over her soft skin, up her throat, and over her jaw, until I take her lips in a hot kiss. She opens to me so sweetly, and I sink into her, our tongues tangling as my fingers spear her hair, holding her just right.

Her nails make claws against my shoulders. I growl in approval that she's not pushing me away. She's trying to draw me closer, encouraging me to rut. I want everything, but I'm also impatient. My hands skim over her body, and one finds her ass, cupping it, pulling her hips flush to me. The other is on a breast, rubbing back and forth over her hard little nipple, making her gasp into my mouth. Her wildness mirrors my own. The higher my frenzy rises, so, too, does hers.

My lips roam her throat, nibbling, sucking, drawing her arousal higher. Her reactions drive me, my cock leaking over the bed, and I shift, trying to stab up, but miss and slide over her clit. Her deep moan tells me she likes that. I pull back, thrust again, and this time, I snag the entrance to her slick little pussy and surge deep.

We both groan together. I pinch her nipple hard, pull out, and plow back in.

The sound she makes is a glorious kind of music to my ears. I want her screaming with pleasure as she comes all over my cock.

Common sense finally pierces the feral nature taking hold in my mind. I still, buried deep, feeling my cock pulse and her pussy fluttering around me. I cup her cheeks, trying to gain her focus. "Look at me, love."

"Don't stop!"

"Dede." I add a little alpha force, and her eyes pop open. Her pupils are blown, the pretty hazel almost swallowed up by the black. I have never seen anything more beautiful than this writhing omega upon the bed. "Dede, look at me, now," I command, and her unfocused eyes find mine.

Her pussy clenches fiercely, and her thighs squeeze around me.

"Have you been knotted before?"

"Please," she mumbles.

"Dede," I warn. "Tell me now."

"No," she says. "Never. Byron... I told him I was a beta. He never...he never did that to me."

I growl at the mention of *his* name, but I also puff with fierce male pride, knowing I shall be the first to take her completely and *knot* her. I brace one arm under her ass, plant the other against the side of her face, and rut her hard and fast, our bodies slapping together, her legs making a cradle for me, arms wrapping around my neck, clinging, pulling me in.

"Please, please, please," she mutters over and over again. "Knot me."

"Fuck!" The thought of knotting her drives me absolutely wild. My hips jerk, thrusting against her, running on instinct, for I've only ever been with a beta and never knotted a lass. The mere thought of pushing all the way into her nearly takes me over the fucking edge.

"I need it," she says.

"I'm going to give it to you. All of it. Every fucking inch."

She whimpers, pussy clamping over my cock in agreement. The urge to thrust deeply into her is near overwhelming, but I fight it. I don't want to hurt her. I know my omega lore. All alphas are taught it, even though few get the privilege of meeting an omega, and fewer still bond with one. Omegas have a second hymen deep inside that can only be broached by an alpha cock once we are buried all the way. She could never get with child, I realize, unless Byron knotted her. Even betas can be taught to accept all of a cock and knot with training and coaxing from a gentle alpha lover, but it is natural to an omega. There is only one barrier in my way.

I begin to move slower, thrusting all the way to my knot, which is only a faint swelling as yet, anticipating the pleasure when I penetrate her fully. With each thrust, I let the ridge bump against the entrance and sink a little way in. She likes that and clutches me closer, her eyes closed, neck arched. It will hurt when I break through the final barrier, but there is no other way.

I kiss her throat, her face, her lips, all the while rutting her but not quite giving her enough. I want her deep into the pleasure before I take the last step.

"Please," she says. "Do not hold back. I need it all. I need all of you now."

My hips seem to snap of their own accord. An alpha can read an omega's needs, or so I have been told, and this drives me forward, arm clasping around her waist so she cannot move.

With my next deep thrust, I feel resistance before I plow all the way in. Her squeal is one of visceral pain. My cock wants to shrink, yet her pussy grips so tightly around me, I become harder still. I kiss her lips, press more over her cheeks and down her throat.

"It's over now, sweet Dede. I am all the way inside."

"Don't stop," she says. There are tears leaking from the corner of her eyes. It breaks me that I hurt her, yet when I tentatively move, slowly rocking, her tears dry up and she issues the most guttural, pleasure steeped cry.

"Fuck," I mutter gruffly. "Does that feel better now, love?"

"Yes," she groans, clinging and shifting impatiently under me.

I growl, hips moving with greater vigor, becoming lost in the sensations as her hot wet sheath welcomes and holds me within. Fuck, my knot is already swelling beyond my experience, and it momentarily scares me how the ridge thickens so swiftly, growing impossibly sensitive. I kiss the dampness of tears away from her cheeks as I slide all the way out, then push all the way back in. We both groan as one, lips meeting, kissing, swallowing up each other's cries as I rut her now with deep, heavy slaps of meeting flesh, driven by animal instinct to fill her all up, to brand her as mine. All the while, my knot swells thicker still, taking me to the point of madness. I am in a state of wonder at how she accepts me, how this tiny little omega can receive all of my cock and knot. Yet she does, joyously pulling me in with every hard slap, her hips slamming up to meet mine, small fingers clutching, kiss deepening and tongues tangling. We are lost in one another and the connection, the wild joyful sensations of being one.

The knot blooms with every stroke until it reaches the point where I must grit my teeth and force past her slippery pussy entrance one last time...and there I nestle so perfectly, just as her pussy locks over me, keeping me there. She convulses in my arms, coming apart, and I follow her straight through, spine tingling, balls rising.

I come deep, filling over and over again, hips rocking against her and my ass clenching with the strain as I try to squeeze out every little drop of seed. Dragging my lips from hers, I shift to the crook of her throat...and there, I bite. Her pussy clenches around me for the second time before falling into yet more of those rhythmic waves, and I keep coming, balls tight, cock jerking, flooding the entrance to her womb.

Breed. The word springs up out of nowhere. She is not yet in heat, and I cannot yet breed her, but I want to.

Mine. That word is a forever word. I will not let her go in any circumstances, not now I have been inside her and marked her as mine. The way she clings tightly tells me she feels the same way.

"You are mine," I say, needing to speak my feelings aloud.

"I am," she agrees. "Until the Goddess may take one of us away."

Her words gentle me, calming the beast clamoring within me.

Whatever comes next is by the Goddess' will. All I know is that this woman holding me inside her is more precious to me than my own life. I have much to make up for, and I intend to spend the rest of my life doing exactly that.

Chapter Twenty-One

Dede

"You are being unreasonable," I say. He has rutted me, knotted me, used my body in every way he might to strengthen the bond between us, swore to me he loves me above all others, and yet he does not have a reasonable bone in his body when it comes to this one thing. "You cannot keep me from him."

His answer is a deep growl.

Having just enjoyed a bath, the first bath in many days, I feel human again. Lulled into thinking he was softening when he let servants in, I dared to broach the subject of Byron.

I tie my sash tighter than I ought to, but my fury has taken hold and my hands tremble a little. Any arguments I make are cut off by the means of a swift rutting, followed by his knot. If the glint in his eyes is any indication, today is no exception. He surges from the chair and stalks over to me, tugs the sash open, and thrusts my gown off. As it pools on the floor at my feet, I squeal my outrage. His grin is one of wicked intentions, and he immediately scoops me up. I rail at him, curse him, beat him with my small fists, straining, arching my back, seeking to force him to put me down. Finally, he does release me...onto the bed.

Given he rarely dresses since claiming me, he needs only dispense with his leather pants, which were not even fastened. He shucks out of them before I can gather my wits.

Hand collaring my throat, he pushes me back to the bed. Shameless hussy that I am, my legs open and I groan with pleasure as he plows me with his cock. The rutting is fast and furious. My body tips straight over into a climax, even before he begins to work in the knot. He slams deep, over and over, growling and snarling over his prize, and Goddess help me, the sensations ripping through me are beyond mere pleasures of the flesh. I am his in every way. He has assuaged his lust upon my gentle omega body. My tolerance for whatever he will do is extreme. The rougher he is, the greater my pleasure, and I always want more.

I cannot begin to understand, I only know I am conditioned to react to him and his handling. The hand around my throat squeezes, and I convulse again, mouth open, guttural cries pouring from my lips. I am little more than a beast, high on his pheromones, and delirious for his slightest touch.

His knot swells, locking us together as he floods me with his cum, seeding his little omega. Although I am not yet in heat, I have every reason to believe he will breed me the moment he can. Maybe afterward, this possessive rage consuming him will ease. Yet a hollow space grows inside me that needs my other mate. Grady purrs for me, and so swiftly, all my troubles implode. I float. I would do anything for his purr, it is the most beautiful sound in the world, but his is not the only purr that has comforted me. I need Byron as well.

He rolls onto his back and positions me to his satisfaction, knot still holding us intimately together, trapping us so that we cannot part, even should we wish to. He purrs, petting me, big hands roaming over my body in a proprietary manner. I am his, and any voicing of dissension, the mere whisper of Byron's name, and Grady will put me on my hands and knees and fill me in any way he can.

He is possessed by demons.

He is unreasonable in every way.

I will need to do something drastic to get through this insanity that has claimed him, but what, I don't know. The bath was today's concession, making me clean only for him to get me dirty all over again. Yet it is apparent to me that I like nothing more than being filled with his knot and cum.

I am yet to make sense of this. Alphas are taught omega lore when they reveal, but there are few omegas and we don't receive the same. A community might have many alphas and one or no omegas. All I have is one herb woman, who has never met an omega herself and merely told me what was passed down to her from her mother and her mother's mother before her, neither of which were an omega nor even met one. It is fair to say what information she has will have lost meaning over time.

Yet one thing she did say has held true—omegas need their alpha and their alpha needs them. Also that some omegas, even here in Hydornia, are throwbacks who need more than one mate. I recognize that I am such an omega, for my scent has not changed. I always presumed Byron had claimed me, but perhaps he did not claim me well enough or it will only work if I am in heat. I need Byron, yet Grady will not entertain such a thought. Tomorrow, he will concede something more than the bath, I hope, for this cannot go on.

"You cannot rut me every time we have a disagreement," I say quietly.

He shifts underneath me, purr taking on a little rattle.

"It might have worked so far, but it will not work forever. I want to see my father and Mia. I want to see anybody who is not in the four corners of this room."

"You have seen Anna," he says. "She came to prepare your bath and brought food this morning."

"I do not like Anna well," I admit. "She and I have not always seen eye to eye." I hold no grudge toward Anna for what happened. Killian could have rutted her for the rest of his life, and it would not have troubled me. It was more the defilement of my personal space, and I dare say the maid had little to no say in that. I can forgive much and forget the rest, but the wounds are still fresh and I desire no reminders.

"Do you want me to find another maid?"

"No," I say tiredly. "That is not what this is about. This is about your unreasonableness." He shifts, big hands spreading over my ass, pressing me down onto his cock. It begins the throb. The knot might be softening, but he is considering rutting me again.

An unwitting groan escapes my lips.

"My mate has needs," he says. "Your scent is still potent. I need to rut you more."

"It has nothing to do with how often you rut me," I say. "It has to do with the fact you are not enough!"

Tension fills the body beneath mine. I have pushed him cruelly, yet he is also cruel to me. Predictably, he rolls, taking me under him and filling me in a single deep thrust, while his eyes hold mine captive.

My body responds, for I cannot help it, yet the pleasure he wrests from my body is only temporary. He doesn't knot me this time, almost like he is punishing me, and I miss the closeness when he pulls out, leaving a wet splatter upon the bed.

He stops beside the bed, standing with his back to me, and I take in the glory of such a powerful male. Everything about him is beautiful, every line of his body. There are a few scars, some are older and some more recent. None detract from what he is. I love him. I hate him at times, but I also love him, and I cannot deny my feelings, for to do so would be to disrespect the Goddess. Yet what he does is also against her will.

He sighs, not looking back. "I am trying to temper what I feel, but he has had you much of the time I was away. I waited for you. I was celibate the whole time we were apart."

Guilt assails me. I have never considered his perspective before, focusing only on what I need. Does he hate me for what I did? There is no anger in his voice, only sadness, and that bothers me the most. What do my actions say about me? "I thought you were not coming back. What happened with Byron wasn't intentional. It was more a friendship that grew steadily over time."

I loved Byron long before I laid with him. Committing our flesh to pleasure was merely a confirmation of everything we felt. I don't tell Grady this. I wish I had the right words to explain, ones that would not cause him pain.

"I do not hold it against you," he says. "I was gone too long. I sent no word. This is my own fault, but I also think it is part of the Goddess' design."

He concedes and shows much with those words. It is the beginning, the first step. I don't need to tell Grady today and now that I also love Byron. For me, sharing intimacy is about more than the pleasure of the flesh. There must also be a deep, emotional connection. I'm still young. Grady is older than me, and our life experiences are very different, yet instinctively, I know it would have troubled me had he been with another woman after making a commitment to me.

"You're an omega. I understand what your unchanged scent means, and I am trying" —his voice breaks a little—"so fucking hard."

I rise to my knees to rest my hand tentatively against his back. I press a kiss to his warm skin, feeling a shudder go through him. His hands clench at his sides, and I press more kisses to his back. I love him, and I am sorrowful in causing this pain. "I wish it were simpler," I say, my voice breaking too. "I wish I loved only one person."

He turns, drawing me against him, pulling my cheek to his chest, purring for me, but a different purr now. He's not rutting me into submission, nor into silence, but listening and accepting.

His vulnerability is stifling, manifesting in the tremble of his body and hands where we touch. No alpha expects to share a mate. It is not in their nature. Across the sea is a land known as the Imperium, where omegas are shared by many, but even so, I expect their journey to understanding must find conflict along the way.

The great clanging of a bell sees my head lift. Grady turns in the direction of the window. "Raiders," he says ominously, then he sighs. "I've spent too much time in this room. It is time for me to resume my duty and become the commander again."

I don't want him to leave. I hate that he will ever be in danger for a moment of his life, but he is the commander and he has been in bed with me for the past few days.

He dresses efficiently in leather pants, belt, a clean under-shirt, full sleeved jerkin, boots, and finally, gathers his sword. I watch him, missing him already, although he has yet to go.

He returns to the bed and presses his lips to mine, the kiss lingering.

"I'll return as soon as I can. Afterward, we shall see about you leaving the room."

Then he is gone, and I stare at the closed door.

Chapter Twenty-Two

Dede

Grady has not left long when the clanging raider bell stops, then the rattle of the gate rising follows. They have gone out to meet whatever foe assails us.

Rising from the bed, I go over to the washstand, pour a bowl of water, and clean myself up. It's not as thorough as a bath, but I feel human again after. Then, because Grady is not here to stop me, I put on some clothes for the first time in many days. The simple dress is a foreign design and decadently soft against my sensitive skin, with a few artfully placed ribbons on the front holding the material together. I wish I had a dozen more, although I could never wear it out of my chamber.

I worry about Grady. He has spent two years battling the orcs, and yet I worry about him in a way I have never done before. There is a connection growing between us, just as one was blooming between Byron and me.

Above all, I long for Byron, to have him hold me and to purr, but also to see with my own eyes that he is well.

Grady has said he will allow me to leave the room when he returns, and I will hold him to that. How difficult this situation must be for him, how a man and lord must struggle with the concept of his mate being shared.

Feeling strangely introspective because there are matters to be resolved, I pad through to the bedroom, coming to a stop before the bed, where Grady's shirt lays discarded on the floor. Pressing it against my cheek, I draw his scent into my lungs.

As my head rises, the urge to place things, to create a safe space, becomes paramount in my mind.

At the bottom of the bed is a chest full of spare blankets and bedding, and I lift the lid to study what lies within. I frown, wondering where I should make my nest. Not the bed, nor on the hard wooden floor. A nest needs to be safe.

My eyes alight on my two closets, one being used for clothing and the other empty, save for some old cases. Opening the door, I decide instantly that this is where I want my nest. I push, pull, sit down, and use my braced feet to shove the unwanted items out. An old rug is laid out on the cold floor to soften it a little before I gather up the bedding bounty and set about making my nest. Plush bedding is layered with cushions until it is blissfully deep. I pet, push, and shuffle things from here to there until I'm satisfied. Then I collect Grady's shirt and give it pride of place.

Wait? Don't I have another... I hurry to my clothing closet, and there at the back on the floor is an old undershirt of Byron's. I draw it to my nose, sorrowful yet comforted by his smell. Taking it back to the nest, I place it beside Grady's, and curl up with it under my cheek, and give in to sleep.

A knock sounding on the outer door rouses me from sleep, and I call for them to enter. It is dark with a glow coming from the dayroom, where someone must have lit a lamp. Anna will likely place my dinner on the table and leave. Footsteps follow, not the lighter ones of a maid, but the heavier tread of a man, pausing and then coming closer, until Declan appears in the entrance to my nest.

I blink a few times, disconcerted to be alone with him. I admit I've always been intimidated by Declan, with his rugged good looks and brawny shoulders that fill my nest doorway. A shock of messy dark hair has fallen over his dark brown eyes, almost like he has just gotten out of bed.

His nostrils flare as he takes in both me and where I am, and as though in answer, my pussy performs a slow clench and a shiver runs down my spine.

"I brought food," he says. I drag my gaze down from his broad shoulders to find he does indeed hold a tray.

"Thank you," I say, lowering my lashes as I scramble to sit. A little of his scent washes over me, and it makes me a little dizzy. Goddess, he is such a fierce male. Grady is very much the son of a king, and for all he is an alpha, he bears a civilized façade. Declan has no civility. He is a raw alpha, *powerful*, and does not bother to temper his ways. He is also wickedly playful. I blush. Where this blush comes from, I have no idea. I am too old for blushes!

"I'll just put it on the table then." He nods his head to the left.

"Th-Thank you," I stammer. Goddess! What is wrong with me? I follow him into the dayroom, a little flustered to be discovered in a nest.

"Grady said he may be out all evening," he says, carefully putting the tray down before walking back toward the door. He shuts it...but he is still on the inside.

My eyes widen slightly as I stand there, nervous...and aroused. I press my hand flat against my tummy, and he turns, eyes locking on the movement.

He raises a brow. "Something troubles you, lass?"

Lass? Nobody calls me lass, except Peter, who is older than my father. The audacity of the man! Yet the word brings a stupid flutter to my heart.

"It's the frenzy," he says. "I told Grady he shouldn't have left you. Said I could deal with the trouble, but he got some foolish notion in his head that he needed to resume his command. Better he dealt with letting Byron see you, that would have made more sense."

He sighs heavily before raking fingers through his messy hair. The movement sets muscles rippling in his burly body, stretching leather armor taunt over muscles. Byron is powerful, yet he does not possess the same deadly air so prevalent in Declan. "I best be leaving."

"Please don't." The request tumbles out before I can stop myself.

The sound he makes is somewhere between a groan and a growl. He swallows thickly, dark eyes glistening in the lamplight. "Tell me to leave," he says gruffly.

I shake my head. He started this by shutting the door, and now I don't want him to leave. We are locked, staring at one another. My belly turns over, and a little slick trickles out.

His throat works as he swallows. "Your scent is enough to drive a man mad."

"You are no weak alpha," I say, a taunting note in my voice. Truthfully, I believe I seek to taunt myself, for his scent tickles my throat and lungs with every drawn breath, but my reckless-ness confuses me. Why do I not order the man to go? Why do I not flee to my bedroom and lock the door?

I swallow. I can admit here and now that I have always

been attracted to Declan...and terrified...and fiercely aroused. We continue to stare at one another. Several paces separate us —a distance that does not seem nearly far enough.

"I don't understand what is happening to me," I say.

"You're an omega," he says. "Your scent has not changed. I should get the lad. Fuck Grady and his stupid fucking rules. There is not always time for a man to come to terms with what must be. Tell me to fucking go, lass."

"No," I say boldly.

"Dede." There is a warning in his voice, one I have heard on Grady's tongue more than once. It stokes further reckless-ness inside me. I wonder what it would be like to be with such a man. I am shameless to be thinking this, yet it does not temper my burgeoning desire.

"You're in frenzy," he repeats. "Lust drunk on alpha pheromones. He has rutted you nonstop for three days, and you could be about to tip into heat. Now, order me to leave!"

I won't, and I can't, even though I see pain on his face. "You are not a weak alpha," I whisper.

"No, I am not, but you are a fucking test of the highest order and I love Grady as much as I love you."

His words shock me, and I didn't think I had any shocks left in me. The casual way in which he discloses this is as unnerving as his vast presence. How can someone be so intimi-dating and yet emotionally verbose all at once?

"How?"

"There isn't a how with love, little lamb. It comes with a will of its own. I loved you from the first moment I met you, but back then, it was a childish infatuation for a noble lass who stood up to men intent on beating me. They changed as feel-ings are wont to do. I cannot help them, and I won't be ashamed of them." He shrugs. "I have spoken plainly to Grady too. There, lass, I have laid all my cards on the table."

It hardly seems possible that the young, scrawny lad, poorly clothed against the cold, went on to become this towering alpha. "When I was younger, and before Grady declared for me, I always thought you and Grady were together."

"It was hopefulness on my part, lass," he says.

"You want him?" My cheeks flush again. Why does the thought of Declan with Grady make my pussy clench twice as hard?

"I do." He smirks, and the old Declan is back—an alpha and the deadliest man I've ever met. He has a coarse accent and ways, nothing like my gentle, sweetly wicked Byron, nor my lordly Grady. Declan is savage to the core. The thought of him with Grady, of them kissing, pressing intimately together, brings a whimper bubbling from my throat.

"Fuck," he growls.

My pussy aches, wanting and needing to be knotted. That is the only way I feel safe anymore. I have been so unsafe for so long, and those brief moments when either Byron or Grady are buried inside me is the only respite from those fears. Hands trembling, I reach for the ties at my throat, pulling the first ribbon free.

The material parts at my breast. Declan's dark eyes glitter as he watches what I do, a low growl rumbling in his chest. He doesn't walk away though, rooted to the spot, and I am caught up in a sensual spell. Suddenly, everything makes sense, and I trust wholly in the Goddess for putting this unexpected man into my path.

"You don't know me," I say. "How could you love me?"

He grunts, riveted by what I do, as I pull the second ribbon free and my breasts almost spill out.

"I have watched you from afar, and we have even spoken many times. Sweet little beta with pretty hazel eyes and kindly ways. Gentle, firm, clever. I love everything about you. You blush so prettily whenever I'm near, but you only had eyes for Grady."

"I noticed you," I say. "I noticed you well."

"Could have fooled me," he says, but he is still staring at my breasts.

As a third ribbon comes free, my breasts spill out, fully exposed to his lustful gaze.

He licks his lips. "I have taken my cock in hand and found relief while thinking about your plump little lips wrapped around me."

The image he conjures rocks me, and I imagine him doing exactly that—fat cock in his fist, jacking up and down until he spills his seed, and all the while, thinking of me.

I want to do that to him, to take him into my mouth. When I pull the next ribbon, the material completely parts, sliding over my shoulders before hitting the floor with a little *whoosh*. I don't experience a scrap of shame as I stand before him, naked.

He wants not only me, though. He also needs Grady, and somehow, that is perfect. I boldly step forward all the way, until I am before him.

Reaching back, he slides the bolt across the door. "I'd like some warning before Grady skewers me."

It's a poor joke that adds a frisson of danger to what we do. Were I sensible, I would release him from this path. I feel tiny standing before him, but I become impossibly small as I sink to my knees and carefully unbuckle his belt.

"Fuck!" he mutters gruffly.

My hands shake, my whole body trembles, but I want to do this more than I want my next breath, to take him in my mouth, just as he imagined, only better.

He doesn't stop me, just fists his hands at his sides and lets me have my way. His pants come loose, and I tug them over his muscular ass and thighs until his cock springs free, thick, veiny, pulsing, ruddy, and leaking with need. The scent hits me, and I press my nose against him.

He growls. "No wonder Grady is losing his fucking mind."

My tongue darts out for the first taste, and he hisses through his teeth. The scent is divine. I run my tongue all the way to the tip before taking my first lick of the pre-cum pooling.

He jerks, hips thrusting forward like he needs more. I glance up at him, take his cock in both hands, and lower the weeping tip to my lips. Meeting his steady gaze, I swirl my tongue around the head. His features turn stark in the lamplight, and I relish every tormented emotion playing across his face. I feel like I'm praying before a god as my hands slide over the thick length, and still holding his eyes, I suckle him.

He groans.

It's not enough... I take the head and half the length all the way into my throat.

His fist closes over my hair, pulling me off when I gag in my enthusiasm.

"Goddess," he says. "No dream nor imagining could ever compare."

I hum, emboldened by his praise, and work my mouth up and down, sucking all the sticky goodness up, feeling the taste slide across my tongue. I want him to come in my mouth before he ruts me in his rough way.

"I'm going to fucking come, lass, going to come all the way down your sweet little throat. Is that what you want? For me to fill my princess all up?"

I suck harder, cheeks hollowing with the need for exactly that, not caring how it strains my throat.

"My filthy, lusty princess, craving an alpha's cock. I'm telling you now, my little lamb, only three men will ever have this pleasure. One of them is Grady, another is now me, and the last one is Byron, but we'll work up to that."

My heart leaps. He embraces and acknowledges everything without hesitation or reserve. My fingers find the ridge of his knot, gliding back and forth, delighting when it starts to bloom.

"I'm going to come so deep and so much, you're going to be choking on it."

I don't care what he does to me so long as he gives me his cum. He may use me as roughly as he wants to. I embrace the moment, push as deep as I possibly can, and then he is coming, shooting into my mouth and filling me with his taste and seed. I cough, but he doesn't let me up. This is not a polite man. This is a rough man. He holds me, forcing me to take more, not caring how the thickness strains my jaw.

His ways make me absolutely drenched. He growls his pleasure, shooting yet more cum down my willing throat.

"Good girl," he says. "Take it all. I know you are greedy for it."

I do take all of it. His legs begin to shake, and his hand shoots out to brace against the door. Still more of his seed pours down my throat, and I swallow, my neck aching with strain of taking him, before finally, he eases out.

My jaw aches, my lips are swollen and sore, and cum is all over my chin, dripping onto my chest. "Clean me up, lass," he says, staring down at me with a heated gaze. "Lick up every last drop until there is none left."

My belly clenches as I lean up and dutifully lick. His hot flesh jerks again, growing hard.

"Good girl." He holds my hair with one hand, the other holding his cock so I can clean him up. When I am done to his satisfaction, he swipes a thumb over my chin and pushes it between my lips. I don't hesitate to suck the offering up. "You'll do better next time, won't you, lass?"

I nod, mesmerized. I am falling into him. He's nothing like

any man I know, neither Grady nor Byron. He is darker and unfettered and will take me roughly.

I want him to.

"Up you get, lass," he says, tugging on my hair.

I rise to my shaky feet, small before this resplendent male, his pants hanging around his muscular thighs. He doesn't care about any of this, and using my hair as a leash, he holds me still as his lips take mine.

The kiss is wet and lusty. He tastes himself on me, tongue delving deeply, setting my skin prickling with heat. His big hand cups my breast *proprietarily* as he squeezes it before taking my nipple between his finger and thumb and rolling it cruelly. I whimper into his mouth. It hurts a little, but in the best kind of way. He squeezes harder as his fist tightens in my hair.

My hands clasp his wrist, but I don't know whether I'm trying to pull him off or make him do more. His lips tear from mine. He stares at me, holding my eyes as he tugs on my sore nipple, squeezing it and then repeating the motion.

My lips part on a pant, and between my thighs, slick begins to trickle down.

"I can smell your pussy. Has Grady come in there?"

I nod slowly, and his eyes darken.

"Good," he says. "Now it is my turn to clean you all up."

Turning me around, he lands a sharp spank against my ass. "On the bed, lass. Legs open and ready for my pleasure."

My naked feet slap against the floor so quickly do I run for the bedroom. I dive for the middle of the bed and lie back with my legs parted, breathless with anticipation.

He takes his time. My ears strain, picking up a faint rustling and a thud. The clutter of things, the dinner he brought maybe, then the sound of water? No, he is pouring wine into a goblet... one he carries with him as he enters my bedroom. Pausing at the door, his gaze lowers to my parted thighs, wet pussy on display.

My breath seizes in my lungs as I take in the ruggedly handsome alpha with a big, burly build. His thick ruddy cock hangs between his thighs, with a thin thread of pre-cum trailing from the tip.

He takes a long drink, then approaches slowly, and leaning over, offers it to my lips. When I lift my hand to take it, he growls, and I snatch my hand down again. I eye him over the rim as he places it against my lips and tips it up. I gulp, but some spills over my chin, throat, and breast. He tips higher and more spills out as I try to swallow it down.

Slamming the goblet against my nightstand, he crawls over me, sucking the spill from my chin before lapping at my throat. His wild savagery sets me on fire. Noisily, he sucks and licks up the spilled wine, working lower until he squeezes my breast in his big hand and takes half the plump mound into his mouth. He sucks hard, and I arch up, mumbled words pouring from my lips, fingers spearing his hair.

His lips pop off abruptly, and he cups both breasts, squeezing them together, capturing both nipples between fingers and thumbs and rolling them. "I'm gonna fuck these tits. Slide my cock between them and come all over your throat before feeding it to you."

I blink at him, dazed, aroused, confused that a man would want to do such a thing, and wishing he would deliver on this promise soon. I do not care where he puts his cock on me, just as long as it goes somewhere.

"But not yet." His eyes lower as he shuffles down, gaze locked on my pussy, grasping my thighs in his big hands and bending me nearly in two. Then his head lowers...and he devours me. His tongue is everywhere, filling me, flicking over my clit, delving deeply, and then lapping the folds. He groans and growls, and I am already high on him. He lavishes me with attention, messy and uninhibited. His fingers slide inside me, moving with unerring accuracy toward my slick gland. He growls as he finds the sensitive spot, rubbing it without mercy, rougher even than Byron or Grady.

I cannot bear the overstimulation. I thrash and strain, but as his lips enclose my clit and begin to gently suckle on me, I explode into a shattering climax. He purrs against my pussy, sucking and petting my slick gland until I splinter again and gush all over his fingers and the bed. His tongue spears inside me, and his thumb finds my clit, petting me as his tongue laps up everything I spill. His savage growl finds an echo within me. I arch up, body on fire, no longer a rational being but something else entirely. I need him inside me, craving both his cock and knot.

Just as I think I cannot possibly take anymore, slick finger-tips slide down and two thick fingers are forced into my ass.

It burns and stings.

It is shocking.

It is absolutely depraved.

And yet it sets off an explosion within me, and I am coming again. My ass flutters, trying to squeeze around him as my body and mind enter freefall.

He stops abruptly, and I lie panting as he surges up, wiping his mouth with the back of his hand, dark eyes glittering—a monster I have willingly unleashed onto my life.

I want him to push his fingers in my ass again.

I want him to eat me like he is ravenous for the taste.

I want every depraved thing he will do.

"Hands and knees, now," he says, tone brooking no argument.

I try, but I am spent, wrung out, and my body defies my commands. He flips me over, drags my hips back, and plows his thick cock deep. I squeal into the covers, feeling every thick inch stretching me just right, throbbing and jerking, his belly flush to my ass.

"Fuck! Your cunt is a fucking test of a man not to spill his seed. Grip me, lass."

Grip?

A sharp spank lands against my right ass cheek, startling another squeal from my lips, making my pussy squeeze over his monstrous cock to the cusp of pain.

"Good girl, just like that," he says. Then he takes my hips in his hands and ruts me. There's no easing me into the coupling, his cock, or knot, he just slams them in and out, over and over again. I am convulsing, soaring, and coming again, all while mumbled nonsense pours from my lips. The roughness of the rutting shakes me about. My body goes up in flames, and everything is spinning. The timbre of his growls, the bruising hands upon my hips, this is not a man nor alpha, who entreats politely. This is a man who takes. That I find pleasure is coincidental in this. He is doing what he wants, and I, the vessel of his lust, am merely along for the ride.

This should assuredly not arouse me, and yet it does. I climb ever higher, climaxing wildly, until finally, with a great roar, he stills and fills me with his cum and locks me upon his knot.

I lose all thought afterward. I could not say what day of the week it was, nor hour of the night, for there is only the feeling of his throbbing cock filling me, dumping cum deep.

Perfectly safe, that is what I am. Despite his rough ways, Declan will keep me safe. He will temper Grady, I know this somehow. As his knot softens, he eases from me. To my surprise, for I half expect him to stalk out of the room, he lies beside me and hauls my limp body over his.

He purrs, and the big hand he places on my ass is proprietary. "There is going to be hell later when Grady returns, but if I'm going to die, I'm going to die in fucking heaven. I'll need to rut you again shortly. Prepare yourself, lass." And he does. Oh, how he does, over and over again, filling my mouth, filling my pussy. He has no shame, forcing his thick fingers in my ass and pumping them in and out until even that makes me wild. He pinches my nipples cruelly and eats my pussy, even after he has come. Nothing fazes him, nothing at all.

Then, in the earlier hours of the morning, Grady returns.

Chapter Twenty-Three

Grady

I t has been a long and exhausting patrol. The attack came midafternoon, and we rode out in force to meet the challenge. They were testing us after we dumped their brothers in the forest, along with Killian. They have lost their source of food and goods and are now desperate men who will likely turn ever more violent. We've killed a few today and will kill more tomorrow, and the day after.

Since Killian assumed control, good men had been steadily leaving Langetta. We are short on numbers now. I have sent word to Tweed Head to canvas any soldiers passing through the port, with a mind to bolstering our number. Likely, there will be increased attacks on the castle, the port town, and outlying farms and villages, and we need to be prepared.

While I have been distracted by my sweet omega mate, life has carried on. Repairs are underway on the castle, restoring pride to the place. Regular patrols ride to all major locations within the kingdom to ensure none are left exposed. Where the raiders once run amok, now they are being harried, turned away, or killed. Likely, they will soon decide there are easier pickings elsewhere. If they don't, I will hunt them down and take pleasure in putting their heads on pikes.

Dawn is breaking as we crest the rise, and as the castle comes into view, potent love and worries rises inside me. Dede is mine now. For her sake, I must resolve things with Byron, and I will, but not today. This is my first time leaving her since I acknowledged her as my omega. I have been a selfish bastard, knowing she aches for her other mate, Byron. A hierarchy will need to be established, and we may fight, if he is so inclined. Much depends on his attitude toward me when we speak.

Some alphas instinctively accept their place, and some do not. It's not our way in Hydornia to share a mate, whether they are betas or omegas, but we are used to an order in our everyday lives, and sharing a mate is not so different, I suppose. I console myself with the knowledge he will rut her only by my command. I can tolerate that much.

The gates open as we approach at a brisk canter, hooves making a drumbeat as we slow to a trot to pass over the wooden drawbridge before entering the courtyard. Men come out to greet us. A few more raiders have been dispensed with, and that is cause for joy.

I don't linger, tossing my reins to a young stable lad, who hastens to take my horse away. The men call out good-natured jeers about rutting as I push through the double doors and stride through the hall, where servants are about. There is always much to be done, but more so now in a castle so recently liberated and which must swiftly prepare for winter.

I take the stairs two at a time, heels clattering against the stone floor. We're going to need to get a bigger fucking bed to accommodate three. With a chuckle, I decide the whelp can sleep on the floor, as I push against the door.

It doesn't budge.

I frown, turn the handle the other way, and put my shoulder into it. Is it locked? Heat flashes through my body. I thump the side of my fist against the door. "Open up!" My mind sinks into chaos. If the whelp is in there, I will beat him black and blue. I have also not seen Declan. Usually, he would be waiting for my return. Now I am worried he has let the fucking lad in here. He keeps talking about me needing to accept it, and I will, when I am fucking ready.

I hammer against the wood. Muffled voices come from the other side—a man and a woman. "Open the fucking door!"

Just as I raise my fist to beat again, the door swings open, only it is not Byron but Declan who is standing on the other side, naked. He casually spreads one arm wide, indicating I should step inside.

"You're late," he says.

Stupefied, I walk in. He is fucking naked! Am I in the wrong room?

He slams the door shut and sighs heavily. My head swings between where Declan stands scratching his jaw, eyeballing the door like he is waiting for...something, then on to the open bedroom door.

"No," I say, shaking my head. "Fucking no."

He shrugs.

"It was my fault," Dede says. Fist drawn back, I'm about to punch Declan, but my head swivels at hearing her voice. My sweet omega, my mate, stands in the doorway to the bedroom with a sheet clasped to her throat. I can't decide what enrages me more—that Declan has clearly rutted her, or that she feels the need to shield herself from me.

I slam my fist into Declan's jaw, and he staggers back a step. I am on him a heartbeat later, pummeling my fists into him over and over. The big bastard just soaks them up.

A shrill scream penetrates the fog, but I am enraged beyond reason. He has betrayed me and my trust. He has put his hands on my woman. My vision tunnels as arms like tree trunks wrap around me.

"Calm the fuck down," Declan snarls. "You are upsetting our little mate."

His poor choice of phrase only makes me see red. I strain, managing to break free, and land a swift jab to his jaw. He grunts, and my vision clears enough for me to see I have pushed the beast too far. He charges me, slamming me to the ground, flipping me onto my belly, and dropping his heavy ass weight onto me. I buck and strain. He drags back one arm, twisting it painfully, then shifts and plants one knee into the center of my back.

The pain in my shoulder and arm is excruciating. The bastard knows how to find a nerve.

"Find reason," he says. "I do not want to snap your fucking arm, but you are acting like an ass and upsetting Dede!"

"I'm not the one upsetting Dede," I snarl. "Get the fuck off of me!"

"No," he says. "I will not get fucking off you until you find a shred of sense."

Long minutes pass, but he does not relent. I curse into the wooden floor, exhausted, mind at sea. "Why?" I demand. "Why would you do this?"

"I asked him to."

My head turns, neck straining, trying to look up. Small naked feet enter my periphery.

"Best not get too close to him, lass," Declan says. "He's having some trouble adjusting."

Dede doesn't pay caution any heed—she has ever been bold —and kneels beside me. I strain, and the tendons in my arm and shoulder feel like they are about to snap.

"He came to bring me dinner," she says, her hand reaching out to brush the hair back from my cheek.

I grunt, wanting more of her touch. His scent covering her drives me crazy.

"I asked him to stay."

"He should not have fucking stayed." I can't process what this means. Has he claimed her now too?

"The man can rally two hundred men in victory against orcs, but he turns into an imbecile where your needs are concerned," Declan says. "Can't see past the end of his fucking nose."

"Is this to get to me, to punish me because of us?" I snarl.

The knee pressing into my back shifts in the most painful of ways. "You're a dick. The lass is a throwback whose scent has not changed. I told her no, but she got down on her fucking knees before me, took out my cock, and sucked it. There is only so much restraint a man possesses."

I don't want to believe him. A throwback? "She already has two mates!"

"Exactly," Declan says. "Two mates were not enough. Can you scent her now?"

I struggle to take in what he says. Scent? I can still scent her, but he is right—it is not the same as before.

"It won't change fully," he says, "until she goes into heat. You've kept her away from Byron, and that will cause some problems too. Dede needs to be claimed by three."

I don't want to hear reason. "Let me up!"

"I'll let you up if you tell me you won't hurt the lass."

I choke out a laugh. "I would never hurt Dede."

"Hmmm... Is this the same man who locked her in a room, waiting for her to bleed? Fucking idiot." He digs his knee into my back for good measure and twists my arm a little more.

The pain maddens me, even as I acknowledge the bastard has a point.

"I have rutted her," he says. "Thoroughly. I've not marked her yet, but I will."

He defers to me in all things, and yet, as I lie prone upon the floor, I recognize for the first time that Declan is the stronger, more powerful male. How can I give him control when everything inside me demands I be her first?

The fight leaves me as I understand where Dede is concerned, Declan is first alpha.

"I'm not taking your place," he says. "But you are not seeing sense where the lass is concerned. It's easier for me. I never had a fucking chance before, and I wasn't expecting this. I was expecting to leave."

"You don't love her," I say.

"Don't I?" His chuckle is dark and swift. A heavy hand slaps against the back of my head, knocking my forehead into the floor, rattling my brains. "I loved her from the moment I met her. I was just a street rat until a sweet lass begged her father to intervene. You think I don't want her, don't care about her? I love her as much as I love you, and that is saying something, though I still think you're a fucking idiot."

He slaps the back of my head again, and I growl as my bruised forehead smacks into the floor.

"Please don't," Dede says. "Let him up now. He needs to be with me. I think he's okay now."

I'm confident I am not okay, nor am I seeing sense. I can't think of anything beyond burying my cock in her pussy, pushing his cum out, and putting mine in.

"I won't hurt her," I say. "But I need to be inside her." I'm hard, cock crushed against the floor. Some of my arousal is for Dede, but some is also from the way Declan has calmly subdued me. I want to deny my response...to fight him and my reaction to him. We have sparred, but now I must acknowledge that he was holding back. Perhaps because of his feelings toward me?

"I am not noble," he says. "You are and are meant to be the leader, just not of Dede. If you fuck up again, I'll pin you to the fucking ground and keep you there. Tie you up if need be until you cool off. Are we good?"

No, we are not good, but I don't point this out. I have a sliver of rationality left, and I have a sweet mate I need and who needs me. "Aye. I understand. I don't like it, but I understand."

The pressure on my arm disappears. It throbs like a bastard. Then his knee lifts, and I'm left lying there on the floor. It takes me a moment to gather myself enough to roll over and heave myself to a sitting position.

A tiny little bundle crashes into me, peppering kisses to my cheeks and throat, small hands tugging on the buckles of my jerkin. "Please," she says, a sob in her voice. "Please Grady, I need you inside me."

I groan, trying to find my fucking wits against the fire she lights inside me. I stagger to my feet with her in my arms, ripping away the sheet she dared use to cover herself from me. Staggering through to the bedroom, I drop her on the bed, loosen the buckle on my pants, and shucking them down enough to free my aching shaft, bury myself to the root. She is wet and open. I growl, smelling him on her, feeling his cum coating my cock as I slam wetly in and out.

"Mine," I growl.

"Yes," she says. "I am yours, Grady."

But she is not only mine. My savage rutting only seems to spur her wild moans. Footsteps vaguely register, and my head lifts, focus shifting from the open panting omega I'm rutting to

Declan, who stands naked beside the bed. Taking a goblet from the nightstand, he lifts it to his lips.

Drinking, he watches me rut my woman. I can't fucking look away from him nor his heated gaze. His eyes lower, roaming down until they settle on the place where my iron hard length is shuttling in and out. He shifts slightly, giving himself a better view. "She has the hottest, tightest little cunt. I have never gotten my cock and knot in a woman like this before. It feels so fucking good. I swore if you killed me, I'd die happy."

I groan, my eyes lowering to where she writhes on the bed. Somehow, him watching me do this sends all the sensations spiraling twice as hard and fast. My lower spine tingles. I'm going to fucking come.

"Clench over him, lass," Declan says. "Like I have taught you. Encourage him to spill his seed."

She does, squeezing over me, making my knot bloom to the point where I cannot pull out. I growl as we lock together, coming and filling her up, hips jerking erratically as I bathe the entrance to her womb, my cum mingling with his, and all the while, Declan is watching me. I don't think I've ever come so hard. It just keeps going, filling her even more.

Then, because Declan is a bastard who has ever been bold, he leans in, grasps her chin, and closes his mouth over hers. Her moans are swallowed, her pussy clenching around me. I stare stupefied, my fingers white against her hips. He is kissing her in front of me, only it doesn't fill me with rage. No, it is the lustiest image I have ever seen.

My hips jerk again, and I spew deeply as a second climax takes me.

I growl my encouragement, eyes shifting to where his big fist is wrapped around his cock as he jacks himself off roughly. I cannot tear my gaze away. Then he rises, and her lips are open, welcoming, as he takes his cock and pushes in.

"Good lass," he says. "I'm going to come quickly. Watching Grady rut you has taken me straight to the edge."

He fucks her mouth, palming her throat as he thrusts his fat cock in and out. I groan, utterly transfixed, as he growls over her.

"Use your tongue. I'm going to come so fucking deep down your throat."

How does this sweet little omega take this huge rough male? Yet her pussy won't stop clenching over me, and I'm caught in a perpetual climatic loop. I grind against her as another small, heady spurt of cum floods her pussy.

"Pet her clit," he says, and it takes me a while to realize he's talking to me. "She will come again. She likes to be used like this."

I move to follow his command without thought, thumb finding her fat little clit, rubbing back and forth, feeling the little bud slide from side to side, and her legs clamp around me.

"Fuck, she really likes that. Does that feel good, little lamb? Do you like Grady's cock in your pussy while I'm filling your pretty mouth?"

Her clit turns slippery under my thumb. My mouth is hanging open, transfixed by this vision before me.

"Fuck, I'm going to come. Gods, her tongue is a test." And then he stills, ass clenching. She chokes a little, cum bubbling around her lips. He doesn't pull out, just holds deep, the hand over her throat moving as she gulps him greedily down. He growls, and she begins convulsing, pussy squeezing fiercely around me.

A shudder ripples through me, and I'm coming again, impossible though it may seem, balls tightening, hips jerking, stars dancing over the room. His cock pops out of her mouth. Her poor lips are swollen and bright pink, her eyes glazed. He swipes the spillage up from her cheek with his thumb and pushes it into her mouth, and she sucks without hesitation, eyes closing in rapture, pussy clenching in waves. She is still coming, I realize.

"There," Declan says, head swinging to face me, catching me in my unguarded moment, "that wasn't so hard, was it?"

Hard? No, it was the most erotic experience of my life, and I already know that I need more.

Chapter Twenty-Four

Declan

I'm pushing Grady past his comfort zone, but I don't fucking care. Everything about this is so fucking right. Dede is the ideal little mate, the perfect balance between us.

As his knot softens, he collapses to the bed on his side, pulling her up so that she lies in front of him. Because I'm a pushy bastard, I go ahead and lie on her other side. She nestles sweetly in his arms, although she sneaks glances at me under her lashes.

I wink, and she bites her lips to stifle her giggle.

"How was the patrol?" I ask.

"You're just going to casually ask me about the patrol?" he says, all surly.

I chuckle, not buying into his bullshit. I saw the expression on his face as we locked eyes while he was rutting her, the lust darkening them as he came again at seeing me fill her sweet little mouth. "You were working through some rage when you

221

first returned. I figured asking you how the patrol went could wait until you were sane again."

He huffs out a breath, hands tightening on Dede, one lowering, fingers probing her slick cunt. She gasps, but her thighs part, giving him better access. As he begins to pump in and out slowly, her eyes lock with mine. Grady has his face buried in her hair, but he lifts his head and my eyes go to him.

"We killed a few of the bastards. A few minor injuries on our part."

Her lips pop open, and a little moan escapes her.

"The slick gland?" I ask.

He nods. "Drives her fucking wild."

"Goddess," she mutters, fingers darting to grab his wrists. I intervene, tugging them away.

"We will need to be vigilant," I say. "But mayhap they will move on and seek easy pickings soon."

"Mnnn!" She twitches, and his fingers begin to make lewd wet noises.

"Good girl," I say. "Let Grady touch you how he needs, lass."

"I'll patrol the nearby villages tomorrow," he says.

"That's an excellent idea," I agree.

"Oh! Goddess help me. I'm going to..."

She comes riding his fingers, gasping, groaning, twitching, and finally falling limp. He pulls his fingers out, and I grab his wrist, bringing his fingers to my lips. His face darkens, but he doesn't look away nor fight me as I suck them into my mouth. My eyes roll back, and my cock jerks with renewed interest. There was only a hint of him inside her earlier, but now I can fucking taste both him and her.

"Fuck!" Grady rumbles. "I'm hard as a rock again."

I release him, redirecting my attention to the limp little omega between us, and take her lips in a sweet kiss, coaxing her, fondling her tit, until she begins moaning into my mouth. Behind her, Grady is already sucking kisses up her throat, his hand on his cock, jerking it with impatient strokes. I want to fucking touch him there, want to suck his cum from the source, but I also want to watch Dede doing that, worshiping him the same way that I do.

I tear my lips from hers. "Up you go, little lamb. Grady needs your mouth on him. Do you want that? To taste his cum while I rut you?"

"Yes, please yes."

He growls encouragement as she rises, scooting down the bed, lips hovering over him and face enrapt, like she is both terrified and wildly aroused. What a fucking treasure we have found. My chest feels full of emotions too potent to contain. I want to shout my love, to tell them both over and over again how much I cherish them, yet I am ever mindful that my feelings are new to them.

So I will show them.

Grady hisses as I take his cock in hand. "Suck it, little lamb," I say. I keep my smile internal. I'm only touching his cock, no need to make a big deal out of it. We haven't done this before, but I have wanted to. Oh how I have wanted to.

Dede leans down and dutifully laps at the leaking tip. "Good girl," I encourage, keeping my hand on him.

It hasn't gone down any, so there's that.

Sprawled out beside him as I am, my cock butts up against his thigh as it begins to harden again. Part of it is the joy of watching Dede tend to him, but part of it is also getting my hand on Grady, finally. We have shared lasses on occasion, and he has been with men in his younger years, or so I have heard, but he has never been intimate with me. I've never pushed it before. I had my own issues to deal with—issues regarding a certain lass who turned out to be an omega. So it was hard for me with Dede and Grady.

Now, you can bet I'm going to fucking push it.

My cock begins to leak over his hair-roughened thigh as I imagine the sounds he would make if I had my dick buried in his ass. I run my thumb over the ridge at the bottom—the knot—in a way I know a man likes.

"Fuck!" he growls. "For fuck's sake, Declan!"

I do smirk now because the ridge is growing, *throbbing* under my thumb, and his cock is stone hard.

I lean in, pressing a kiss to Dede's temple, breathing in *his* scent with hers. Her lips pop off, and she looks at me, cheeks flushed, lips swollen and a little damp. Fist full of her hair, I share a lusty kiss with her, all the while toying with Grady's cock.

He rumbles a low sensual growl as he watches us, dick leaking pre-cum all over my fingers like someone opened a tap. Then casually, so casually that no one would suspect my intentions, I break the kiss and slip my mouth over his cock...and suck. It's over as quickly as it started, and I'm back to kissing Dede.

"Declan," he says. There is warning in his voice, but he's still rock-hard. Only now I have the taste of him, and I know I want more.

But not today. I've been a patient man for a long while, I can be patient a little longer. This time when I break the kiss, I redirect Dede's lips to the prize, roll to my knees, and come up behind her. There is no preamble, she is drenched with arousal, and my cock slips inside like it is being welcomed home. Fuck, she feels so fucking good. Such a needy little delight, hungry for cock any way she can get it. Hands braced to her hips, I take a couple of leisurely thrusts before lifting my head from the arresting sight of my hard length shuttling wetly in and out.

My eyes meet and hold Grady's. "Work your fingers over the knot, little lamb, as you have just seen me do."

She hums, and Grady groans. Fuck, I am not going to fucking last.

"This cunt is fucking amazing." I tear my gaze from Grady's eyes, lowering to where my cock thrusts in and out. "It's like you are sucking me in."

Chapter Twenty-Five

Byron

I'm an outsider, where once I was a part. Days have gone by since Declan liberated me from the cells, and with every one, my temper rises. I have it on good authority from Barnaby, who has heard from Mia, that both Declan and Grady are now rutting Dede.

My blood boils whenever Declan calls me to the practice pit, but the bastard just grins. He is as hard as fucking nails. I'm a big alpha, arguably the biggest in Langetta, but he fights mean, and I spend more time on my back than putting up a credible challenge.

"Your heart's not in it today, lad," he taunts, grabbing my forearm and heaving me to my feet. I spit out a mouthful of blood. The fucker does not hold back.

"I want to see her," I say, my frustration spilling out.

"It's not up to me," Declan says, knees bending and fists rising, ready for action so he can pummel me again. It's cold at this time of year, but we are both shirtless and sweat makes rivulets in the dirt smearing us.

"Then who is it up to?" I demand. "Why wouldn't she tell me herself if she doesn't want me anymore?"

"It's not about that." He takes a jab at my nose. Distracted, I don't block the blow and end up sitting on my ass in the dirt. I pinch the bridge of my nose as blood squirts all over the fucking place. Losing my last shred of patience, I surge to my feet with a roar and tackle him to the ground. The bastard is both strong and fast. Flipping me onto my back, he is on me, pinning me to the fucking ground. I arch, strain, and rock this way and that, trying to toss the heavy fucker off, but he just puts all his fucking monster weight on top of me and I only wear myself out.

He grins down at me with bloody teeth. I guess I landed one good blow.

"Are you fucking hard?"

He chuckles. "Something about subduing a man or woman does it for me."

"Get the fuck off me!"

"When I'm ready," he says.

The clang of the raider alarm distracts us both. Declan exhales a heavy sigh and heaves himself off of me before helping me to my feet.

"I don't want your fucking help," I grumble, shaking off his hand as soon as I'm standing. My nose is fucking throbbing and bleeding all over the place.

"You are not pressing in the right place," he says, frowning, making like he is going to help me.

I take a step back, scowling at him. The alarm is still clanging, so somewhere, the kingdom is under attack.

"Is it true?" I ask, feeling reckless, growing ever more

desperate to see the woman I think of as my mate. "Are you both rutting her?"

His face softens, and I know even before he nods that he is. I would go at the bastard again if I had any energy left. "It is not my fucking decision. Grady is being an ass with me, but he struggles more with you because you had her first. For all the while he was away, he remained celibate, thinking he would return and claim her, only to find she was with you."

I am stunned by this admission, such that I don't notice Declan nearing to shift my fingers on my nose. He is gentle, hand steady on the back of my head, lips pursed like he is troubled. He squeezes over my neck briefly before he steps away.

The clatter of horses being readied redirects our attention. I turn to find Grady striding from the courtyard for the practice pit. He stares at Declan and then me. "Mount up," he calls, looking over the few men present...and me. "There are reports of raiders near Little Meade. We ride."

Declan nods his head at me. "The lad is injured, best we leave him here. He is in no state to ride and battle raiders."

I have not yet patrolled with Grady. Maybe he is seeking to finally acknowledge me. I go to voice my protest—it is only a fucking nosebleed, and further, has now stopped. Declan places a hand on the back of my neck again, shocking me into silence. Grady looks between us, a tic thumping in jaw. Growling, he pivots and stalks off.

The hand drops, and Declan winks at me. "Sometimes, you need to push a man to do the right thing."

Then he is striding off after Grady, snatching up his leather jerkin and sword from where they lie on a low wall and hollering to nearby men who are dawdling.

I stare after him, heart thudding. Was Grady's inclusion of me more about keeping me from Dede, and was Declan giving me the go ahead? I think he was, and if he wasn't, I am fucking taking it as such. Grady worries me, but he is not a badass bastard like Declan. Although I don't trust Declan much, I trust him not to get me killed. From the very start, he has acted as a go-between, removing me from danger, tempering me while Grady got his head out of his ass, as Declan says.

Somehow, I contain myself enough to act casually until they mount and ride out of the castle, listening for chains rattling as the gate rises and the sounds of hooves clattering.

When I lower my fingers, my nose is no longer bleeding. I go to the barrel where the water is kept, fill a bucket, and wash off my hands, face, and upper body. There's a stack of rags nearby, and I use one to wipe myself down. My nose throbs... It takes them fucking ages to ride out the gate, then comes another rattle as the gate lumbers down.

I take a fast diagonal path across the practice pit for the backdoor, into the kitchen, past busy cooks and maids, out the other side, and into the corridor at the back of the hall, heading straight for her room, bare chested and a little damp but not fucking caring. I'm getting tunnel vision at the thought of being with her once again, and I take the stairs two at a time before skittering to a stop at her door.

It's just the fucking door, one I've walked through many times, yet the emotions that assault me from being separated from her these two weeks past are deep and complex. It was never easy to be with her while Killian was a threat, but they were precious moments, every one of them.

When I revealed as an alpha, the change was swift. I grew nearly two feet in the space of as many weeks. The pain was excruciating, and I spent much of the period on poppy milk. I remember Dede, tending me with gentle hands. I wasn't expecting anything, being with her never crossed my mind. Killian and his madness just pushed us together. I wanted to protect her, and then...well, love happened.

I have thought only about how I feel being separated from Dede, but now I have seen the other side of it. I can only imagine how hard it was for Grady to come back, not just to Killian's tyranny, but to find another man in Dede's bed.

My pa is a baker, my ma too. They've done that all their lives. Mayhap if I'd revealed as a beta, I would have been a baker too, but I'm an alpha. I see things differently and understand the pain an alpha experiences in sharing his mate with another. I fucking love her, would give her anything within my power, even if it were only my life, and I've missed her far more than I thought possible.

Now Killian is gone. The bastard needed to die, only I wasn't the man who could do that. Grady did and I'm grateful to him, but as Declan says, Grady has spent enough time with his head up his ass and now he needs to fucking learn to share.

The cool metal of the handle gives, and as I turn and push, the door creaks open. It feels strange to be here, like I have been away forever, rather than two weeks.

"Grady?" she calls.

My gut twists at hearing her sweet voice call another man's name. Next comes the patter of footsteps before she appears in the bedroom doorway.

She stops as she sees me, fingers flying to her mouth as a little gasp escapes. She is wearing a long blue gown tied with little ribbons that experience tells me come undone easily by my fingers.

"It's not Grady," I say. The place where my heart beats for her becomes hollow, but then she runs to me sobbing, throwing her arms around my neck, and the sense of emptiness disappears, replaced by a great swelling of joy. I hold her close, burying my nose in the crook of her neck, sucking her scent in, hands trembling where they hold her as I lift her up into my arms.

"Byron, Byron, Byron," she says, pressing little kisses over my face, my shoulders, against my throat. "Byron!"

In my wildest dreams, I could not wish for any more than this moment, and her obvious joy soothes my tired heart.

"Oh, Byron, I have missed you."

"I have missed you too, my Dede, my princess." Somehow, I kick the door shut and stagger forward toward the bedroom with her still in my arms. Their scent is all over the space—Dede's, Declan's, and a less known to me one belonging to Grady.

Strangely, although I do not expect it, the urge to rut her is tempered by a simple need to hold her. I sit on the edge of the bed, pulling her close. She clings, arms and legs wrapping around me like a little monkey, and sobs. There are tears trickling down my own cheeks. We don't move for the longest time. I can hear her heartbeat, can feel the wild flutter of the vein at her throat where my lips are pressed. I want to be inside her, but I want to hold her more.

Her impatience breaks through this stoic barrier that grips me. As her kisses gain urgency, my eyes lift and I frown. "Is that a nest?"

Her head pops up and swivels around to see what I'm staring at. She glances back at me, cheeks damp, and I brush the tears away with the pad of my thumb.

"Yes," she says. "I made a nest. Would you like to come in?"

"I would, more than anything." The castle has been aflutter with news of her being an omega. I suspected it once a few things fell into place, but her new status is talked about openly now. An omega nest is sacred. An alpha must ask permission before he may enter. It is a place where she will be rutted when she goes into heat and rest when she wishes to feel safe. It is only on the omega's approval that a male may step inside.

She slips down from my lap and I miss the touch, miss her,

but as she takes my hand in hers, coaxing me from the bed, I rise gladly. Her hand is so tiny within mine, a clumsy giant beside a tiny sprite. On reaching the doorway, she stops, glancing shyly up at me. Is she seeking my approval?

"It's beautiful," I say, and truly, I believe this must be the most beautiful nest in all the world. Clothing nestles between the blankets, cushions, and pillows, some I do not recognize, and I can only presume they belong to Grady or Declan. But there, in the very center, is an old undershirt of mine.

"Is that mine?" I ask.

She nods, grinning. "I found it at the back of my closet. I wanted something of yours in here. You are the first to enter. I refused to let the others in until we were reunited."

I don't fully understand what happens next. One moment, she is standing beside me with her tiny hand in mine, and the next, I am trying to consume her, one searing kiss at a time. "Tell me to rut you in the nest," I say, sucking kisses down her throat before nipping at the place where I marked.

"Please, Byron, rut me in my nest."

Growling, I wade in, suffering her hiss of displeasure when I displace a few cushions at the edge. I'm impatient, charged with arousal the likes of which I have never known before. Lowering her to the middle of the nest with her head upon the shirt that once belonged to me, but is given willingly to my little omega mate, I come down over her. "I need to be inside you." My hands shake as I divest her of her dress.

"Yes, yes, yes," she says, as impatient as me, small fingers on my buckle, tugging it open before pushing my pants past my hips, frustrated when they bunch at my ankles and snag in my boots. She giggles as I finally kick everything off, but it turns into a groan as I suck her tit into my mouth. My cock is leaking and wants nothing more than to be inside my sweet Dede. "I can't wait," I say.

"I don't want you to," she says. "I need to be rutted properly."

I still my mouth against her plump tit, head lifting. "What is a proper rutting?"

A blush creeps over her cheeks, but she doesn't hesitate to place a hand against my chest, pushing me back a little way so she can wriggle out from underneath me before rolling over and rising up onto her hands and knees.

"Fuck," I mutter gruffly, placing my hands tentatively upon her hips, spreading my fingers wide and gently squeezing. She throws a glance over her shoulder at me, and I could drown in that look. "Is this what you want, Dede? For me to take you from behind? To rut you in your nest?"

"Yes, Byron," she says. "That is exactly what I want, and I don't want you to be gentle about it. I want you to rut me roughly, to fill me with your cock and knot."

Rough? Knot? My mind turns to white fuzz and my fingers go to my balls, yanking them down, the pain doing little to take the edge off my fierce arousal. Fuck!

She bites her lower lip, waiting while I get myself under control.

"I will do that," I say. "But you must tell me if I am being too rough."

"You won't hurt me," she says, but then her eyes lower to my cock and the knot, which is always in a half formed state around Dede.

"Goddess," she whispers before turning back and burying her face in the nest. "I had forgotten about your knot."

"What about it?" My fingers skim over her ass, fumbling in the wet folds, getting all up over her clit before delving into the hot wetness of her pussy. She is so tight, seeming to suck my fingers in.

"It's...it's very big," she finally says.

"I'll go slowly," I say as her ass cants, giving me better access to her slick pussy.

"Please, Byron, I need you inside me!"

I pause to lick up all the juices from my fingers, reveling in the taste of her. She is an omega, meant to take all of me.

"I will go slowly," I repeat.

"I don't want you to! Have you not listened to a word I say?"

She is an impatient little thing, and if I'm honest, I don't want to go slowly either. But I force myself to, taking my cock in hand, sliding the sensitive tip up and down her wet folds, mumbling a chant to myself not to come. She whimpers, pushing back, body trembling with the same desperation possessing me. I snag the entrance and sink a little way in.

"Yes!" she says. "Byron, it feels so good."

I ease deeper and deeper, and she groans, trying to push back, but I take hold of her hip and still her wriggling lest she take too much too quickly and hurt herself. Tight, wet, welcoming me in, I've never felt anything as heavenly as this. I surge all the way to the knot.

She emits a little squeal, and I still. "Did I hurt you?" I demand.

"No, Byron. Please, it feels good. Don't stop."

I growl, fingers sinking so deeply into her ass that they turn the flesh white. I can't temper myself anymore, I am too far gone. I begin to rut deeply in rough thrusts, my knot already swelling, making me panic a little.

Head thrown back, neck arched, she groans her pleasure, mumbling nonsense as I fight to temper my need to slam my knot in, but it is not fucking easy. Knots are not supposed to swell until they are being worked in, I know this. My cock looks obscene as it bludgeons her tight little pussy, I can't work out how my knot will go in as well.

"I need more!" she cries.

"I'm going to fucking come," I say, sweat breaking out all over my body as I become caught between needs and fears, sinking the swelling knot against her slippery entrance, trying to force it inside, and yet consumed by a worry that it is somehow dangerous to her.

Then she's coming, squealing with pleasure, her pussy milking my length. With a groan of frustration, I sink my fingers into my knot, squeezing it as I spill inside her, waves of pleasure yet tempered by my failure to knot my mate as she asked me to.

Only my cock is still hard, I keep thrusting, and if anything, my knot grows.

We rut, falling upon one another over and over again. Her needs are insatiable. If I stop, she growls her displeasure and nips me with her teeth.

And I can't fucking knot her. It gets worse with every coupling, until I am sure I am about to lose my fucking mind.

Then, deep into the frenzy as I teeter upon the cusp of madness, I hear a savage growl before hard hands tear me from my mate.

Chapter Twenty-Six

Grady

The ten-mile ride to Little Meade is spent wondering about Dede. There wasn't time to argue with Declan when he said the lad should stay behind, but jealousy roars within me and I worry that in my absence, Byron has gone to her.

Barely had I come to terms with Byron when Declan crashed into the situation, and now I must share her with not one, but two men. I admit, I have come to enjoy watching her with Declan, to realize it is not a case of losing something but of gaining more. Yet it is still difficult to extend such intimacy to a man I do not know.

Declan is also fucking pushing me. I know what he wants from me, what he needs. I have been with men before, for it is the nature of young men to experiment and there is no shame in it. I determined long ago that I wanted a woman and children in my future, yet there is something about Declan's touch

239

that reawakens me to those different pleasures. Now it is no longer a case of losing one or the other. With Dede, I can have a sweet, lusty mate and children...but I can have Declan too, if her reaction to him handling me is anything to go by.

I need to step up and be a leader, both to the wider community of the kingdom and in my personal life, but today I am distracted and can't shake off the suspicion that a silent communication took place between Declan and Byron before we left. They have trained together daily since the castle was liberated, forming a relationship...establishing an order.

I am still brooding over these matters when we arrive at Little Meade to find the raiders are gone. A nearby farm has been ransacked, cured beef and grain taken and a couple laborers injured, but that is the worst of it.

"We best track them," Declan says.

It's the right thing to do, but I'm thinking about Dede. "Aye," I agree.

We follow the route the raiders took and so begins a merry chase that takes us all fucking day and leads us to a small camp. It doesn't matter that they have twice our numbers, I charge straight in, hacking, cutting, slicing, and punching my way through every bastard until they are dead upon the ground.

It is only as I stand, chest heaving, splattered in their foul blood, that I realize I have dismounted to better cut them down.

Declan is eyeballing me from the vantage of a horse, smirking. "Mayhap the rest of us can take a nap next time." I glance around at the bodies, then over to the men accompanying me, noticing how they fidget, watching me with wary expressions. I have not entered the white rage since I fought the Blighten.

"He's going into rut," one of the men says.

"Aye," Declan says. "Mayhap he is."

Rut? I shake my head, trying to clear the fog. How can I be in rut? Doesn't it need an omega heat to trigger it? Then I remember the increasing frenzy gripping me of late, how I haven't resolved things with the lad... Dede must be going into fucking heat.

"We need to return," I say.

"We do," Declan agrees casually. How can he be casual at such a time? I've just slaughtered a dozen men from the looks of it, mostly single-handed. *What am I going to do to the lad?* I don't realize I have said this last part aloud until Declan replies.

"I'll be there," he says. "I'll make sure nothing happens. She's not yet in heat, but given you rutted her nonstop for days even before I entered the mix, I sense it is close. Blood, killing, dealing with the raider scum, and rutting an omega between. Little wonder we aren't all tipping over the edge."

Only Declan is calm, and I realize I trust him to keep me true, to stop me from a course of action that I will regret for the rest of my life. I've never felt a trust like this before, one deeper than the more familiar trusting of a man to watch your back in battle. It is the kind that transcends words.

We gather up the supplies we find in the camp, along with a couple horses, load up, and leave. Declan and I ride on for Langetta Castle, while the remainder of our party return to the village with the recovered goods.

Now our duty is done, my thoughts circle back to Byron and my suspicions that he has gone to Dede. I think this might be part of my rage, knowing he is balls deep inside her, putting his mark on her throat...the one I tried to obliterate with my own. And our sweet, lusty omega will be begging him for more.

"You are growling," Declan says as we crest the rise that brings the castle into view, the sun sinking behind it. "Temper it. If I need to take you to the practice pit, even at this time of night, I will. Tell me you are in control, and I will allow you to go to her room."

I snarl at him, but he growls right back, prepared to back up any threat.

The rattle of the chains heralds the gate rising, and our horses' hooves make a clatter as we pass through into the courtyard. Despite the onset of dusk, many people are about and hasten over, concerned when there are only two of us and me splattered in blood.

"All is well," Declan announces as we dismount. "We found a camp. A dozen raiders were killed, and goods recovered. The other men are staying on at Little Meade tonight."

This news is greeted with cheers from those gathered. Any word of raiders being killed or moving on is a source of celebration. The small crowd parts, and Declan steers me in the direction of a water barrel. "Clean yourself up. You look like a one-man army of death."

I pull the buckles free, yank off my leather jerkin, and dunk my head, shoulders, and arms deep into the barrel. With the turn in weather as we approach winter, the cold water is shocking. The sharp breeze on my wet skin dampens the heat inside me and cools my urge to run up the fucking stairs to rip *him* from her, because I must let Declan lead this. "He went to her, didn't he?"

"He did, but you'll let me deal with this."

I realize then that it's time for me to trust Declan, to accept and give the woman I love everything she needs. "I will," I say.

Declan

At my insistence, and to Grady's displeasure, we strip before entering the chamber. Grady glares at me like he's thinking about ripping my head off, but as we've already established, he can't, and so he does as he is told.

We enter, dropping our clothes and boots beside the door... and find Byron in the nest with Dede. Given she has allowed neither Grady nor me access, I feel the slight as keenly as Grady does.

I don't give Grady a chance to react, just wade in and wrestle Byron out. Grady snatches up a protesting Dede, a deep growl emanating from his chest as he takes her to the bed.

"Don't hurt him! Oh, please, make them stop!"

Byron turns feral as I grapple with him. He throws everything he has at me, but I spar with the lad for a reason and I'm as familiar with his moves as I am Grady's. The lad thrashes and strains, but I don't give a fucking inch. The tussle between us, the ripe scent of Dede's slick and his cum, all has a predictable effect on me. I am hard as a fucking rock, which only enrages him more.

Dede cries and makes sobbed demands from the bed, where Grady holds her. I don't spare him a glance, all my focus is on bringing Byron to heel. Somehow, he ends up on his knees with me behind him, one arm braced across his throat. The other snakes around his waist, pinning his arms. My hard length pushes up against his ass.

"Get the fuck off of me!" he hisses.

On the bed, Dede is silent, riveted by our show.

"Stop fighting," I say. "You can't go to Dede like that. You'll hurt her."

But Byron is beyond reason, and he only strains and struggles harder, rubbing my cock in the most arresting way. Then I glance down and notice what he's packing.

"The fuck is that?" Grady says gruffly. I'm in a similar state of shock.

"Have you knotted her yet, lad?" I demand, tightening my arm around his throat.

"No!"

Thank fuck! "Her pussy will surely be ruined once his monster knot is forced inside her. Grady and I will need to thoroughly prepare her first. Work our knots in and out, so she is open enough for you." His body contorts as he fights for freedom. I shouldn't provoke the lad, but as Grady will attest, I struggle with boundaries and common sense.

"Please," Dede says. "Let me touch him."

Grady growls, holding her easily as she strains to get down. The lass is lucky she hasn't gotten a dick in her already. It would certainly calm her down.

Byron's body is a mass of quivering rage. He is the strongest alpha I have dominated. While much of my arousal is for the final culmination of our claiming of Dede, for the woman I have admired from afar, another equally compelling part relates to gaining Byron's full submission. My dick is hard, throbbing, leaking, and ready to take the last step. "If you want to be part of this, you need to earn your place and submit to me. Outside of the bedchamber, Grady is first, but in regard to rutting Dede, that will always be me."

"Place?" Byron snarls. "I will not take your fucking cock."

But his dick has not softened, so he is not as averse to the idea. An alpha can read an omega, but I have always been able to read men as well, to gauge their interest or lack thereof. The timing was never right with Grady, but I sense it is approaching. Perhaps Byron's submission will prove the trigger for Grady.

"Please," Dede begs. "Let me go to him, touch him."

I nod to Grady, who carefully releases the wriggling bundle. She scrambles off the bed and falls to her knees before Byron. He hisses as her small hand closes over his throbbing length. She glances at him, eyes wide and lips parted. It won't be long before her heat takes her. She is insatiable, always willing and eager for our attention. I have touched Grady on occasion, and she shows no sign of stress or jealousy, and it heartens me further to see her enjoying what I do with Byron.

"Do you like this, little lamb? Watching me master Byron?"

"Yes," she says, eyes lowering to where her hands pump up and down his cock.

"Calm yourself, lad," I whisper in his ear. "You do not want to hurt our little lamb. Let her tend to you. It will take some of your rage."

The smallest amount of tension leaves his body, although he strains still. I shift, sliding down and then up so that my cock springs to nestle between his thighs. He jerks, thrusting forward, as a small hand encloses my cock as well. Two hands are pumping together, squeezing our cocks close, spreading the sticky pre-cum all over the lengths. I'm ready to blow my fucking load. "Have you ever had a cock in your ass?" I ask. He grunts and turns rigid, so that probably wasn't the best thing to ask. "Your dick hasn't gone down lad, so I'll take that as indication that you're not against this. There needs to be hierarchy and order."

Byron growls, but he is no longer straining, for the little omega leans down and begins lapping at our cocks, and this garners all his attention. Her wet tongue brushes over the top of both, his, mine, his, mine, twirling around the top, pumping them in her small hand. She's barely aware of anything besides getting the cum inside her. Grady falls to his knees behind her. Byron hisses, his focus torn between the omega tending him, and what Grady is doing. There is no preamble on Grady's part. His cock is hard and ruddy with arousal, and he is interested only in slaking his lust.

Grady's eyes lower first to her ass, then on to where she

tends to the two of us, before rising to meet mine. I smirk. Grady enjoys my dominant side. "I'm going to rut you well, lad. Maybe I'll let her suck you while I'm doing it. Maybe I'll let you rut her? Or maybe I'll just fuck you and make her watch?"

Byron growls, jerking against my hold, while Grady swallows. I sense he is coming to accept this side of me. Then his eyes redirect to the omega before he lines up and thrusts deep.

Dede groans, deep, guttural. A few deep thrusts, and she is closing her lips around Byron's cock, hands mashing us together, pumping with firm strokes that send pleasure rising.

"Fuck!" Byron hisses.

"Indeed, lad," I say. "She has a sweet little tongue. I have enjoyed her tending to me very much over the last few days." Byron thrusts his hips forward, trying to get more of her attention. "Feels good, doesn't it? An omega was meant to take cock. See how enthusiastic she becomes while Grady is rutting her. He doesn't hold back, does he?"

The heavy slaps commence as Grady pounds her, jolting her lips over our cocks. Her small body quivers from the impact, while her sweet groaning tells me that she likes what he does. "Have you ever seen a more arresting sight?" I say close to his ear. "Tiny little omega being rutted by a big savage alpha."

"Fuck!" Byron growls. His body jerks, and then I am coming too. Dede convulses with her own climax, groaning, sucking, trying to get as much cum in her as she can, even though it is going fucking everywhere. My cock is lower and a bit behind, so it sprays all over her tits, belly, and spews across the floor.

"Squeeze his knot, little lamb."

Small fingers rub erratically against my swelling, mashing our cocks together within tiny hands as she rubs and plays and licks.

Claimed by Three

Grady's hands turn white over her hips, holding her still, head thrown back, ecstasy written on his contorted face and the corded lines of his arched neck, muscles taut, hips jerking as he fills her all up.

Chapter Twenty-Seven

Grady

What has happened to my life? I remember a simpler time when I was a lad, expecting to grow up, get married, have a couple of whelps, and hope to watch them flourish as old age took me. Then I came to Langetta, and the castle—and a certain young lass—weaved their magic upon me. Roll forward, and here I am on the floor, having rutted that same lass from behind while she sucks the cocks of two other men. One I know well, the other, not so much. Yet we are all bound together to serve one woman who will become our mate.

I recognize that I am sinking into my rut, but it is only now as it bears down upon me that I understand what this means. Inhibitions have gone out the window and are floating into the distance. We are all caught up in the same spell.

Dede is locked on my knot, and as I draw her back against me, Byron leans in to gather her face between his hands and kiss her. Declan rises, staggering to his feet and striding from the room.

It should be hard for me to see them together, yet the coming rut holds resentment, anger, and petty jealousy at bay. He is so gentle with her, nothing like Declan or me. In this euphoric state, I can admit the sight of them here, before me, while she is still locked on me, is deeply arousing. My hands move over her, gentle in this brief interlude before the storm comes for us. If I live to be a hundred, I shall never tire of her lush, giving body.

The knot softens, and I ease from her warmth, sending a gush of our cum spilling out.

As I gain my feet, they break the kiss and cling together, her legs wrapping around his waist as he gathers her in close.

I can't tear my eyes away. They are so fucking sweet together, giving each other gentle kisses and touches. Were I not so hyperaware, I might presume that she had forgotten I exist. Yet she hasn't, she's merely renewing love for the man who claimed her first.

Declan comes to stand beside me. My eyes lower to his hard cock before returning to his face. Smirking, he wiggles his eyebrows. "You're next."

"Not to-fucking-day," I say.

"No," he says. "Maybe tomorrow then." I hear the smile in his voice as we both turn our attention to the young alpha and omega, seeing all the tenderness present there. If I had to pick a third, I could not pick someone better. I remember the quiet baker's boy, who wasn't really part of my circle when I was the commander. Upon my subsequent return, I find a young man and alpha taking on the impossible task of protecting Dede against Killian. I still cannot think of that monster's name without wanting to go on a rampage, but he is gone now, and I'm ever grateful Byron was here in my absence. There have been only good reports about Byron, who is well liked and respected by everyone, and a strong alpha in ways beside his obvious brawn.

He is one of the best.

"She needs all of us," Declan says, reminding me that we must be aligned in purpose and agreement.

"Aye," I say. "But she better not need anyone fucking else."

Declan chuckles. "Best we get this over with. I sense the lass is close to her heat."

Declan

I place the bottle on the table. Byron looks between the bottle and me. Our little omega, who is nestled on his lap, similarly eyes the bottle before pressing urgent kisses to Byron's cheeks, down his throat, and nipping at the strong column. Her hands turn a little feverish, petting him, trying to calm him, for she knows what this is about.

"What's that for?" Byron asks suspiciously, his hands possessively cupping her ass. She nips at his throat again, bringing a groan to his lips.

"You know what it is, lad. Your respite is over. Before you knot her, your place must be established."

His deep growl follows as our sweet mate's kisses weave magic upon him.

"Please," she says. "Let him do this. I want to see you like that."

He is going to come so hard and hot, he'll see stars, but he's also nervous. Most men are the first time. This isn't only about him, though, nor any of us individually. It's about all of us bonding together in a way each of us needs. "You will take it," I say, "because I want you to. There will be other times when I want and need you like this."

He growls softly under his breath. No alpha likes to be dominated, but sometimes, it needs to be done. My cock is hard as stone. I take it in hand, jacking up and down. He watches, nostrils flaring. "I won't submit easily," he says. "I can't."

Dede slides her hand down his chest and over his stomach, until she dips between them and grasps his dick. It's hard and leaking—for her or for me? I don't know. I don't fucking care. It'll be hard for me before I am through, and then he will come because I tell him to. "I hope that you won't." My grin is all teeth because I recognize he's all in. He knows it too. If he wants Dede to be part of this, he must accept.

"What if I subdue you?"

I chuckle. "An alpha knows his place. Sometimes he fights it. Sometimes, if the alphas are closely matched, no hierarchy is established. In this case, we both know."

Byron is young, so maybe one day he will best me, but I don't believe he has the disposition to claim first alpha place.

I take up the oil, pour a good measure into my palm, and slather up my dick. "Best prepare yourself, lad."

Only he doesn't. The little lamb on his lap is making wet slapping noises as she jerks her small fist up and down his cock, while he leaks like a fucking tap. He swallows.

"Let the lass down, let her go to Grady."

She hisses at me, the little brat.

"Dede." I add a little force. Her hands pop off his cock, and she throws a look at me. "Go to Grady."

She nods, wriggling down from Byron's lap, her small feet making a patter as she darts across the floor to the bed, where Grady rests propped against the pillows. There is no hesitation as she nestles sweetly upon his lap. Our eyes follow, for both Byron and I have placed her in the center of our world. Whenever I see her with Grady, love swells within my chest. To see them together and be part of it, an equal part, is a truly heady experience.

The lad turns to me. My cock is well oiled, and even if a little of it comes off in the inevitable tussle, it will ease the penetration. I lie, he is going to grunt like a pig when I fill him, but soon after, his dick is going to spew in ways that will blow his mind, and if we are both lucky, he'll take well to it.

I grin as I take a step toward him. That's all it takes. His arm shoots out to slap against my shoulder and hold me away, but I push into it and he pushes back. Goddess, I love the challenge. The alpha in me enjoys this so very much. I can't tussle like this with an omega, for Dede is tiny and precious. But I like the fight, and the way adrenaline crashes through me as I subdue another dominant male, the sensation of overpowering them, of being the ultimate one, feeling their asshole give as I force my way in, the tightness...everything about it, up to and including their final surrender. I knock his hand away, grab his arm, and twist it, but he twists out. I take a punch and taste blood as he tries to kick my legs out. I hold firm and twist, and we grapple. Everything inside me roars to life.

I have dominated men many times in my life and do not prolong the battle. With a savage growl, I take him by the throat and force him down on his knees before the bed. He arches, but it is already too late as I pivot behind him and kick his legs apart before thrusting him face first into the bed. His elbow swings, and I pin it to his back, eliciting a sharp cry.

"Submit," I say. "We both need this if we are to move forward."

I sink down behind him. My cock nestles between the cheeks of his ass, and I slide it backward and forward in a prelude for what is to come, relishing his fiery growl.

My smirk only grows broader. Here, right here, I feel alive.

Then I do the one thing he is not expecting—I completely release him.

§

Byron

One moment, I'm fighting to protect my virgin ass, then the restraining hands are gone.

Is it over? Was that a test? I heave a gusty breath. I'm on my knees at the bottom of the bed. Before me is Dede nestled on Grady's lap, watching me with open-mouthed, glassy-eyed lust. I understand that she is falling into heat, just as I am sinking into rut.

When I throw a glance back, I find Declan is standing over me with a wicked gleam in his eye, and I swallow. This is not over. My cock throbs, pre-cum leaking from the tip. In this heightened state, I have clarity of thought, understanding at a deeper, more primitive level the necessity of bonding to Declan, my first alpha, in the way he needs. Only then can I be with Dede, whom I love.

Declan crashed into my life like a whirlwind, demanding attention. Grady has yet to earn my trust, respect, and love, but Declan is halfway there. I turn forward. "Get on with it then."

Declan chuckles. "Was that a *yes, Declan, please rut my ass?*"

The bastard doesn't give an inch. He doesn't only want to wrestle me into submission like he does in the practice pit time and time again. Now he wants my whole submission—body, mind and soul.

"It is," I say.

"Look at Dede, lad," Declan says.

As I lift my eyes and watch the sweet lass who owns my

heart, her hand skitters down and her fingers dip between her thighs to play in her pussy. Behind her, Grady barely notices what she does, for he's staring at me in my state of submission before he turns his gaze away toward Declan. Latent emotion brims in that exchange. The preexisting relationship between the two men often made me wonder if they were together. Maybe they are now? No, there is yet some barrier in the way. I sense what we do here is part of it, connected in some way.

"Get on with it," I say through gritted teeth. "Before I lose my fucking nerve."

I hear footsteps... Declan is leaving? I glance over my shoulder, but he's gone to the bottle and brings it back with him. Fuck, my stomach turns over, and I swear my balls try to crawl up into my ass, but my cock is still hard. Swallowing past the lump in my throat, I turn back to the front. I can't look at Grady, and I can't look at Dede, I just stare at the fucking bed. I hear the pop of the cork before cool liquid trickles over the crack of my ass. I clench as his fingers follow, swiping down and up, pausing over the entrance to my ass. I'm so fucking tense. His other hand slides over my back all the way to my hip. He squeezes my hip gently, nothing threatening about it.

Then he grips tightly and sinks two thick fingers slowly into my ass. I hiss, jerking forward. It is fucking slippery, and my ass just gives as I twitch. It's not unpleasant...not unpleasant at all. Men do this. They take pleasure in it. I never had any interest in it myself, but as he teases his fingers in and out, all the nerves inside me awaken. "Fuck," I mutter gruffly.

"Indeed," says Declan. "We are going to fuck."

Whimpering draws my attention. Grady has shackled Dede's wrists so he can take over fingering her, thrusting thick digits in and out. Her thighs part before me, giving me the perfect view of what he is doing. Everything swirls up together,

her scent, the wet sticky noises as he plays with her, the rippling sensation as nerves I didn't know existed awaken.

Then she is there, right in front of me, and my mouth is on her, feasting on the plump, swollen folds, just as Declan twists his fingers inside me. My hips jerk. *Fuck!* I'm going to come!

"There we go," Declan says. "Relax, lad. It's gonna feel so fucking good when I get my cock in here."

I'm trying not to think about his cock going in there... Also, I'm trying desperately not to fucking come because that would somehow be embarrassing, given he has not yet fucked my ass. Sweat pops out across the surface of my skin. "Fuck! Fuck! Fuck!" I mumble into Dede's pussy as he delves his fingers deeper into my ass. I shudder as a gush of stickiness ejects from my dick. Goddess, the man knows how to do this.

A shiver courses through me as his fingers slip out, and because I know what this fucking means, I get my tongue deep into Dede, burying myself under the dark blanket of pleasure, letting her moans and twitches settle me.

Then something bigger is taking their place, fat, blunt cock pressing and pressing, terrifying me, yet I'm so deeply aroused, I can't think straight as it sinks slowly in. *Fuck!* My cock is leaking all over the bed. I want to grab it, to squeeze it, to ease this ache. My spine tingles, my balls tighten, wanting rise and fucking empty.

I drag my mouth from Dede's pussy. "I'm going to come!" There I've said it, admitted it.

"Not gotten half of it in yet, lad," Declan says just as his fat, rippling rod drives deeper into me. "Breathe through it."

Breathe through it? Is he fucking insane? The sounds I make are inhuman, my body shudders, my mouth is on her pussy, sucking her clit, because I need something to ground me as the sensations clamor, wild and out of control. I feel like I'm being stuffed with a fucking pole, like he's rearranging my insides one inch at a time. Finally, I feel his hairy thighs and crotch nestle against the back of my legs and ass.

It stings and burns. Fuck, how it burns.

"Fuck, you're tight," he says.

I jerk my hips. Shouldn't he be fucking moving already?

An arm reaches around, slicked fingers cupping my balls and rolling them. I try to jerk away, but his other arm holds me fast and all I can do is endure the torment, wanting to empty my load all over the bed. A tingle skitters over my body, rippling over my skin, and more pre-cum gushes from my cock. I'm about to lose my fucking mind.

My ass clenches. I can't stop it, like I'm trying to push him out.

Dede is moaning and humping up into my face, I think she might be coming, but I'm so out of it, I can't gather enough wits to work the details out.

Then I'm being taken by the hips, and the thick burning rod filling me draws all the way out. *Ah!* He slams back in, and everything turns to sparkling dots.

"Fuck! Hold it, lad," Declan says, voice a rough growl.

Hold it? I don't know what the fuck I'm doing or where the fuck I am. I'm just existing, caught on the cusp of monstrous pleasure and pain as Declan begins to rut my ass, fast in, slowly drawing out, fast in, slowly drawing out, then becoming faster. My ass is burning, my skin igniting, and deep inside, every time it pushes over a sensitive spot it causes a body racking shudder. Spine tingling, balls clenching, I'm going to fucking come. I'm going to come...

Another shudder ripples through me, and sweat pops, saturating the air with pheromones, and I feel like I empty my soul onto the bedding. Dede moans wildly, gushing cum which I greedily lap up, groaning, lost in the euphoria. His monster cock continues shuttling in and out of my fucking ass, and my entire body is on fire. My dick spits more cum, my knot aches, and the thrusting rod takes me over into another savage climax. I pant, I groan, I lose all command over my body. The great beast behind me keeps plowing into me, until finally, as I become a gibbering, twitching wreck, he stills. His cock throbs, grows, the burn increases, and he roars as he comes, dumping a hot gush inside me. I'm clenching over him, ass contracting in waves of white-hot bliss as a final savage climax tears me apart. I'd collapse but for the arm anchored around my waist, holding me still, holding me to him.

"Fuck!" Shaking uncontrollably, I press my forehead to Dede's thigh. Fingers are in my hair, small, gentle fingers belonging to the woman I love.

Declan chuckles gruffly and sighs. It is full of contentment, and I can't help but grin too.

"I'm gonna ease out now."

That's all the warning I get, and I shudder yet again as the dark rippling coaxes another small ejaculation from my cock. My ass is sticky and sore, but I don't even fucking care.

I collapse, head on Dede's belly, utterly spent, balls drained. I don't think I'm ever going to be the same again. Distantly, I hear Declan move off, cleaning up, I presume, then footsteps, a door opening, and the low mumble of voices before the door closes again.

Blissful, untroubled sleep pulls me under.

Dede

Watching Declan rut Byron was the most brutally perfect experience of my life. The sounds, the scents, the utter savagery, and the tormented pleasure upon my sweet mate's face, all conspire to send me reeling.

His head is heavy on my belly, but I don't mind, taking comfort from the weight. I yawn, sleepy. It's dark in the room, with only a little moonlight spilling in, but I'm unable to tear my gaze away from Byron's sleeping form. He looks so peaceful, a big alpha all sprawled out with his feet dangling over the edge. Beyond the closed bedroom door, I can hear the rumble of Grady and Declan's conversation.

They haven't tried to take him away from me, and further, have left us here together. I feel my heart lift inside my chest with wonder and joy. So many times, all I had with Byron was stolen kisses and heated lovemaking in the still of the night before he was forced to leave me, sneaking out lest he be caught, and underlying it all was the guilt and love I still harbored for Grady. For once, there is no sense of guilt nor betrayal, nor is there reason for Byron to leave. He may rest here, nestled against my belly until he is ready to rise.

My fingers play in his silky hair, and I wonder what the two men are discussing on the other side of the door.

Byron shifts, hissing and groaning, as he rises and heaves himself up the bed, pulling my back to his front and throwing a heavy thigh over mine, half smothering me as he buries his nose in the crook of my neck.

"Byron?" I whisper. "Are you all right?"

"Yeah," he says, sounding sleepy. "I'm...um...a bit sore."

I giggle. He nips at my throat.

"The fuck are you giggling about?"

I giggle harder because he sounds cute and growly all at the same time, and if I were to tell him, it would be sure to make him grouchy. "I love you," I say, and that quickly, I feel tears sting the backs of my eyes. While I am wrapped up in his arms, knowing Grady and Declan are on the other side of the door, keeping us safe, I feel my love for the three of them spill over.

"I love you too, so fucking much." His arm tightens around me. "I think I might love Declan too. That was fucking wild."

I giggle again, but it fades because I'm thinking about them together, the raw emotions on Byron's face, the absolute determination on Declan's, his power and domination. Dark, otherworldly danger lurks under Declan's, at times brooding and at times playful, façade. I think I'm half in love with him too. "That was the most amazing thing I have ever seen. I can't stop thinking about how you looked when he was rutting you."

Byron groans. "Don't. I must have looked weak."

"Weak?" I am genuinely shocked as I twist to peer back at him through the gloom. "No, not at all, not even slightly. You looked beautiful together, powerful, the both of you. He was so rough with you, and yet you took everything. You gave him all your trust, and he cherished it, read you and your needs perfectly, and never looked away from you once. His focus was absolute. I think...I think some men need that, need your trust and submission, but it doesn't make either of you less. Would you...would you do it again?"

He groans and presses his lips to mine. "Fuck, I don't know. My ass might need time to recover before he goes at it again."

I smile, settling back and content as he nestles behind me.

"He grew up on the streets of Knoll, an orphan, stealing for food. The city watch was going to hang him, but my father agreed he could come back to the castle with us. I think Declan is different in more ways than only that, and he needs to hold control. He kept pushing Grady about letting me see you. I know Grady would have relented, I wouldn't have stood for anything else, but it was hard for him to do the right thing."

"I know," Byron says. "And I understand now. I've been training with Declan every day. Well, he pummels the hell out of me under the guise of a training session, but now I realize he was preparing me for this, to share you, for Grady to accept. For all of us to be together."

The Goddess is ever mysterious, and through Declan, she has provided the perfect mediator between Grady and Byron, the perfect mate to ensure no one oversteps the mark.

A rumbly purr emanates from Byron's chest. His purr.

I sink into sleep.

Chapter Twenty-Eight

Grady

It's hard for me to leave the warmth of her body, but I know I must. Also, Declan's glare says he's going to drag me out if I don't do it on my own terms. I stagger out of the bed in a state of shocked arousal after what just went down. Declan is all business as he cleans himself up and slips on a pair of pants, while I do the same. He doesn't make mention of my rigid cock, nor my muttered curses as I fight to stuff it into my pants.

Before I shut the door, I take a lingering look at the bed. The lad is sprawled out over Dede, dead to the world. Raking my fingers through my hair, I close the door on them. It's still dark outside. The lamp has burned down low, and I go over to turn it up. Declan is standing at the table, rifling through the plate on the tray, helping himself to whatever's on there. I should eat too. We've had a full day riding and a battle with raider bastards, followed by a rutting.

"I can't believe she let the lad into the fucking nest," I say.

Declan chuckles. That's the man I know and love—yes, I can admit that much—finding amusement in everything.

"I'm jealous of the whelp" he says around a mouthful of bread and cheese. "She has freely declared her love for both of you. I'm the one who is still an outsider."

"You're not," I say. I hadn't considered his side of things. Declan is so steadfast and forthright, one might be forgiven for forgetting he has needs beside his obvious lust. His happiness is important to me, I realize. Declan is the final piece that makes everything perfect. "She will come to care for you." *I already do.*

He sits beside me on the couch, close but making no move to touch me, yet I sense he wishes to. How do I bridge this gap that I have created between us? I know what he wants, what he needs—me on my knees, taking his cock the way Byron did. I swallow thickly. Fuck! I can't get the image out of my mind.

I have watched him with Dede, ruthlessness and determination etched in every line of his face as he holds absolute control. Yet somehow, he never does too much, never more than the recipient of his lust can take or cope with. He gives them exactly what they need.

He side-eyes me. "Don't overthink it," he says.

I glare at him. Chuckling, he holds his goblet up as though in toast before drinking deeply. I watch his throat move as he swallows. *Powerful.* Declan is everything an alpha should be, yet he has other admirable characteristics, the mental ones that separate us from ravaging beasts. He is strong in his heart and his mind, and his body is merely a reflection of all that.

"She will go into heat soon," he says.

"I'm surprised she didn't tip over tonight."

He shrugs. "I did wonder. The lad is good with her. You know that, right?"

"He is also too soft with her. It's a good fucking job we returned."

"Mayhap I like the lad exactly how he is." Declan's grin turns wolfish, and he points his thumb in the direction of the closed bedroom door. "Did you notice?"

"Notice what?" I'd been too busy watching him rut Byron into ecstasy to notice much of anything. Declan smirks like he knows what I'm thinking about, and as if to confirm it, his eyes lower to my cock bulging against my leather pants obscenely. It will only amuse the bastard further if I try to adjust it.

"Her scent. Even before her heat and full claiming, her scent has changed."

I frown, then raise my brows. "Thank fuck, because I wasn't going to share with anybody else."

Dede

When I next wake up, I'm tangled with Byron on the bed and daylight is streaming in through the window. A comforter has been placed over us, although it is not needed, for his warm body blankets mine and is throwing off heat like a furnace.

This is the first time I have woken up beside him, for he always had to sneak out in the past. As I wriggle to turn onto my back, the wall of firm flesh untangles from mine. I blink about the room. "Where are Grady and Declan?"

"Declan is on patrol, and Grady is doing whatever lordly things he does. They said we should sleep in. Well, Declan said as much. Grady looked like he had swallowed a lemon, took his stuff, and stormed off. Declan winked at me before following him out. I get the impression the two of them might be engaging in a sparring session later and Declan will pummel some sense into him."

I press my hand over my lips to stifle my giggle. Byron smirks, and the big hand tucked around my belly slides up to cup my breast.

"No," I say, putting on a sulky voice and wondering what he will do.

Grinning, he squeezes it before rolling onto his back and stretching out like a lazy cat. With sandy brown hair, blue eyes, and a blond beard, he is a brawny, handsome alpha, whose gentle, caring ways make him an easy man to love. Leaning onto one elbow, I stare down at him.

"How do you feel?"

"Like I was fucked in the ass."

I laugh, seeing the mischief shining in his eyes. "Does it hurt?"

"No, just tender." He raises a brow. "You know lasses do that, right?"

"They do not!" I say, scandalized.

"They certainly do...and with alphas." He is grinning again now, and I can't decide if he is telling the truth. Heat burns my cheeks. "Do you want to do that, Dede?"

I shake my head, but I am thinking about how both Byron and Declan have pushed their fingers in there while rutting me. Suddenly, I am convinced Declan, in particular, will want to take me in such a way, and further, will likely tease me until I beg him to do so.

"You're thinking about it," Byron says smugly. His palm, resting on his firm belly, slides down, displacing the covers, until he encloses his thick cock. Fisting it, he pumps slowly up and down.

My eyes are riveted, and he knows I am weak for his beautiful cock. Now that I have seen other men's, I realize how huge

Byron is...especially the knot. Last night, I missed out when he came on the bed. I feel his eyes on me, watching me watch what he does, and I send a quick glance his way before heaving myself up. He groans as I nimbly roll over him until I am kneeling in between his splayed legs. He doesn't stop pumping, just keeps sliding his hand up and down.

"You said no, Dede. I have no choice but to take care of matters on my own."

I hiss my displeasure. He knows the scent of his pre-cum leaking out weakens me. "I wasn't saying no to everything."

"What if I say no," he says, reminding me that for all he can be sweet and loving, he is also wicked at times and not averse to taunting me.

My mouth waters at seeing the pre-cum leaking all over his tip, and my eyes flash to meet his. "Will you?"

"I'm not fucking stupid." He gives one final rough tug before placing both hands behind his head and grinning. "Have at it, little omega."

He has never called me an omega before, I am yet new to it, and it is strange to acknowledge what I am. "I love you," I say.

"I love you too, Dede." He nods his head at his cock. "Now, put me out of my misery. Wrap those sweet lips around my cock and suck it until I come."

This playfulness is new to me, and I like how it fills me with warmth and reminds me I am loved. Smiling, I close my hand around his cock. I don't think I've ever had the opportunity to study it like this in daylight before. The ridge at the bottom, the knot, is already inflamed, and I am no small amount intimidated by the thought of him eventually working it inside me. As I pump my hands slowly, he groans and more sticky pre-cum spills, making me feel all tingly inside.

"Fuck!" he hisses as I swipe my thumb over the tip. I can't wait any longer—my lips lower, and I begin to lap up all the stickiness. We both groan at the same time, caught in the spell, while I bob my head up and down, sucking as much as I can, lashing my tongue over it.

"Fuck, that feels so good," he says. "I could wake up to this every day."

I hope that we will too as I worship him, showing him how much I care.

"I'm going to come," he says gruffly, and he does, filling my mouth. I swallow it down, spilling a little, feeling it fizzle upon my tongue. Joyfully, I lap up every drop before lifting my head to gaze up at him. There is a little on my fingers, and I'm considering licking them when he snatches me up and drags me over his body. My squeal is silenced as he spears his fingers in my hair and takes my mouth in a lusty kiss.

Using my hair as a leash, he drags me off, blue eyes holding mine as our gusty breaths mingle. "Is it still no, Dede?"

"Assuredly, it is yes."

"Good," he says. "Climb on up. I want to eat your pussy out. Come and sit on my face."

I gasp in shock. Does he mean...? "Why would you want me to do such a thing?"

A sharp spank lands upon my bottom.

"Ow!"

"That did not hurt," he says. Okay, so I might have overreacted, and I do like the stinging feeling that emanates from my ass cheek. "You've had your breakfast. Now it's my turn."

A blush spreads from my cheeks, up to the roots of my hair. I'm feeling needy, my pussy slick just from tasting his cum. It doesn't matter what my mates do to me, my body craves more. A flutter kicks off in my belly, and I'm aroused all the time. So although I feel a great deal of embarrassment in doing as he asks, I do it anyway.

It is a little awkward as I scoot forward, but his big hands palm my ass and he hauls me up to where he wants me. Then I'm there and his tongue is inside me, and from his first lick, I am lost.

Groans pour from my lips. I twitch and try to lift, but the hands on my ass tighten, keeping me placed to his liking. Hands braced against the wall, I submit to the pleasure of his tongue lapping all over me, poking up inside my pussy before swiping up to circle around my clit. My hips move a little, rolling, trying to get more, thighs trembling, and that quickly, I am ready to come.

As his lips latch onto my needy clit and begin to suck, I lose all control, and then I'm coming, tumbling over, groaning and moaning and rocking my hips, sure I would collapse were Byron not holding me.

He doesn't stop, and I wriggle. "Please, it's too sensitive!"

"Uff!" I am tossed onto my back beside him, and he is on me again, kissing me, his tongue tangling with mine.

"That," he says, "was a perfect morning."

He rises, and I stare after his beautiful body, rippling with muscle, as he strides across the room. Byron is a stunning male and alpha, and I am filled with pride that he is mine. As he snatches open the door to my dayroom, I hear a squeal on the other side.

"Thank you kindly, Anna," he says. "Appreciate the breakfast." I am up off the bed, feet making little slapping noises, ready to smite the hussy who would dare look at my naked mate.

The outer door slams shut on her retreat, but I am far from satisfied. Perhaps sensing my deadly intent, Byron snags me around the waist. I fight, intending to charge the door. "Whoa!"

"She is not to look at you. I will scratch the hussy's eyes out if she dares to look at you again!"

"Peace, Dede," he says, a smile in his voice. "She has gone. See, breakfast is waiting for us."

My tummy rumbles. I don't know what came over me, but the moment I think about Anna, my temper rises again. Chuckling, he scoops me up and carries me to the table, where he takes a seat with me on his lap. I like this very much, feeling his naked thighs against my bottom and his warm chest against my side. "You are an omega in all ways, now the herbs are gone."

"When did you know?" I ask, pulling the tray forward and already dismissing Anna, who I decide will no longer be servicing this room.

"The day of the battle, when Grady retook the keep. I suspected something, but then Barnaby let it slip."

"Mia?" I shake my head. Given she admitted to sharing gossip with the lad, I should not be surprised.

He snags the buttered bread and stuffs it in his mouth. "Aye," he mumbles around the food. "She is sweet on him and near feisty as you should another lass look at him."

I chuckle. I cannot be angry at Mia when she has done so much for me.

We eat breakfast over companionable conversation. Everything about the experience is wondrous and new. After, he cleans up and dresses before heading out for a patrol, but before he goes, we share a lingering kiss, which reminds me how lucky I am. We are barely at the beginning of this, and I am filled with joy at the thought of the many years to come.

Once he is gone, I take a leisurely bath. I'm finishing dressing when my dearest friend Mia pokes her head around the door. She squeals as she sees me, hurrying over and throwing her arms around my neck. She kisses my cheek. "Dede! Finally, my constant sneaking around the corridor has paid off. Your men are insatiable."

I laugh. "They are," I agree.

"Are you fully claimed?" she asks. "Are they all your mates?"

"Not quite," I say. "I have not yet gone into heat."

"Are they... Are they okay with one another? Do you rut them all at the same time? Or do they take it in turns?"

I blush. "Mia, I do not want to discuss it."

She makes like she is fanning herself. "I think they take you together."

"They are very impatient," I admit, blushing. "It is hard to make any of them wait."

She hugs me again as we both giggle.

"Your father was asking about you. He is much improved, leaving his room most days. In the mornings, he can be found having breakfast at the high table with the new chancellor. In the afternoon, he visits various locations within the castle, the barracks yesterday, the stores the day before, and even a tour of the battlements. It gives the people much hope to see him thus."

"That is wonderful news."

She nods. "Truly, it is, but it is not the only change taking place in Langetta while your mates closeted you. You will be amazed!"

"Show me," I say. "Take me that I might see."

We leave the room together, moving along corridors and out into the main hall. My father is indeed there with a man new to me. Mia slinks off after spotting Barnaby stacking wood beside the fire on the far side of the hall.

I am introduced to the new chancellor, a slim faced man with a long wiry white beard and bald head. He bows politely before excusing himself with a promise to speak to my father later in the day.

"He is from the Borne estate. Given his excellent under-standing of law from serving for a time in the king's court, I'm hoping he will stay on," my father explains. "Grady sent word to his brother for support, and the chancellor is not the only arrival. Goods and tradesmen arrived yesterday. Next week, soldiers are coming by ship."

"This is wonderful news!" I am shocked by how greatly my father has changed... He reminds me of the time before the Goddess called my mother to her side.

"I am so sorry, my love," he says, eyes shining with love and a little sorrow. "I was a fool, and I made poor decisions while lost to my grief. Your mother was the strong one. She would have been furious with me for my failings."

"She would," I agree, but I smile to soften the blow. "Then she would have forgiven you, as I do. I missed you. It has been a terrible few years."

"I miss your mother," he says. "Every day.

"As do I," I say.

"She would be proud of you. An omega... Who would have thought it?"

"Not me," I say.

"Grady is a good man," he says. "But I have heard some rumors that not only Grady claims you?"

This is an awkward conversation to be having with one's father, but there is no avoiding it. "They are true, Father. It is not only Grady who will claim me, but Byron and Declan."

His brows crawl for his hairline. "Three? You are going to be claimed by three?"

"I am." A smile spreads across my face at his shocked expression. "It is not so bad, Father. I love Byron. My feelings have grown for him over the two years, first as a friend, and then as a protector, and finally as a lover."

"And Declan?" my father asks. "I can still remember the scrawny street urchin giving us attitude. I thought for sure I would end up hanging him. He bends to no man's rules."

"He is a fine alpha and is strong" —I place my hand over my heart— "in here, and will keep my other two mates true, ensuring the bond between us remains steady."

My father's hand reaches to cover mine, and he gives it a squeeze. "If you're happy, my sweet Dede, then I am happy for you."

"I am happy," I say, feeling it in my very soul. There are sure to be bumps in the path before us. I am not yet fully claimed, and I am certain all of us will need to work hard with such a complex relationship. But with love, and the blessing of the Goddess, I believe anything is possible.

A bowing servant approaches with a message in his hand. "Go on," my father says. "I see Mia waiting for you. This is your first venture out in many days. Take some fresh air, even if it is chilly at this time of year. We can talk later, my love."

Pressing a kiss to my father's cheek, I go to join Mia.

"Come on," she says. "I can't wait to show you!"

Beyond the grand double doors is the courtyard...and a hive of industry as workmen are busy at repairs. The sky is clear and blue with a hint of frost in the air.

"Lord Borne sent them, along with food and equipment. Did your father tell you?"

"Yes," I say, staring about. "So I just heard."

Stone masons, carpenters, and laborers are busy making repairs. Weeds that once littered the cobbles are gone. The slow creeping death calling to Langetta is being scrubbed away, allowing for new life. The air might be cold, as winter's chill approaches, yet it feels like a new beginning for the castle.

I am ashamed that I ever thought to abandon my ancestral home and kingdom. "Let's go up on the battlements," I say. I want to feel the wind in my hair as I gaze out across lands that will one day be mine.

"You are not dressed for the battlements, my lady," she says.

"I do not care," I say.

She laughs, as do I, and we hurry up the winding stairs, past guards who give us wary looks. One shouts out to be careful.

Then we are at the top, and I fill my heart and soul with the view. The Tyne River is closest to the castle on this side, cutting a wide meandering path through the trees. Forests stretch in every direction, but to the north, beyond the sweeping hills, I can just make out the sea, before which is a jostle of houses, taverns, and all manner of buildings that make up the walled port town of Twin Heads. I can even make out tiny fishing boats, or perhaps sailing ships.

"I'm disappointed," Mia says beside me.

"Why?" I ask, frowning.

"Because omegas are claimed, and I was so hoping for a grand wedding."

I had not thought about that before. "We shall have a feast instead," I say.

Mia claps her hands together in glee.

"Yes! We are long overdue for a proper feast. It will be the most splendid feast ever. Grady's brother generously gifted us food and other supplies. It seems many of the southern kingdoms sent support to him during the war. The high king himself sent goods and soldiers, or so I have learned." She winks at me. "I heard Grady sent stern words to his brother for being kept away so long."

I chuckle. "It is the least he can do for taking Grady away from me."

Her face softens. "I was so worried about you. Even after Killian was gone. Grady was a bear with Byron...and everyone.

But Declan, he is a bit of a surprise. The lasses of the castle were devastated when they heard he has claimed you."

I growl at the mention of lasses coveting my mate, ready to storm the castle and smite any hussy who dares to look at my men, only tempering it when Mia's laughter penetrates the red haze.

"You are truly an omega. It is the first time I have recognized you as such." She slips her arm through mine. "I cannot wait for the babies! I hope there will be many for me to coo over."

So do I, I realize with a smile.

Chapter Twenty-Nine

Grady

"I don't have time for a fucking sparring session," I say, eyeing Declan with a measure of trepidation. He has just returned from a patrol, his dark hair a little wild, and there is a telling gleam in his eye.

A week has passed since I resolved myself to sharing, and it would be fair to say I still struggle to fully embrace the situation at times. Declan likes that I struggle because it gives the bastard an excuse to put me in my place...and force me to submit.

"I couldn't give a fuck," Declan says, grinning and cracking his fucking knuckles.

Oh, this is going to hurt, and the bastard is going to enjoy every minute.

"Don't mind me, my lord," the engineer I was talking to says. "I lived a goodly number of years in the Imperium lands, and sparring between bonded mates is a natural and healthy way to settle things. Even after, some find it beneficial to settle tempers."

I raise a fucking brow. Declan chuckles, and the engineer, perhaps sensing I am not in the best frame of mind, slinks off.

With no choice now, I follow Declan to the practice pit.

"You are jesting with me," I say. There is a fucking crowd gathered! Right at the front is Byron, a smug grin near splitting his face. Fucking whelp! Is it not enough that I let him snuggle with my mate?

Our mate, I amend. This sparring session is about me accepting that I must share.

"I never jest about rutting or fighting," Declan says, wasting no time stripping his leather jerkin and tossing it onto the low wall. I follow his lead. I do not have a fucking choice.

Byron

Watching Declan pummel Grady is an unexpectedly joyful experience, even if I wince on occasion when Declan lands a particularly savage blow. Having been on the receiving end of those monster fists, I know exactly how they feel. The crowd cheers and shouts their encouragement as the two men punch, wrestle, and wear each other out.

It is quite a thing to have an omega claiming, and by three mates no less. Dede is a throwback, a coveted reminder of our barbaric past. News of her will be spreading throughout the kingdom. Omegas are rare enough, but it is not the way of our people for them to take more than one mate. I anticipate a procession of visitors over the coming weeks and months...as long as there are no more fucking alphas sniffing around.

Flat on his back among the dust and dirt, Grady finally lifts a tired hand in indication of submission to the cheer of the crowd. He is well beaten, while Declan, as per usual, is perky and only a little winded.

Declan reaches down to clasp his forearm and heaves him to his feet before pulling him in for a hug. The touch does not linger, yet it holds much emotion as Declan places his hand on the back of Grady's neck. They have words I cannot hear from here.

It is a strange dynamic to navigate, three men and one woman. There is no rule book for such things, not in these lands anyway. Even in the Imperium on the other side of the Lumen Sea, I expect they must likewise need to learn to navigate it in their own way. I feel like an outsider, for the two men have known each other for many years.

Yet we are all also grappling with our own sense of inadequacy. For Declan, it is a worry that he will never claim Dede's love. For Grady, it is remorse that he left, and in his absence, she bonded with me, sharing both her love and her body. There is much to work through during the months and years ahead of us. Life is a journey, but ours is just a little more complicated than most.

The two men turn, and Declan's eyes alight on me. He grins and motions me over. As I approach, he throws his arm around my neck.

"Get the fuck off," I say. He is sweaty, filthy, and smeared in Grady's blood. Declan only squeezes harder until I feel the muscles on my neck strain. Then he releases me, chuckling. Strangely, I do not feel like an outsider anymore.

"Come on, lad," Grady says, patting me on the shoulder. This is the first time he has touched me, and it furthers my sense of inclusion, even if it grates on my nerves when he calls me a fucking lad. "We've got an omega that needs to be rutted."

That quickly, my cock rises to attention.

"About that," Declan says.

"What part?" Grady demands. "My legs are weak and my body aches from head to toe, but I know the moment I get in the room, I'll forget everything but Dede."

"We need to make a plan for monster rod, here." Declan gestures in my direction.

The fuck?

Grady chuckles. "The lad is not normal, that's for sure."

"Why am I not fucking normal?" I scowl between them, although I am now aware that my hardened cock is somewhat larger than average...especially the knot.

"Does the knot get any bigger?" Declan asks, gaze drifting down to where my cock tents my pants.

"I don't know," I say, feeling a flush creep over my cheeks. "It just always rises when my cock does."

"Don't worry about it," Declan says. "Mayhap the lass just needs some training before she takes it, that is all."

He winks at Grady, who shakes his head, although he is laughing too.

"She'll be more limber when in heat," Declan states matter-of-factly. He grabs a rag and rubs down his chest before tossing it to Grady. Grady glances down at himself before stalking toward the barrel of cleaning water. He curses as he douses himself in the frigid water not far off being frozen at this time of year. Both Declan and I laugh.

"Good thing she's an omega," Declan says. "They are Goddess sent to take cock, and the lass is beyond lusty, from what I have seen. A blessing, given she has three hale mates who all want and need her."

I swallow. "Do you think she will soon go into heat?"

"I do," Grady says as he approaches, wiping himself off. He is shivering but looks better for cleaning up. "I can't believe she let you into her fucking nest."

I grin smugly, and Declan clips me on the back of the head.

"Fuck!"

"You are the first one in the fucking nest," Declan says. "Allow us to be a little pissed. Come on, let's go find our little mate. Time to begin the training."

Dede

"Goddess! What happened to you?" I demand as the men enter my chamber. I spend my days burning with anticipation for their arrival, but tonight, when they finally arrive, Grady is half naked, wet, and shivering, covered in bruises and a few cuts.

Also, they are all here together. Usually it is Declan and Byron or Grady and Declan. This is the first time all three have arrived at once.

"Declan pummels me every fucking day," Byron grouches.

"Declan did this?" I ask, turning toward Declan, who is the last in and busy shutting the door. "I thought you had been attacked by raiders!"

Declan grins, while Grady shrugs his big shoulders before making a grab for me.

I squeal and dart out the way—he is covered in goose-bumps, and I don't want his frozen hands upon me—only to slam into Byron. "Uff!"

"Gotcha," Byron says, snaking an arm around my waist. His hand is in my hair a heartbeat later, then his lips are on mine, and I melt into the kiss. His cock is hard and pressing against my belly. His scent washes over me, and I drown in it, even as I go up in flames

A savage growl penetrates the euphoria. Byron's lips pop off, and I throw a look over my shoulder to see Declan with his palm planted in the middle of Grady's chest. It is Grady who is growling. That is as much as I see before I am shoved behind Byron's towering bulk. I peer around him.

"Get used to it," Declan rumbles. "He is going to have his cock in her later, and you will need to get used to that as well."

"Let me go to him," I say. My tummy is in a state of riot with both their aggression and pheromones filling the air.

"No," Declan says. "Not until he calms the fuck down. You will kiss Byron until he is satisfied, and then you will kiss me, and after, when Grady has learned not to act like a whelp, you may also greet him."

My pussy clenches at Declan's stern voice, and a needy whimper escapes my lips. All three men swing their heads my way. Goddess help me, being the object of their attention is a thousand times more intense today.

Byron scoops me up and strides for the couch, where he takes a seat with me straddling his lap. Then his lips are on mine again, and all other thoughts fly out of my mind. My hands grip his hair, our tongues tangling, my clothing a frustration. His hands burrow under the hem of my dress, and he groans into my mouth as his big hands cup my naked ass.

On the other side of the room, I can hear Grady's low growl, and it only drives a wildness in me.

Another hand finds the back of my hair, pulling my lips from Byron's, arching my throat back before Declan claims my lips.

"Fuck!" Byron mutters gruffly. Another hand, Declan's, yanks my bodice down, tugging roughly until both breasts spill free. Then lips are on them, sucking, nipping, and all the while, Declan claims my mouth and Byron palms my ass.

I groan, utterly lost that swiftly. On the other side of the room, the growling continues. Declan is taunting Grady, reminding him that he must share, and that there will be consequences if he does not. A part of me hates Grady's suffering, but another part remembers how he locked both Byron and me up, how we all suffered, and I decide that he can wait a little longer.

Declan's lips leave mine and I suck a deep breath in trying to find ground.

"Does that feel good, little lamb?" he asks.

My eyes lower to where Byron, cheeks flushed, suckles on my nipple. To the other side, Declan toys with my other nipple, pinching and petting it cruelly, making my pussy gush slick and ache to be filled.

"So good," I say.

"I'm going to let Grady rut you first," he says before taking my lips in another kiss. Byron growls, his teeth nipping against my throat. His fingers are skimming down, dipping between my ass cheeks to find the wetness pooling from my pussy. A bite stings my throat, just as he plunges two thick fingers into me from behind.

It's too much, the sensations of being trapped between these two dominant males, their scents, their hands, their lips... A great shuddering climax ripples through me, and I groan into Declan's mouth, riding Byron's fingers, wanting more.

Heads lift, and I am left gasping for breath. Distantly, I hear thuds and rustling, but Byron is still pumping lazily into my pussy, and that captures all my thoughts.

"I think she enjoyed that," Declan says.

"Aye," Byron agrees.

Chapter Thirty

Grady

Not only has the bastard beaten me black and blue, now he is making me wait. Seeing her come apart for them has me teetering on the edge. I have watched them with her before, have shared her with both men, but somehow, my ability to endure today is hard won.

Stripping is done as efficiently as my shaking hands and body will allow, divesting myself of boots and pants before tossing them to the floor. Noticing Declan watching me, I fist my cock. His eyes lower and nostrils flare. Two can play the taunting game.

He smirks, releasing Dede's hair. "She is all yours," he says.

She flings herself into my arms, and I stride for the bedroom, where I toss her onto the bed. "Strip!"

Her fingers fumble with the buttons at the back, but I can't wait for that. I push up her skirt, grasp her thighs, and haul her down the bed, where her glistening pussy is in perfect alignment for my cock...then thrust deep.

We both groan.

"Fuck! Your pussy feels good."

There I rut her, watching her tits jiggle about with every deep slap of our joining bodies. My knot is already growing. I am not much better than the fucking whelp! "I'm going to knot you. Tell me to knot you, Dede. Tell me to ruin this pussy. Tell me to rut you until you are open and ready for Byron's knot."

My words spew out. I have experienced genuine fear at the thought of Byron thrusting that abomination into her cunt, but now I am ready to spill my load thinking about exactly that.

"Please rut me. Please ruin me. I don't care, just make me come."

I sink, losing myself in her heady pheromones and the rapture written upon her face. Then she comes, but I am fucking determined not to give her my seed or knot yet, so I grit teeth against the pull of her wild clenching, her moans of pleasure, and rapture contorted face. My knot is growing, swelling, but I take hold of her hips and continue to slam in and out.

And heaven help us all, she takes it and begs for more.

Byron

Grady is on the bed rutting Dede, and I can't fucking wait. Having stripped, I am caught, watching enrapt, as the alpha and omega lose themselves to lust. Declan has sent for food and drinks and is in the dayroom sorting that out after ordering me *not to fucking interfere*. But I am nearing full-blown panic as the great swelling of my knot blooms bigger than ever before.

I think I am fucking broken. If I don't get it inside her soon, I fear I may damage myself.

The bedroom door opens, and a naked Declan enters. He

glances only briefly at the bed, where the wild rutting continues, before coming to stand behind me, muscular body blanketing mine. I jolt as he places a hand on my chest, sliding it down until he grasps my cock. I hiss but don't fight it. He has had his dick in my ass, so I reason his hand on my cock is of small consequence beside that. He's a possessive bastard with all of us. I get the impression he considers it his right to touch us however the fuck he wants, and damn, even the light relief of his hand stroking up and down my shaft, spreading the pre-cum around, feels fucking amazing. He rubs his thumb all over the leaking tip, making my hips jerk, and all the while, my eyes are locked on the bed, on the image of Grady forcing his growing knot in and out of Dede's pussy. Her wild moans of pleasure find a direct line to the hand pumping my cock.

"Does that feel good, lad?" Declan asks, voice a growl beside my ear.

"You know it fucking does."

He chuckles and surprises me by taking his hand away. I'm disappointed. What the fuck has he done to me that I'm disappointed?

Then he kneels and takes my cock in his hand again... guiding it toward his mouth.

I nearly blow my load with the first swipe of his tongue. The vision of this powerful, dominant male on his knees tending to me is utterly captivating. "Ah!" He sucks, taking me to the knot in a single motion. Fuck! That is so fucking good. Hot, wet lips slide over me, fingers rolling over the inflamed knot. I curse because I want to fucking last.

A wild moan comes from the bed, and my eyes jerk in that direction. Dede is on her hands and knees now, head thrown back as Grady knots her. She's so tiny, so lusty, so desperate for cum, and the joy on her face is a thing of wonder.

Fuck! My eyes snap down as Declan thrusts one thick

finger into my ass and sucks me deep. It burns so fucking good. My hand shoots out to grasp the nearby chair, my legs trembling and my knees threatening to give. A second finger is forced in beside the first, delving, finding that magic fucking spot.

"Fuck!" I come, shooting down his throat, ass clenching in waves over his thick fingers as he rubs the gland, and my cock spews another heady rush that has me seeing stars. Nose to my crotch, cock tunneled down his throat so that my knot butts up against his lips, his arm clamps around me, holding me to him, because I'm shaking and spasming and coming so fucking hard, I fear I might collapse.

I shudder as his fingers slide from my ass and his lips pop off my cock. More cum ejects from the tip to splatter against the floor.

Declan smirks as he rises to his feet.

I love him, I realize, a development I did not expect. His steadfast way, his generosity, and his calm no matter the situation, all tell me he is a man I can rely upon to keep me true for the rest of my life. The feeling rocks me. It is unexpected and humbling.

His smirk has gone, and something deeper takes its place. "I love you," I say. Heat flares in his eyes, because those simple words mean much to this complex man I am yet coming to know. His rough ways and speech are a façade over many layers. Then there is his complete lack of sexual inhibition or boundaries that blow my fucking mind.

Leaning forward, I kiss him, just a light press of lips, but he fists my hair and kisses me back, *aggressive* and full of his dominance. That fast, my cock is hard again.

Declan

Grady has just taken a turn with Dede and is now lying sprawled out beside her, watching Byron rut her. The lass is still in her dress, skirts rucked up and tits bouncing with each thrust. Somehow her being clothed makes the scene even more debauch.

Grady appears tempered, but I am ever aware that he is not yet fully submissive to me. I need his complete surrender before Dede goes into heat.

"Don't fucking knot her!" I call to Byron.

Byron groans, but he will do as he is told. It's going to be a rough day for him, given we need to work her up to taking his knot and the poor lad is desperate for that step.

We have all bitten her, and the bond is growing stronger daily. It won't complete until we mate, but I sense her heat is near. I'm hoping today will be a trigger, because we need this, especially Grady, who still fucking struggles.

That burgeoning bond is both a blessing and a curse at times, battering us with emotions, sensations, and pleasure, whether we experience it directly ourselves or not. An alpha can withhold feelings to an extent, but I'd expressly ordered Byron to *project* today, and he is.

With or without using the bond, it's fair to say we have a triggering effect on one another and are all fucking impatient when it comes to getting time with our mate...which leads to other things that are pleasurable, just in different ways.

Byron is open with his affection and can go all fucking night and take it all fucking night. He's not fussy about who is doing what, so long as he is getting some relief and can touch Dede, or at worst, keep her in his line of sight.

Grady... Grady is getting better, but not yet there.

Byron collapses to his side with Dede before him. Grady

takes her other side, sharing a lusty kiss, one hand on her plump tit, squeezing the flesh. Her scent is absolutely divine, which only adds to the potent mix.

Collecting the bottle of oil, I place it on the nightstand with a *thunk* before coming down behind Grady.

Byron chuckles. Grady drags his lips from Dede's and glares back at me. Getting my body—and hard cock—right up against his, I take his chin in hand and kiss him.

Dede's groan turns into a moan, and I let her obvious pleasure wash over me, amplifying my own as Grady accepts the kiss. Because I'm a pushy bastard, I close my fingers around his cock and jack them slowly up and down.

"Fuck!" Grady exclaims with a growl, tearing his lips from mine. He doesn't stop me touching him, just returns his attention to Dede, kissing her with open-mouthed hunger, swallowing her moans, groaning as I tease his beautiful, fat cock with my fingers.

"You know what I want," I rumble against his ear. His hips jerk, but not to pull away. No, he is thrusting into my hand as Dede's rich scent weaves a spell on us. He is comfortable with me touching him or sucking him and has even pleasured me. We have kissed often, but we have yet to take the final step. "I want your submission, your *full* submission, and you're going to give it to me."

My cock leaks all over his ass as I grind up against him. Our little omega is squished between Byron and Grady, kissing one while the other plays with her clit. If her twitching and moaning is any indication, she is about to come again.

She does. I release Grady's cock and grab his wrist before he finishes the job himself. He growls, and I growl back.

"Goddess!" Dede gasps out in pleasure.

"Fuck! She won't stop fucking coming," Byron mutters thickly.

"Good," I say. Holding eye contact with Grady, I grind my cock against his ass again. His body trembles with tension and a desperate desire to come. My lips tug up.

I nod to Byron, who removes his hands from Dede. Grady snatches her up with a growl.

I let him.

🙐

Grady

I know what he's going to do, but I'm too far gone to care. Dede's scent takes me to my fucking knees, while her sensual high is battering me through the bond, but this is not only about her. I've watched Byron, slack-jawed, as Declan ruts him into pleasure, and I want to do this, to be fully part of what we all share.

Dede is under me, her cunt open, wet and sticky with their cum, as I rut her. Declan is busy coating up his cock.

I jolt as a broad palm plants itself on my lower back, pinning my hips flush to Dede.

I suck a sharp breath in as the blunt tip of his cock nudges the entrance to my ass...and sinks in.

All the way fucking in, forcing me to give, to yield, setting sweat popping the length of my spine. My ass clenches and those dark, twisty nerves flare to life, and all the while my mind and body flip back and forth between pleasure and pain.

"Fuck!" I hiss. The bastard took his time with Byron, but I'm getting no such fucking care. Damn, it feels so good, though, like hot burning pleasure and pressure, so much pressure.

"Hold it," he rumbles.

Hold it? Before me, Byron is tangling tongues with Dede.

Behind me is a wall of strong muscle belonging to a supremely dominant male. A big hand skims up the back of my neck before enclosing my throat and squeezing, reminding me that he's the one controlling this.

It doesn't matter what the rest of me thinks, my cock is all in.

"Fuck, just move already," I grit out.

Then he does, guiding me in and out of Dede in shallow thrusts while his iron hard cock is wedged deep in my ass, every slow thrust making me clench around him, my knot swelling, adding to the sensation overload. The double stimulation is white-hot and all-consuming...until he begins to thrust with me. Slow then faster, and with every stroke, nerves I forgot existed are brought to savage life.

A shiver ripples through me, and my balls tingle with the onset of an imminent release.

Dede squeals with pleasure, her climax tearing my own from me via her clenching pussy and the bond. My knot locks, and I dump a river of cum deep inside her.

My ass is set on fire as Declan begins to slam in and out, stoking those nerves and inner glands until I am a twitching, convulsing wreck, ass walls spasming. Declan's ragged groan accompanies him driving deep and stilling with a savage growl. A hot flood fills me.

My vision is coming through a tunnel, ass, cock and knot throbbing in blissful waves. The bond flutters in my chest as I feel both Declan's satisfaction and completion.

He loves me.

I did not understand how much before, and I am humbled beyond words.

Lips press against my throat. He nips lightly, making my cock flex. My arms begin shaking so violently, it's all I can do to stop myself from crushing Dede.

Declan must retain enough wits to realize this too, and we collapse to our side, me hissing as Declan eases his cock from my sore ass. It's sticky and messy, and Declan leaves the bed to go and clean up.

Dede nestles between Byron and me. As my knot begins to soften, I ease out, to her hiss of displeasure. I purr, Byron purrs, and she settles again. I'm in the hazy stage of trying to recover my wits when a deep guttural cry comes from the sweet lass between us.

"About time," Declan says ominously as he strides back for the bed.

Chapter Thirty-One

Byron

My vision swims as her sweet scent hits me, and I blink. Grady has Dede on her back, her chin in one hand, while his other skims over her rippling belly.

"What's happening?" I ask.

Her face contorts, twisting up, and a horrifying groan of pain erupts from her lips. Her knees curl up.

"Hold her legs," Grady says.

"What? Why?" I mutter.

"Oh! It hurts."

I take her leg, as does Declan, holding her down to still her thrashing, my gut clenching at her terrible whimpers and moans that are assuredly not pleasure. Her pussy ejects a great flood of clear, sticky liquid, and I stare at it, transfixed but confused that my cock can be so fucking hard all of a sudden when the woman I love is in such pain. I *am* fucking broken!

"Good girl," Declan says, rumbling a purr. I purr too, then Grady takes up the call.

What the fuck is happening to her? Why is she in pain? Did Grady do this? Was he too rough?

"Heat," Declan says gruffly. "She's going into heat."

Dede

"Hot," I say, fighting to escape the restraining hands. Flames burn my skin, while deep in my womb, a tiny fist is savaging me. "Too hot. Make it go away."

"Breathe, little lamb," Declan says. It's his stern voice, the one I want to obey, only it's hard when a force of nature is ripping through me. Tears leak out the corners of my eyes as I fight weakly against their hold. I want to curl up into a ball. Why won't they let me?

"We need to get her out of these clothes," Grady says.

"Aye," Declan agrees.

"She won't keep fucking still!" Byron hisses.

"Cut the fucking things off," Declan says. "What the fuck was wrong with you, Grady, rutting the lass half dressed."

Soft rumbly purrs wash over me, their faces a blur through the tears, but I feel their hands and I scent them. Yet the more I breathe, the harder the tiny fist abuses my delicate insides.

A glint of metal, then a slow whoosh, and the constrictive clothing disappears.

I pant. That feels a little better. "Ahhh!" Another savage contraction takes my womb. "Please make it stop, I cannot bear it!"

"She needs tipping over," Declan says. "She will suffer until she does."

I thrash my head from side to side. I don't care what they do. I need something...more.

Their purrs deepen, then turn to growls that I feel all the way inside my chest. A hot splash hits my breasts, like rain drops only heavier, then yet more sprinkles over me. The scent hits me a moment later, and I thrash as more scalding splashes coat my thighs, belly, chest, arms, and throat. One spray hits my chin and lower lip, and instinctively, my tongue darts out.

Cum. The taste explodes across my tongue, my groan cutting off as fingers are in my mouth, pressing more inside, and I suck it down greedily.

Gentle fingers smooth over my right cheek and through my hair, and I lean into it. "Is that better, little lamb?"

"Much better," I say, only now my skin is tingling and my tongue feels heavy. I'm panting. Why am I panting?

A sudden spasm grips my pussy, but not pain. No, this is pleasure, a blinding kind of pleasure every bit as demanding as the pain. "Please!" My legs are parted, and a cock fills me just right. I arch up into it, nails raking over the bedding as he slams in and out, my body coming alive in a way it's never done before. Hands are on me, holding me still for the rough rutting.

I blink, coming to full awareness. Declan, my dark protector, cups my chin, his eyes on me, watching the rapture play out across my face as all the internal nerves zing to heavenly life. To my side, Byron toys with my nipple, handsome face similarly captivated.

I feel a connection growing between us, especially as things resolve and I find what I need. Past dangers drift from my mind until there's only the feel of the man above me—Grady, my first love, the man who stole my heart and then he left for distant war. There was a time I feared I would never see him again. Now he is here with me, rutting me, holding me, filling me with his cock, the knot blooming once again as he works it in and out, stretching me until I begin to sink into the dark madness again.

"Mnnnnn!" My climax sideswipes me. I grunt and pant, no longer a lady, but a wild cat with claws.

"No!" My screech of displeasure accompanies the cock jerking out and hot cum splashing over my belly.

A hand closes over the front of my throat, and my lips are taken in a kiss by Declan, first and most savage among us, the one who will retain control.

❦

Declan

I squeeze gently over her throat, and she arches, moaning into my mouth. Reluctantly, I tear my lips from hers and meet her glazed eyes as we share gusty breaths. "Tell me what you want, little lamb."

"My nest," she says. "I need to be in my nest."

"You want us to rut you in the nest?" I don't give her a chance to answer before taking her lips again. My needs have been barely tempered by coming over her.

"Please," she groans. "I need you all in my nest."

Gathering her into my arms, I stride for the sacred place. She hisses as feet made hasty by need, trample the outer wall. "Don't mind it, lass. We're going to ruin it as we make you perfect for us."

The others growl their approval. We are all sinking into rut, our human minds regressing, allowing the beastly side we keep locked up to rise. Once, back in our ancient history, we were shifters with a beast. Now the beast has melded with the man, but here, in times of heat and rut, that animal clamors to the surface. Mine is dominant. What Grady and Byron glimpse during normal times blazes to the fore as I settle the sweet, needy little omega into the nest.

Her chest rises and falls in unsteady pants, and a fine sheen of perspiration covers the surface of her skin. *Pheromones*, rich and potent, call to my long dormant beast.

We move as one, flipping her onto her hands and knees, coming down around her, crowding her, hands skimming over her body, cupping, pinching, *biting*. Here, I am first alpha and I take my first alpha rights, sinking behind her, fingers testing the openness of her slick pussy before lining up my cock, probing and testing again before slamming deep. Her clenching pussy demands my cum, hot and slick, and welcomes me as I slam wetly in and out.

Her groan is one of pleasure. My growl is one of possession.

Grady and Byron hold her for me, keeping her still as I begin the deep rutting needed to prepare her to be fully claimed. They share kisses, pet her needy clit, touch and pinch tits and nipples, driving her lust higher. She is already covered in our cum, but more splashes to join it. A cock thrusts between parted lips, and she is greedy for that too.

I give myself over to my beast, trusting him to know better than I what the omega I will soon mark and claim needs.

Marked, rutted, knotted, and bred, he tells me. In this, we are perfectly aligned.

Dede

Everything about this is perfect—the dark safety of my nest, my mates holding me, tending to me, the place where they are claiming me.

Declan knots me with a savage growl that finds an echo in

me. Deep inside, I feel a hot flood as he fills me with his seed. I snarl back at him over my shoulder, sinking nails into the nearest male. Teeth are at my throat, biting. I taste blood, though it is not my senses, but an echo of Declan's as he marks and claims me. I convulse around him as an awareness lights up inside. Pleasure blooms and crests as blissfully sharp contractions ravage my pussy.

"We're going to breed you," Declan says, his voice a growl against my throat as he laps at the wound. I push back, my body spasming around him, encouraging more of his seed.

His cock jerks inside me, spilling yet more cum, fingers bruising on my hips, holding me flush to him. His complete domination only makes me wilder.

"We'll both need to work our knots in and out to fully prepare her for Byron." Declan's words barely penetrate the hazy fog.

A growl sounds, Byron's, but it holds only desperation and agreement. Fingers press between my lips, filling me, making me gag and salivate all at once. A mouth is against one breast, sucking and lavishing it with a tongue. Another hand palms the other side, squeezing it, pinching the taut nipple, then rolling it. More fingers slide back and forth over my engorged clit, coaxing another savage climax from me.

The fingers bite into my hips, and the thick swelling of Declan's knot fights to pull free. Instantly, I try to clench, to hold him in, but with a snarl, it pops free, sending a gush of slick and cum splatting over thighs and nest. Fingers probe my pussy before pumping roughly, twisting, two, three, no four, stretching me, fingers sliding over my clit, circling round and round. I moan around the fingers in my mouth. My breasts, my pussy, my body tingles on the cusp but never quite reaching the summit.

Fingers slip from my mouth, and Byron is there, kissing me,

teasing me, and I chase his lips, panting and blinking up into blue eyes.

"Come for us, little lamb," Declan says. It rolls through me like a great wave, crashing over me, sending me tumbling as my eyes lock with Byron's, with sounds like an animal pouring from my lips. My gentle mate is gone, and this one is every bit a savage. My eyes lower to his cock, latching upon the swollen, veiny mutilation at the base that is assuredly not a normal knot.

He is going to put that in me.

My eyes snap up to meet his as I tumble straight over into a climax again, crushing the fingers filling me. Byron sees it all, my fear, trepidation, and arousal, and a dark smirk lights his handsome face. "Do you want my cock?" he asks, taking it in hand and brushing the slick tip back and forth over my lips, making me chase it with my tongue.

Then I am shifting, the nest sliding as I am tumbled onto my back. My legs are parted as Grady and Declan hold me spread wide and begin to probe me with fingers again. Byron's cock is back at my lips, and he slides his length in, brushing from tip all the way to the mutilated knot before sliding back until the wet tip reaches my parted lips, then he pushes inside again. I hum around the thickness, lavishing it with attention.

"She is beautifully open," Grady says. Fingers press into me, pulling me open, playing in the slippery slick and cum.

"She is becoming perfect for us," Declan agrees.

Then another cock is filling me with an ease that ought to scare me but doesn't. They take turns, first Grady then Declan, knotting me and pulling it out, then forcing it in again until they come, over and over. They bite me, mark me all over my body, and cover me in their cum.

I rise higher, a wildness tearing through me that, impossibly, wants and needs more. I beg, for I am not yet joined with my sweetly wicked Byron, and that is the only thing that matters now. I snarl my displeasure at the other males who dare to take me, to try to breed me and fill me with their cum.

"I want Byron!" My voice is a hoarse croak, for I have said as much a thousand times before. Just when I feel the desperate hopelessness that I shall never have my dues, he is there, big, beautiful body and terrifying cock rising over me, only I am no longer terrified. Now I need him with a desperation that knows no bounds.

Hands hold me still as the thick cock presses, slowly sinking into my entrance. I am near delirious with pleasure and joy. "Fuck! I'm not going to last." There is a desperation in Byron's voice, one I feel echoed in me.

"You will, lad," Declan says, that voice brooking no argument, expecting absolute obedience. "And our sweet lusty little omega will take it all."

A cock is presented to my lips, and there is not the slightest hesitation as I dutifully open and accept. I welcome the distraction from the thick club filling me, craving the taste and the feel of it forcing its way between my lips, and the ache for it complements the wildness consuming me. Declan surges deeply, straight to the back of my throat, making me gag, before pulling out again. "That is good, little lamb. You know this is what you need." And I do. His utter domination is something to behold.

Byron begins to thrust, his groans and growls drawing me as surely as the sweet sensations of nerves flaring to glorious life, while his thick cock slides in and out.

"She can take your knot," Grady says, and Declan growls his approval.

"Ah!" I feel the frustration and hope in Byron's guttural cry. His cock surges in and out, going ever deeper, the monstrous knot breaching me a little way. My focus is split between sensations—the fingers, the lips upon sore breasts and nipples, the cock surging in and out of my throat.

Panic blooms. It's too big, it won't fit. It *can't* fit.

"Take her fucking pussy, lad," Declan barks, slamming the force of his will into it. "Take her fully, or I will take your fucking ass and force you fucking in!"

His cock pops from my mouth just as Byron surges all the way in, tearing a squeal of white-hot pleasure from my lips. Cum bathes the entrance of my womb, the impossible thickness locking us completely as Byron comes with a savage roar that cuts through the air. I convulse, welcoming the teeth sinking into my throat, clinging, wrapping arms and legs around the man who claimed me first and now also claims me last. I sob with joy, the force of the emotional storm almost too much to bear. He is inside me, all the way, and I want to hold him there forever.

Safe.

Loved.

Sweet purrs fill the nest, and inside, deep in the center of my chest, an awareness blooms.

Love, more love than I thought the world contained, rains down upon me. Warm bodies draw close until I don't know where we all begin and end.

I bask in the moment, the blissful perfection, but not for long.

Need rises, pussy clenching over the great cock and knot, womb fisting in a demand for more.

"Our mate has needs," Declan says.

And so it begins again.

Grady

We rut, gratuitous and debauched, without limit or reservation, until we finally fall into a sleepy tangle around Dede. We have claimed the woman, but she has likewise captured our heart and now owns our cocks. The connection is a revelation, a window into each of us, our souls bared. Byron is trusting and open, and I envy the ease with which he gives his love and body to not only Dede but Declan as well. Dede, her beauty, her strength, her giving ways, the woman I have loved and left and, through the light of the Goddess, have found again. Declan, complex, ruthless, and yet unreserved in his love, his depth rocks me.

I love them all, even Byron. After seeing his patience and determination as he waited to fully claim our mate, trusting in Declan to guide him through what could have been a horrifying experience with a weaker alpha, how could I not?

Declan stirs where he lies sprawled over Byron, his arm curved around his body and over Dede, until his hand rests against my hip. The big hand tightens briefly on me in a comforting gesture before it slides back to rest against Byron. He pushes his hips forward, stirring Byron, who has slept with his hand splayed over Dede's belly.

Byron blinks, groaning, hand sliding down to cup the mound of Dede's pussy. He turns his head back to study Declan, who leans over to take his lips in a kiss that heats as his tongue spears into Byron's open mouth. I thought my cock was dead, but that hot kiss lights a fire of longing in my belly. Declan's eyes lift, and he pins me with a look as he holds Byron's chin to his and plunders his mouth.

Dede groans, and her legs popping open tears my gaze away, only to find Byron is playing in her slick folds.

"How does your pussy feel, little lamb?" Declan asks.

"Goddess! Don't stop, please, I need to come."

My fingers are beside Byron's, sliding into her wetness.

"Fuck, she is so hot and open," Byron says in wonder.

"Given you have rutted her with your monster fucking knot, that is hardly a surprise," Declan says dryly. "Go and tell the servants to prepare a bath, lad, and have fresh food and drinks delivered."

The lad grumbles but does Declan's bidding. Then Declan kisses our sweet, well claimed little omega as I gently coax her to come. After, she snuggles into my arms as Declan crowds her other side, and then, in what feels like the most natural thing in the world, he cups the back of my neck and presses his lips to mine for a kiss that lifts my heart.

Epilogue

Dede

L angetta's hall is bustling with preparations for the feast, for tomorrow morning, I will be crowned as the queen. My father, after much deliberation, has decided to abdicate. I tried to persuade him not to, but he said it was time and that he had made too many mistakes.

"After the raiding and pain of the last two years, the people need a new hope," he said when we spoke earlier this morning. *"You are an omega, with three mates who will make excellent consorts. Now you are with child, it's time for change. Besides, I am looking forward to watching you flourish and being a grandfather until the Goddess takes me to join your dear mother."*

And so I am to be a queen and a mother and a lover to my three amorous mates. Yet it does not feel burdensome, nor do I worry when I have three perfect alphas to stand by my side. Grady, with his experience as a leader, will be my advisor, and in those times when mothering duties take precedence, he will act in my stead. Declan will step up to the position of commander, while Byron will both assist Declan and take the role of my personal guard where circumstances require. Given all three of them take my safety and well-being extremely seriously, I dare say those occasions might be rare.

"Young Derick will break his neck!" Mia gasps. We are making winter garlands ready for tomorrow. Pine cones, conifer, and ivy spread out before us where we sit at a table with a handful of castle womenfolk.

Turning to look over my shoulder, I similarly gasp.

"What the fuck are you doing?" Declan says as he snatches the young lad off the table where he is stood balancing on a stool.

"I am putting the decorations up!" Derick says, the skinny five-year-old dwarfed in the big alpha's arms. "We were having a race!"

"You will be washing the fucking dishes instead of feasting if I see you up to mischief again," Declan says sternly. He puts the lad on the ground and ruffles his hair.

My heart softens at seeing this exchange. Derick is an orphan, and as I only recently discovered, Declan is a mentor to a few orphans here, making sure they find good placements with families and following up regularly afterward.

Steadfast, that is the word that comes to mind when I think of Declan. He's like a great boulder, standing against the churning sea of life.

As the young lad scampers off, Declan turns, and his eyes narrow on me. My tummy clenches, and I emit an entirely different sort of gasp. The bond between us blazes to life, and his needs and hunger pummel me, setting my pussy clenching in anticipation.

Mia chuckles. "Looks like us ladies will be making the garlands without Dede!"

As Declan strides toward me, I fear Mia is right. Collective flutters of appreciation follow him scooping me up into his arms.

"I was busy! And I can walk!" I protest.

"Let me carry you, lass," he says, smirking, as he strides from the room. "You are small and no trouble to carry thus. Also, I like feeling you here. Is your pussy making a mess? Do I need to clean you all up?"

"I...Goodness," I say weakly, face flushing as he makes a beeline for the nearest door—a stockroom full of jars and cured hams. A flustered servant flees when Declan barks, "Out!"

"What? Oh!"

I am dropped on to a sturdy wooden table, and my skirts are thrust up. He taps my thigh when I don't open my legs fast enough for his liking.

"We are in a store room!" I say, scandalized.

He smirks down at me, dark eyes hungry, hair a little messy, like he has just rolled out of bed, a savage alpha with a playful side. The man is neither ashamed nor limited when it comes to his sexuality. It hardly seems possible that the young boy who stood before me beaten and bloody, poorly clothed against the winter, should have grown into this mountain.

"I love you," I say.

His eyes darken as his hand goes to my hair, then his lips are on mine, tongue plundering my mouth. Declarations of love have an extreme effect on Declan, one that results in enthusiastic rutting. His head lifts again quickly, dark eyes boring into mine as he sucks in a gusty breath. I'm tipped back and my thighs thrust open before he buries his head between them. My fingers spear into his hair as my heart rate surges, pussy clenching and eyes rolling back as his wicked tongue is put to good use.

He is noisy, feasting with satisfied growls that raise me from simmer to boil so swiftly, I'm seeing stars.

Declan is an alpha who takes what he wants, not only from me, but from Byron and Grady as well. But he also gives. As he feasts on my pussy, driving me delirious with his lips, fingers, and tongue, that is about his pleasure, for his pleasure is derived from mine, driving me toward climax so he can further gorge on my slick.

I do come, twice, before the faint chink of his buckle signifies my imminent rutting, which he does—hot, fast, wild rutting that sets the jars and pots on the table rattling and clanking and the table creaking with the strain.

"Goddess!" I say as I rouse myself from the delirium of Declan at his most intense to find my sensitive nose assaulted by a repugnant smell, a testament to his skills at distraction. "Please do not knot me in a room full of cheese again!"

He chuckles. "I make no promises, lass. The room is handy."

Byron

"I don't know about this, son," my pa says gruffly as my ma fusses over my new uniform. "Looks a bit fancy. I'd be worrying all the time about getting mud on it."

"I've already gotten mud on it," I say dryly. "Declan insisted we christen it in the practice pit."

In his wisdom, Declan decided that we must find out if the fancy new leather armor improved my skills at all. It didn't, and I spent the usual amount of time on my ass, but the buttery soft leather is flexible and the finest clothing I have ever owned or worn.

"I like it," my ma says. "But the lad better not grow anymore!"

My five sisters all giggle, making a gaggle around me, wanting to know what we shall call the babe when he or she arrives. A baby! I'm going to be a father! Well, one of three fathers, but I'm ready for this next step and not much younger than my pa when I arrived. My only disappointment is that Dede won't go into heat again until after the baby is born. I can't fucking wait!

I feel her before she even enters the room, an awareness in the center of my chest that is attuned to all things Dede. A hush settles over the bakery where we are gathered as my mate and soon to be queen walks in.

"Goodness!" she says, blushing prettily as my family hastens to show respect. "Please do not bow!"

The girls soon swallow her up, taking her over to inspect the sweet pastries they have been preparing for the feast, beaming when Dede tries a bite of the samples baked and emits a groan of pleasure...that takes my mind straight to other things.

I tear my gaze away from the woman I love more than life, lest I find myself in an embarrassing situation before my ma and pa.

My ma waves me to lean down so she can plant a kiss on my cheek. "It's been a terrible few years since the late queen died, but there is hope here. The lass was ever a wonder as a princess. I shall never forget how she helped in your care when you went through the change. She will make a fine queen, and we, the people of Langetta, will be richer for her steady influence over the coming years."

"She will," I agree.

My feelings for the young woman who suffered so much has not wavered once. Finding my place with her and her other two mates was a bumpy ride, where the future was far from certain. Yet when I see us all together, I see the Goddess' hand at work.

"Please excuse us," Dede says, smiling to my parents as she slips her arm through mine. "We have business to attend to."

"Business?" I ask, my mind immediately heading south, even as we wish my family farewell. "The ceremony is not until later."

Her lips tug up in a smile that sends blood rushing to my dick.

"True." She blushes a pretty shade of red.

Grady

Dressed in all her finery, Dede is a sight to behold as she emerges from the hallway, her long golden-brown hair perfectly curled into an up-do and wearing a forest green gown with gold embroidery that sets off her pretty eyes. Flanking her are Declan and Byron, both donned in fine clothing as befits their new ranks as mates to a queen.

Her smile is nervous, but she *is* about to be crowned the Queen of Langetta. Beyond the double doors, an assembly of dignitaries and castle residents are awaiting her arrival.

Riddled with guilt for how this gentle young woman suffered while I was at war, I resolve myself to dedicating the rest of my life to her as I take her hand in mine and bring it to my lips. "Are you ready, love?"

She nods and takes a deep breath. "I am."

I purr, the others take up the call, and our precious omega mate instantly calms.

Love pulses through the bond, not distinct, but a combined love that wraps around us all.

When I first returned, I went through a great deal of adjustment. First with Killian and the threat he presented to Dede, then within myself and my understanding of love. The situation here changed and continues to do so. Dede's affection for Byron, followed by Declan, all conspired against me as I battled to accept a future so wildly different to my prior expectations.

It was fair to say I had difficulty letting go.

In my mind, Dede was mine, and I wanted her to love me and only me, believing that sharing with her would diminish my value in her eyes. Yet a heart has limitless capacity to love, and the more it is fed, the more it blooms. Dede is blooming under the care of us three mates. She shows us with her ways, her open joy, and giving body, how she loves us all, and I am humbled by this revelation.

I am humbled by all that has come to pass.

Not only do I get to share the rest of my earthly life with Dede, but with Declan and Byron as well. I can admit, from this side of the journey, that I have been a fool. What I once viewed as unorthodox and untenable is now natural and right.

As the double doors swing open and a fanfare heralds our entrance into the next chapter of our lives, I reflect that I would not wish my life to turn out any other way. Our sweet, resilient, mate, soon to be queen, has been lovingly claimed by three.

Did you enjoy Cliamed by Three? Please consider leaving a review. Authors love reviews!

How about some spicy eight mate pack with an alpha, a beta, and six shifters... in Bound to the Pack!

For free short stories and links to join my mailing list, please check out my website www.AuthorLVLane.com

Enjoying the Coveted Prey Series? You can find more stories on my Patreon www.patreon.com/LVLane

Also by L.V. Lane

Coveted Prey

The Controllers

The Awakening

Taking Control

Complete Control

Deviant Control

Deviant Evolution

Deviant Betrayl

Ruthless Control

Absolute Control

Deviant Games

Savage Control

Mate for the Alien Master

Punished

Ravaged

Avenged

Gifted to the Gladiator

The Girl with the Gray Eyes

The Girl with the Gray Eyes

The Warrior in the Shadows

The Master of the Switch

Darkly Ever After

Owned

Owned and Knotted

Verity Arden

Enjoyed L.V.'s books? You might also enjoy her contemporary pen name, Verity Arden!

In His Debt

Make Her Purr

Good With His Hands

Rough Around The Edges

About the Author

In a secret garden hidden behind a wall of shrubs and trees, you'll find L.V. Lane's writing den, where she crafts adventures in fantastical worlds.

Best known for spicy adventures...Magical and mythical creatures, wolf shifters, and alphas of every flavor who give sweet and feisty omegas and heroines a guaranteed HEA, she also writes the occasional character-driven hard sci-fi full of political intrigue and action.

Subscribe to my mailing list at my website for the latest news: www.AuthorLVLane.com

f facebook.com/LVLaneAuthor

X x.com/AuthorLVLane

instagram.com/authorlvlane

a amazon.com/author/lvlane

BB bookbub.com/profile/l-v-lane

g goodreads.com/LVLane

patreon.com/LVLane